The Heart of Jacob Wilson

THE LAREDO SERIES BOOK 4

LEE ANN SONTHEIMER MURPHY

This is a work of fiction. Names, characters, places, and incidents are products of the author's imagination or are used fictitiously and are not to be construed as real. Any resemblance to actual events, locations, organizations, or persons, living or dead, is entirely coincidental.

World Castle Publishing, LLC
Pensacola, Florida
Copyright © 2025 Lee Ann Sontheimer Murphy
Hardback ISBN: 9798273956414
Paperback ISBN: 9798891264885
eBook ISBN: 9798891264892
First Edition World Castle Publishing, LLC, November 24, 2025
http://www.worldcastlepublishing.com

Cover: Cover Designs by Karen
Editor: Karen Fuller

CHAPTER ONE

Autumn 1878

Every persimmon that Jacob had cut open had a spoon, not a fork. The woolly worms that the children found predicted a harsh winter. Onion and corn skins were thicker. Moses counted more fogs than usual on August mornings. The few walnut trees were heavy with nuts, and acorns on the rare oak trees were numerous. Boone said there'd been a ring around the moon since October, and the birds that flew south for the winter had gone. All the signs indicated an early and cold winter, something Jacob of all the Wilsons didn't mind. There were times he missed Kentucky and the cooler climate there, although not enough to return.

After two years in Texas, it had become home. Veteran of several cattle drives and known for his ways with horses, Jacob fit into ranch life like a well-made shirt. He was the only one of his brothers in Texas who lacked a wife. Back home, as far as he knew, Garrett hadn't married.

After Ezekiel and Katie wed and moved into the small cabin, Jacob had spent his evenings in the bunkhouse with the other hands for the company. Most of the time, he took his meals with one of his brothers' families, but he liked knowing he could eat at the bunkhouse anytime. Once Boone's new home, a shotgun house, was finished, then everyone changed homes once more. Moses and Mattie remained on one side of the dog trot cabin while Zeke and Katie moved into Boone's former abode. Jacob returned to the small cabin that had been built for him and Ezekiel to share. He preferred sleeping there to the bunkhouse for the privacy and for the proximity to the rest of the family.

The shotgun house lay about twenty feet beyond it, back toward the main ranch house, as well as near the vegetable garden. Built in the classic style, it boasted five rooms, one after another.

. The largest, at the back, belonged to Boone and Rachel. The other two lay behind the kitchen, one for the boys and one for the girls. Unlike the cabins, it had as many windows as Boone could afford. When they were all opened, as well as the doors, the house breathed as the wind blew through. That made it cooler than the cabins or even Liam's main house. Sometimes the wind whistled and moaned beneath the eaves, making odd music. It also sat a few feet above the ground so that snakes couldn't get inside.

Jacob treasured the memory of Sally Ann, his late wife, although with each passing year, he accepted that life continued even though she hadn't. He could recall her dark brown hair, as close to black as it could be, and her brown eyes that sparkled when she was happy. He missed her touch and the small things, whispering about the day just past in bed at night, the first cup of coffee, the pies she would bake, or the leather britches beans she cooked.

Until he came to Texas, he'd never paid much attention to blonde women, but when he first saw Moses' wife, Mattie, and then her sister, married to Liam Rafferty, founder and original owner of the ranch, Jacob noticed. Both women were beautiful, with delicate features, eyes bluer than a summer sky, and hair as golden as sunshine or corn silk. When he arrived, both sisters wore their hair in braids pinned up around their heads like a crown. Now, Maggie still wore that hairstyle, but Mattie sometimes did her braid in a figure eight on the back of her head or as a simple bun. He'd come to regard Mattie as a sister, and he had become friends with Maggie, as much as a man could be friends with a married woman. Moses knew Jacob found his wife pretty, but he'd never said much about it. If Boone or Zeke were aware, neither had they. He thought Boone might suspect he had an affection for Maggie Rafferty, but if so, he never mentioned it. Since Maggie was a married woman, he could do no more than admire her from afar and be a friend.

Maggie, for her part, seemed to accept Jacob's friendship, and he liked that. In a different world and situation, he would have courted her, he thought. She wasn't his Sally Ann, and there wasn't much similarity between the two women, but he thought he could have loved Maggie if the timing had been right.

Liam had sent their two children off to school in San Antonio, to his in-laws, and Maggie missed them fiercely. In their absence, Jacob had done all he could to help keep that loneliness at bay, although he couldn't fill in for her babies.

Jacob enjoyed being an uncle and figured he would remain the bachelor uncle. He missed his daughters, but it'd been so long since he'd seen them, almost three years, they had become fond but distant memories. He had always been close to his brothers, and that had deepened since coming to Texas. Only Garrett remained in Kentucky, and if he ever saw him again, Jacob expected the bond would still be there. The one he missed most back home was his mother, Jemima, who swore she'd come to Texas, but so far had not.

"I wish she would come," Boone had said the previous week when they gathered to celebrate his wife Rachel's birthday. "She could take the train as far as San Antone, then we could fetch her from there. I'd like her to see my children 'fore they grow up."

He had four now, the youngest born during a snowstorm in January last year. His oldest girl, Mima, named for their mother, was now seven, Rob was five, Benjamin would be two come this January, and the baby was Sarah Rose. Moses had his daughter Ellie and another baby on the way. Ezekiel and Katie had yet to produce a child, but Jacob suspected that it might change in the next nine months or less.

"It's still a hard trip from there," Jacob told Boone. "Ma's getting on in years."

Boone laughed. "She ain't sixty years old yet, and I wouldn't let her hear you say that."

"I hope she does come," Ezekiel had added. "It's been eight years since I saw her last."

"More than that for me," Boone returned.

Jacob wondered what it would be like if Ma ever came to Texas. The trains now were as close as San Antonio, which left no more than a five-or six-day ride to the ranch. That trip would be easier than the way each of the Wilson men had come to Texas and made it a real possibility that Mrs. Jemima Wilson could one day arrive.

With just days left in October, Jacob had been checking the hooves of every horse on the ranch, one animal at a time. A couple of hands assisted, including Mac and Jacob's brother Ezekiel. Liam had also acquired six new horses, bought from a ranch south of Laredo on the Rio Grande, and all were unbroken. During the less busy fall season, Boone, Moses, and some of the other hands would break them. Jacob did his daily work at the main horse barn, beside the largest corral on the ranch. He preferred the work to trailing cattle to market, but when it came time for the spring drive, he didn't complain either.

"I've got my eye on the gray mustang," Liam said with admiration. "He'll make a fine mount once he's broken."

"He's the wildest," Jacob replied. "Got a crazy look in his eye. I pity the man who breaks him – I reckon he'll end up on the ground more than once."

"The wildest horses make the best mounts," Liam said as he tried to stroke the gray's nose. The horse flinched and snapped his teeth, barely missing taking a hunk from Liam's hand. "That's what I've always heard."

Jacob didn't agree, but he kept silent out of friendship and respect.

"He's loco," Boone commented from the edge of the corral. "He'll be a hard one to break and dangerous."

Liam laughed. "If you're frightened of him, Boone, I may just break this one myself."

"You're welcome to it."

"Gettin' to be a scaredy cat in your old age?"

"Not quite, but I hope I've gained some wisdom," Boone said. "That mustang could be a killer, and I'll not take the chance to find out."

"I don't plan to ever grow old, but I will ride this horse or die trying," Liam boasted. The man could be a bit of a braggart at times, but Jacob liked him well enough.

His words bothered Jacob, though. He'd never been one to claim any fey ways or have premonitions, but he did believe in both. If it wouldn't disturb Ezekiel's red-haired Irish wife, he'd ask her, but she might tell or she might not. Katie was contrary, but he liked her fine. She made his youngest brother a good wife, and she had healing ways. He wouldn't call her a witch, but the woman had talents he didn't begin to understand. Jacob hadn't forgotten the eerie episode last Halloween when Katie claimed the unearthly howls they all heard had been a banshee or that Katie's young brother, Connor, who had become a dependable hand on the ranch, died a short time later when he ran afoul of a nest of rattlesnakes.

Because of the mustang's unpredictable nature, Jacob kept him separated from the other horses for safety. After Liam had gone, Boone turned to him. "You're welcome to come for supper if you want. Rachel's not got anything fancy, but it'll stick to your ribs. You're looking skinny as a fence rail these days."

Jacob laughed. "Hard work and a long, hot summer,

Boone. I appreciate the invite, but I think I'll go fix myself some of those frijoles. I borrowed that Mark Twain book Moses has and thought I'd read it for a spell."

All the Wilsons could read and enjoyed it when time permitted. As adults, they seldom had much opportunity, but Jacob had little else to do in the long evenings and had been rediscovering reading for pleasure.

"*Roughing It?*" Boone asked. "It's a fair read. If you ain't comin' to eat tonight, come for Sunday dinner tomorrow. We'll eat chicken and noodles at my house, although Mattie's making the noodles and Katie promised bread of some kind."

"I will, then." It sounded delicious, and Moses' German wife made the best noodles he'd ever put in his mouth. "Hey, Boone?"

"What?"

"I got a bad feelin' about that gray mustang," Jacob told him. "Promise me you won't ride it, nor let Ezekiel or Moses neither."

Boone nodded. "I don't plan to get within biting distance of that animal," he said. "I don't rightly know what we'll do with the horse, but I give you my word, Jacob. I won't try to break him, and I'll see none of you do neither. Might keep him for breeding, I don't rightly know."

"I'd get him off the place first chance you get."

"I do believe that would be wise," Boone said. "I'll study on how to get rid of the mustang. Come around dinnertime tomorrow or before. You're always welcome at my house."

He knew that, but it was good to hear. "I'll be there, Boone. G'night."

Over Sunday dinner, a delicious spread that included the chicken and dumplings, light bread as well as Irish scones that Katie contributed, leather britches beans seasoned with bacon, and raisin pie, no one mentioned the mustang. Instead, they talked about autumn, cooler than usual for this far south in Texas, and the winter.

"I reckon it'll be a cold one," Moses said. "My old bones ain't looking forward to that."

"You're not old," his wife Mattie said with a nudge and smile.

"Naw, it's Boone that's old," Ezekiel said with a wink.

Two years older than Jacob, Boone turned thirty-four in September. Other than a few gray hairs mixed with the brown and a few lines cut deep into his face, he hadn't aged much. He remained fit, heavier than Jacob, but then he was too slender. On occasion, Boone's back pained him, but he was a long way from old age.

"I ain't so old as that," Boone said. "Liam's a good five years older, if you're countin'."

That put the man at almost forty, Jacob thought. His wife, the pretty Maggie, had to be younger. "Is his wife as old as that?"

Mattie frowned at him. "She's not, although she's older than me," she said. "If I remember right, she's thirty-one, hardly an old crone."

Jacob had marked his 32nd birthday last January. In the coming year, he would be 33. Maggie was just a bit younger, closer in age than he had thought. If she weren't Liam's wife, she'd be a spinster, but of an age right for him. Since she was married, he dismissed the thought as those gathered laughed.

"I'm less than two years younger than Boone," he said. "I surely don't think of myself as an old man."

"You're not, and neither am I," Boone said. "Let's have some pie."

His youngest, Sarah Rose, grunted as her tiny face turned red and she filled her diaper. A powerful stench radiated from her, and although Rachel took her from Katie's arms to change it, Katie's pale face turned a greenish hue.

She gulped, then, without a word, bolted outside. Ezekiel tossed down his napkin and followed, but she didn't go far. The unmistakable sound of retching could be heard even with most of the windows closed. Mattie handed Ellie to Moses and wet a rag. She followed Ezekiel, who returned before the women.

"Is she sick?" Moses asked.

Ezekiel beamed. "Naw, she's with child," he replied. "She wanted to wait to say anything, but she gets sick like this a good bit. I reckon I'd best take her home, though."

Boone rose and opened a window for fresh air. As he did, Mattie and Katie returned.

"Ye needn't do that," Katie said. Her face was white, and she dabbed at it with the rag Mattie had brought. "I'll be right in a moment."

Zeke pulled out a chair for her. "I'll take you home if you want, pretty girl."

She shook her head. "I want to stay, Ezekiel. I suppose ye told them why I boked."

He grinned. "I did."

"He's proud as if he did this on his own," she said. "Ye'd think no man ever would be a da before him."

Seven-year-old Mima smiled. "Z's gonna be a daddy?"

Katie nodded. "That he is."

"I like babies," the little girl said. "I'll help you tend it when it comes."

"Good thing you're fond of them," Boone said. "We've plenty in the family now. She's good with the little ones, though, Katie, even at her age."

"Aye, she's grand. I've seen her with the wanes. 'Twill be a spring baby, that I know."

"You need to write Ma," Ezekiel said. "She'll be glad to hear the news."

Although all of them could read and write, Boone, as the

oldest, did most of the letter writing. Sometimes one of the other brothers might add a postscript or note, but he handled the family correspondence most of the time.

Rachel returned with her youngest daughter and handed her to Boone. "I've got to clear the table and wash the dishes."

Mima held out her arms. "I'll take Rosie-Posey."

That was the little girl's nickname for her sister. Her father put the child in her arms.

"Sit in the rocking chair with her, then."

"I will."

Since it was Sunday and he had the time, Boone got out paper and pen.

Dear Ma,

I hope this letter finds you and the family well. It's now November, and so things have slowed down on the ranch. We are all well, although Ezekiel and his bride have a bit of news. They will bring a baby into this world come spring. That will make six grandbabies here in Texas that you've not seen, my four, Moses' daughter, and now a new Wilson. Our partner Liam Rafferty, who you may recall from previous letters, has two, so there will be eight little ones on the ranch. Rachel has taught the ones who are old enough to read and write. My little Mima loves to read and has a storybook she likes. She likes to hear stories, too, and no one tells them the way you do.

I think of you often, Ma, and of old Kentucky with fond memories. I doubt that I'll ever return as I thought I would, but it would do my heart good to see you once more.

If you come to Texas, you will be welcomed by your four sons here and our families. You can bunk with Jacob in the small cabin, so there's room for you.

Give Garrett our regards and love.

Your son,

Boone Wilson

Each of them added their names below his: Jacob, Moses, Ezekiel, Rachel, Mattie, Katie, and even Mima.

"I'll send it next time I get to Laredo," Ezekiel said.

Jacob shook his head. "After what happened to you there last year, I'll take it myself," he said. "Or at least accompany you."

"Ain't necessary," Zeke said, although he looked down while he spoke.

"I'd say it is," Boone added. "Now that you have a wife and a child on the way to raise, you might ought to take more care."

Their kid brother had returned from what was meant to be a routine trip to Laredo the previous year, beaten and stabbed. If they hadn't tracked him down and found him where he'd fallen from his horse on the way home, he would have likely died. Ezekiel had recovered from the beating, but the worst of the stab wounds had festered, requiring Boone to take extreme measures he'd learned during the war to treat it.

Jacob stayed until dark, talking, smoking, and singing with the family. Rachel fed them leftovers come supper time with freshly made biscuits. Jacob enjoyed the time with his family, and until he came home to his small, dark cabin, he'd all but forgotten about the berserk horse.

Out in the separate stall where he'd locked it, the animal threshed and kicked, causing a ruckus that had the other horses riled.

His earlier unease about the horse returned and kept him awake for a long time, smoking and wondering why it disturbed him so. Jacob trusted Boone's opinion, and his brother also had issues with the mustang. He wasn't sure what Boone would have done with the animal if Liam hadn't been so set on breaking it, but if it were up to Jacob, he thought he'd get the creature off the ranch before anyone got injured or killed.

CHAPTER TWO

In November, Ezekiel managed to shoot three wild turkeys, which would become the centerpiece of the Wilson Thanksgiving dinner. Liam had plans to butcher a hog, then roast it for the hands as he'd done in other years. Cookie would fix other dishes, and it would be a feast.

Maggie had offered to host a meal for her family and the Wilsons, connected to the Rafferty family through her sister Mattie, now Moses' wife. Liam had also been a friend of Boone's for years, first serving together during the Civil War, then going west together. It had been Liam who started the ranch and persuaded Boone to stay. Jacob had heard the stories many times as the last of the four Wilson brothers to call the Double Deuce home. His brothers were partners in the operation and had urged him to put some money into it as they had. So far, he hadn't.

Boone turned down Maggie's invitation and asked the Raffertys to join them instead.

Jacob had contributed a dozen squirrels he'd shot for the dinner, and Mattie said she would also make pies. Katie promised Irish stew, so there would be a well-rounded menu.

The week before Thanksgiving, though, the weather warmed in a brief Indian summer. Jacob went about in shirtsleeves instead of wearing a coat and long underwear.

On the Tuesday before Thanksgiving, he awakened early to hear wild hoofbeats along with shouting in the corral and rushed outside to see what the ruckus was about. He found Liam in the corral with the gray mustang, a rope in one hand, facing the crazed stallion.

"Liam, I'd not recommend being near that horse," Jacob

said. "He's a danger."

"He's not," Liam replied, shaking his head until his unruly black hair flew in every direction. "He's just spirited. I still hold that he'll make a fine mount and a sturdy horse. I've little else to do with the holiday this week, so I decided I'd come down and break him today."

Jacob shivered as a cold chill shuddered through his body, what Ma had always called someone walking over your grave. "Don't, Liam, he's likely to hurt you or worse."

Ezekiel arrived, out of breath from running. "I heard all the noise. What's the fuss?"

"Liam means to ride that gray mustang," Jacob replied. "It's a poor idea and I have a bad feeling about it."

"Boone said none of us were to attempt to mount that hell stallion."

"I made him promise we wouldn't, but that didn't include Liam. Fetch Boone and hurry. Maybe he can talk him out of this notion."

Liam circled the mustang, talking in a soft voice as the animal rampaged. It reared and galloped, kicked, and rushed toward him. As Jacob watched, the stallion bit Liam, tearing a chunk from his arm. Blood poured from it, but Liam ignored it, intent on mastering the beast.

"Whatever ye do, don't get close." Katie stood at Jacob's side. "I'll tell ye what I told my man – that horse will bring death."

Jacob nodded. "I believe that."

Her voice was unbelievably soft as she said. "I've seen it. 'Twill be today, Jacob."

"Dear Lord." Boone had arrived. He approached the corral but stopped short of entering it. "Liam, don't be a fool, man."

Rafferty offered a rakish grin. "I'm not, but I'll tame this horse and show you all. And you said Wilsons were good with horses."

"We are, and not one of us would take the chance with that devil," Boone replied.

Liam laughed. He managed to get a rope around the stallion's neck, but the beast reared high and knocked him down in the process. Liam cussed and came to his feet only for the horse to knock him hard against the fence. When the horse retreated, Jacob could see that Liam's left arm hung at an odd angle.

"His arm's busted," Boone said. "I cain't see how he can hold on, but he's doing it."

Jacob shrugged. "They say where there's a will, there's a way.

The determination on Liam's face changed to anger. He flushed crimson as he came at the mustang. In one swift motion, he vaulted onto its back and dug his uninjured hand into the mane. From where he stood, Jacob could see Liam's knuckles grow white with the effort of holding tight. The horse reared, then began to buck in a wild frenzy. Liam held his seat for a few moments, then flew into the dirt and landed hard. He stood up, chest heaving with the effort, and came at the horse. Once more, he managed to climb onto his back, but the beast tossed him again.

Liam rose, staggering, and came toward the stallion, his fist clenched as if he intended to hit the creature square between the eyes. The horse caught Liam with its lashing hooves and put him down. As the man fought to rise, the stallion came down again and struck him three times. Liam lay still, face down in the dirt, and didn't attempt to rise.

"He's hurt," Ezekiel said.

The animal stomped Liam again, striking the back of his head with a flying hoof, then kicked him.

"He's dead," Boone stated with sorrow in his voice. "I fear Liam is dead."

The mustang twirled in circles, still kicking like a

whirlwind, moving in every direction at once. His eyes rolled back with the whites showing, wild and crazed. He roared, a far deeper sound than a whinny, and to those watching, it sounded like a shout of triumph. Then he rushed toward the fence, toward where they stood.

None of them moved until Boone, his face a grim mask, drew his Griswold and shot the rampaging creature between the eyes. When it screamed but didn't go down, he fired again. The horse landed beside Liam's unmoving body, thrashed, then died. Blood from man and beast blended into a red puddle that soaked into the Texas dirt.

Jacob rushed into the corral, followed by Boone.

"Stay right there," Boone growled toward Ezekiel and Katie.

Boone turned Liam over with a careful hand, but there was no mistaking that he was dead. The back of his head had been bashed in by a stray hoof. His sightless eyes stared upward, so Boone shut them with one finger. He removed his hat, and so did Jacob to show respect. Katie made the sign of the Cross.

The shots brought Moses and several hands. They halted at the sight of Liam's body, then their voices rose with questions and shocked outcries.

"What happened?" Moses asked after he reached Ezekiel.

"He was hellbent on breaking that mustang," Zeke told him. "Paid for it with his life."

"He's dead?"

"Stone cold."

"Who killed the horse?" Moses said.

"I did after he killed Liam," Boone said. "The crazy horse could have hurt or killed someone else, and God help us if he'd got out of the corral. He would've wreaked havoc on the ranch."

The word of Liam's passing spread like wildfire to the hands. One by one, they arrived at the corral, some still buttoning their shirts. When they saw the boss lying still, they doffed their hats to show respect. Boone asked Deacon Lee and Mac to get a group to carry Liam's remains home. Like him, they'd served with Liam during the war and followed him to Texas. Then he asked another of the hands to tell Spider Webb that they'd need a coffin made. Once he'd assigned tasks, Boone came out of the corral.

"We had best go tell Maggie about Liam," he said. "She needs to know."

"I'll go with you," Moses said. "Maggie'll need Mattie, but my wife's gonna need me."

"Davy or Beau, go tell my wife what's happened," Boone said. "Ezekiel and Jacob, you'd best come with me, too."

"I'll come," Katie spoke up, although she had turned paler than fresh fallen snow.

"I'd rather you mind Moses' baby," Boone told her. "Take Ellie to your place. Will you help lay Liam out when it's time? I don't reckon his wife will feel able."

"I will. 'Tis a task I've done before."

Mattie met them at the cabin door, eyes worried. "I heard the shouting and the shots," she said. "I was worried."

"We're all fine," Moses told her as he picked up Ellie and held her close. "But Liam's not."

"Is he hurt?"

"He's dead," Boone told her. "That crazy horse kilt him. Katie, here, will take care of Ellie, but I reckon your sister will have need of you."

"*Ach der Lieber Gott,*" Mattie said. "I imagine that she will. Let me get my shawl, and I'll come."

Moses handed his daughter to Katie. "If she gets hungry, bring her to Maggie's if Mattie's not back."

"Aye, I will."

Jacob tapped Boone's shoulder as they headed toward the

main house. "If you want me to go make sure Rachel's heard the news, I can go over there."

"Naw, one of the hands should have already done it. I need you with me."

His voice carried deep sorrow, and Jacob recalled that Boone first met Liam when both were Confederate soldiers in the war. Their close friendship didn't end when the war did. Boone trailed to Texas after Liam, worked together with him on several cattle drives and ranches, then came to work for Liam when he bought the place. Although in Jacob's eyes, Liam had changed from the man he must have been, but he'd still been a friend to Boone and a good one.

Jacob would have gone to tell Maggie even if Boone hadn't insisted that all the Wilsons go. He considered Maggie a friend, and though he'd never shared his other feelings about her, he wanted to be on hand to offer what help and comfort he could.

They walked the short distance to the main ranch house. He heard Maggie singing inside the house as she baked. The delicious aroma of cookies wafted toward them as they approached, and although he didn't speak German, he recognized the song as "*Du, Du, Liegst Mir in Herzen*". He'd heard it sung, and from what Mattie had once said, it wasn't quite a love song but more a lament that longed for a deep love, one that was lacking.

She didn't hear their approach on foot, and most were silent. Boone went around to the kitchen door, the others falling behind, and knocked. Normally, he didn't, not if Liam was at home, but this was different. The song stopped, and Maggie came to the door, her pretty face flushed from baking. Although she wore an apron, flour dusted her skirt, and her welcoming expression turned wary when she saw all four Wilson brothers and her sister.

"*Was ist los?*" she asked.

"I've got sad news for you, Maggie," Boone said as he

removed his hat. Jacob and the others followed suit. "I don't reckon there's any good way to say it but..."

Maggie paled. "Liam's dead, isn't he? I can't think of another thing that would bring you all here, your faces so serious and my sister with you."

Boone nodded. "He is, and I'm right sorry. That gray mustang killed him, and I've got the hands bringing him home to you. If you want, I'll send someone off to San Antonio to tell your family and bring your children back so we can lay Liam to rest."

She stepped back and let them all enter, then sat down at the kitchen table. Maggie shook her head. "*Nein, nein. Jawohl,* send word to my parents, and they can tell the children, but we can't wait for them to come. It takes almost a week, and we can't wait to bury my husband."

So far, the woman hadn't cried, but her face was haggard. Ma had always told them that folks grieve in different ways. Mattie sat down beside her sister and took her hands.

"Maggie, we can wait if necessary."

"No, we mustn't. It may be cold, but it's not cold enough to keep Liam from stinking. Who'll make the coffin?"

"Spider will," Boone said. Then he must have realized Liam's wife, now a widow, might not know the hands by nicknames. "Otis Webb, the trail cook, makes such, and I've already sent word for him to get started. Some of the hands will bring Liam home, but I'd advise you not to look at him. He's mighty busted up from the horse."

Maggie lifted her head with dignity. "I must see him. After all, I was his wife, and I'll have to lay him out."

"Ezekiel's wife Katie will do that task for you," Jacob spoke, his voice gentle. "Boone's right. You'd be better to remember Liam as he was, Maggie."

Her dark blue eyes met his. "Do you truly think so, Jacob?"

He nodded. "I do."

The way the back of Liam's head had been crushed was liable to give him nightmares, he thought, and it would be far easier if Maggie didn't have that awful image in her mind. Liam had died in pain, face contorted with it, and although Boone had closed his friend's eyes, the man looked far from at peace.

"Then I'll take your advice," Maggie replied. "It's hard to believe. We sat here at this table this very morning, although he said little. I watched him drink his coffee and eat a bite of bacon, then he went, eager to work with that horse he found so appealing. He didn't kiss me goodbye nor look back."

Mattie tried to hug her sister, but Maggie sat straight without yielding. "Sister, he had no idea he wouldn't be back."

"I know." Maggie's tone was hollow. "I've no notion what to do first. So many things to do."

Boone knelt before the new widow. "I'm here to do whatever you need me to do. Liam and I have been friends for years, served together in the war. I wouldn't even be in Texas if it hadn't been for Liam. Deacon Lee and me followed him down here. Tell me what you want done and I'll do it."

"Any of us will offer our help," Jacob said. He still stood near the kitchen door, Moses and Ezekiel flanking him.

Maggie sat still, like a wounded creature, and said nothing for a few minutes. Then she sighed. "He'd want a priest, I think, so we must send for one. That priest, the one who did Katie's brother's funeral, what was his name?"

"Father Leveillee," Ezekiel told her, speaking for the first time since they arrived. "I can go fetch him."

"He'll need to know when the burying will be," Boone said. "I reckon you'd best decide on that first. Once you have, we'll send for him and anyone else you might want. If the weather stays cold, and I think it will for a day or two, you don't have to make a rush."

"There's no need to wait," Maggie said. "I'd rather it be

done than not. I'd like to have Liam's funeral on Thanksgiving."

"That's just two days, sister," Mattie said. "I don't know if that's enough time."

"It must be," Maggie stated. "We planned a feast, so we can eat that food for the dinner after."

"You need black dresses, a widow's veil, and such," Mattie told her. "We can send to Laredo for some, although I doubt they have any readymade. They might in San Antonio. Our parents could bring the widow's weeds when they come if you'll wait."

"No," Maggie said. "I won't wait. If there's none to be had, then we'll dye some of my dresses black."

"I reckon we can find something black in town," Boone told her. "I can send one of the hands to find out when they go to fetch the Father. Even if it's cloth and veiling, my wife and the other ladies will sew a dress if there's the need."

"*Ja*, then," Maggie said. "You ought to send someone today, Boone, so they can go and return."

"I will," Boone told her. "Deacon Lee will likely go to Laredo. He can visit his wife whilst he's there, and I reckon Jack would go too."

The delicious aroma of baking was replaced by the sharp stench of cookies burning. Maggie gasped when she realized and started to rise. Jacob, closer to the stove, grabbed a rag and pulled out the sheets with ruined cookies. He burned his hand a bit doing it, but said nothing. He stepped to the door and tossed the black discs into the yard.

"I burned the cookies," Maggie said. "Oh, dear."

"It's only cookies," her sister told her. "If we need more, we'll bake them."

"Who will take word to San Antonio?" Maggie asked and looked at Boone.

Jacob knew his brother wouldn't leave his family long enough for that trek, especially not in the current situation. He parted his lips to volunteer, then realized he would rather be on the ranch to help Maggie rather than gone.

"Mac will go," Boone replied. "If you want, I'll write a letter with the news for your folks."

Maggie shook her head. "I will do that, although I appreciate the offer. You can't write in German, and I can."

Jacob made coffee, and Mattie fixed biscuits with sausage and gravy.

"I can't eat," Maggie told her, staring at the food.

"Someone will," Mattie told her. "Tell Boone who needs to be brought from Laredo besides Father Leveillee."

Maggie listed them, writing each name down on a fresh sheet of paper. There was Judge Masters, she thought he should be there, and possibly the current sheriff, although no one really knew him. She added the names of the livery stable owner, a few other businessmen, two lawyers, and two other veterans who served with Liam in the war.

"That's all I can think of at the moment," she said and handed the list to Boone.

Mattie took it and added nine to ten yards of black material as well as black veiling and thread. "It's enough for one dress," she said. "Maybe he should buy enough for two."

Boone set out to see what progress Spider had made on the coffin. Liam's body, covered with a sheet, remained outside in the wagon that had carried it home from the corral. With Mattie's help, Maggie chose garments for Liam to wear: a black broadcloth suit, a good shirt, and a jacket.

Then she took pen and paper to write the letter with the news. Maggie wrote in German, but her sister read it to them all in English.

Dear Mama and Papa,

I, your daughter Magdalena, write with sad news. My husband, Liam Rafferty, was killed in a mishap with a horse this morning on the ranch. I made the choice to bury him in two days' time, on Thanksgiving, here on the ranch he loved.

There was no reason to wait until you or the children could come. Please tell Grace and Seamus that their father has died and bring them to the ranch to pay their respects.

I would like them to remain with me afterward, and I will not return to San Antonio. This is my home and where I will stay.

Do not send Gunther Hammerschmidt to this ranch. If he shows his face here, he will be removed.

I look forward to seeing you, the family, and my children despite the sad occasion that will bring you to the ranch.

With love, your daughter Magdalena Rafferty

"Is that enough?" Maggie asked. "I don't know what else to say."

"It's fine," Mattie told her. "It says all that needs to be told."

She had yet to shed a tear, but Jacob saw the ravages of grief in her face – that and something more.

CHAPTER THREE

His steps were slow. Boone's thoughts were both deep and dark as he walked home from delivering the news that Liam Rafferty, his friend, his compadre, and boss, had died that morning. Liam's widow had taken it hard, but that was to be expected. He'd stayed to offer a helping hand and a steady manner, but he craved his home and family.

Images from then and now haunted his thoughts as he walked, memories from the war years when he first met Liam, and they'd served together through the long conflict. He'd come to Texas with Liam, his imagination fired by tales of the distant land, and stayed. Once Liam bought a ranch, he'd gone to work for him until all these years later, he and his brothers were partners.

He'd barely finished his coffee when he heard the commotion at the corral and was gone before Rachel could serve him sausage and eggs. There hadn't been time for lunch, and the truth was, he hadn't been hungry. Now that old Spider, the trail cook, who also could do carpentry, had finished the coffin, Boone headed home.

His house lay no more than 100 feet from the dog trot cabin, but it seemed longer as he walked it. When he was almost within sight, he thought he heard someone crying. *Must be the children, fighting or fussing about something.* When Boone drew closer, however, he recognized Rachel's sobs as well as Mima's.

His heart pounded and his belly twisted into a knot. Boone hurried, and when he approached his home, he saw his wife sitting on the porch, weeping into her apron. Mima sat beside her, face blotched with tears as she cried. His two sons stood behind them, faces as serious as a sentry on duty.

Mima glanced up, and when she saw him, her face shifted. "Daddy!" she screamed. "Daddy!"

She came off the step in one motion, braids and skirt flying, and ran to him. When she had almost reached him, she leaped into the air, and he caught her. Mima locked her arms around his neck and kissed his face over and over. "Daddy, you're home."

Rachel stood up and stared. Then she ran across the few feet between them, still weeping. Boone, fearing some new tragedy, set his daughter down. "Go tend to your brothers," he said. "Rachel, what's the matter?"

"Boone, oh, Boone," she cried as she reached him. "I thought it was you. They told me it was you."

For a moment, he failed to understand, and then he did. "Who told you what?"

Rachel clung to him, and he pulled her into his arms. "Davy, that kid, that hand, Davy," she sobbed. "He came and told me you were dead, that the horse killed you."

"It was Liam," he told her, his voice gentle. "Liam got killed. He told you it was me?"

"He said that the boss was killed. You're the top hand, and so I thought it was you," she said. "Some of them call you 'boss,' and he didn't give me any details. And when you didn't come home, I thought…"

She began sobbing, and he cradled her close. "Hush, honey, hush. I ain't dead and I'm sorry you thought I was. I had to tell Maggie the sad news, and then I've been there, helping see to things. I come home as soon as I could. If I'd thought for a cotton-picking minute, they'd make you think it was me, I'd have sent Jacob or Ezekiel."

"I love you, Boone, so very much," Rachel said. "I'm so glad you're alive. I didn't think I could bear to be a widow."

"Honey, I love you more than anything, and you ain't a

widow," Boone replied. His heart ached for her, suffering through hours when she believed him dead. He'd been terrified when she had difficulties bringing Sarah Rose into the world, certain he couldn't live without her and could only imagine how she must have felt.

Eight years married come December, he loved her more than ever. Like most married folks raising a family, they'd fallen into new routines, and their life revolved around the babies. Rachel had the work of the children and the house while Boone spent his days on the ranch, often from daylight to dark as the top hand. Still, they always found time for a caress or kiss. He savored their quiet moments alone in bed, snuggled up and talking as much as intimacy, maybe more. He had been convinced he was dying when they met, and so was everyone else. A gunshot wound to the chest had made that outcome seem likely, but Rachel refused to accept it. She'd nursed him through and had removed the bullet with her own hands.

As if their love hadn't been tested enough, he'd been arrested for a murder he didn't commit and spent the first few months of their marriage in jail, with the gallows waiting. Liam had worked to free him, but it'd been his brother Moses who found the truth. Boone had intended to go home to Kentucky, taking Ezekiel, who was just fifteen, with him, but once he learned Rachel was expecting, his plans changed. They'd come to the ranch and been there since.

Boone didn't think all married folks displayed their affection openly. His parents had, he recalled, but it had been subtle. Moses and Ezekiel were still newlyweds, still in the honeymoon phase.

Today, he needed to give Rachel some time and his attention to make up for the terrible misunderstanding. Boone kissed her, for once, not minding the children would see, and held her close. She clung to him, her arms tight as if she'd never let go. She began to shake in his arms, and her legs trembled so hard he could feel it. He figured it was a delayed reaction, but so she wouldn't fall, he lifted her up in his arms. Her arms locked around his neck, and he started for the house, pausing at the sight of the children. They were together, his boys sitting on either side of Mima, with tear-stained faces, but they smiled up at him.

"Where's Sarah Rose?" he asked his daughter.

"In the cradle for her nap," Mima replied. "Do you want me to fetch her before she wakes?"

"I do," he told her. "Will you mind her for now? I need to see to your mama."

"Is she sick?" Rob asked.

"Naw," Boone said. "Just scared and agitated because she thought I was a goner. She needs me right now, and your sister will tend to you."

"I will, Daddy," Mima promised.

Once she'd got the baby, Boone carried Rachel through the rooms to the last one, their bedroom. She didn't protest or say a word until he put her down on the bed. Rachel sat on the edge and gazed at him, eyes still brimming with tears.

"Are you feelin' alright?" he asked her. He undid his belt, putting the pistol and holster aside. Then he removed his jacket and vest, though it was cool in the room.

"I was heartbroken when I thought you were dead," she said. "I'm fine now."

"Are you?" Boone questioned. "You don't look it, honey."

Rachel sighed. "My head hurts."

He lifted one big hand to push the hair away from her face, then he rubbed her forehead. When she sighed, he almost smiled. "That feel good?"

"Yes, Boone."

"Then I'll keep on," he said, sitting next to her on the bed. "Then if you want, I'll brush out your hair and braid it."

It was something he seldom did, but that they both enjoyed. "I'd like that. Will you sing to me?"

A slow grin spread over his face. "I will, honey. Then, you're gonna sleep for a bit, and I'll make supper."

She lifted an eyebrow at that and smiled a little for the first time since he'd come home. "Will you?"

"I can cook a bit," he said with a grin. "Fed myself through four years of the war over campfires and plenty of times since. Besides, I reckon Jemima Ann will help me if I ask."

"She will," Rachel said as she reached up to undo her hair. "My hairbrush is over on the table."

Once she let down her hair, Boone caressed it with his hands, marveling at the length of it. Then he brushed it with slow, soft strokes, touching her every chance he had. When he judged that she'd become relaxed, he divided her hair into three sections and braided it, neat and tight.

"I never knew any other man who could braid hair the way you do," Rachel told him. She sounded sleepy

He wanted a smoke, but not enough to leave Rachel. "I ain't never braided any other gal's hair but yours and Mima's."

"Don't ever, Boone, except maybe our Sarah Rose's when she's older."

He laughed. "Are you ready to lay down for a spell?"

As he spoke, he slipped off her shoes and undid the knot that tied her apron around her waist.

"I shouldn't," she protested.

"It's been a hard day," Boone told her. "You could use the rest. These next few days are gonna be rough around the ranch."

"Stay with me and sing."

"I intend to," he said. "I'll stretch out there beside you for a bit if you'd like."

She fumbled toward him with a kiss. Boone tucked her into bed and covered her with a quilt. Then he lay down beside her on top of the covers. Rachel rolled toward him, and he put his arms around her. He sang to her in a low voice, not the same songs he sang to the babies at night but love songs, some he'd sung to her before they wed. She fell asleep in a few moments. He kissed her face and held her close, but couldn't sleep. Too many thoughts whirled around in his head like a dust devil dancing on a windy day. There were too many things yet to be done for Liam, and he'd just become the ranch boss by default.

After an hour, he rose and put his boots back on. He walked with quiet tread to see the children and found them at the table, eating cookies and drinking milk. Mima held her baby sister in the rocker. He picked up a chair. "I'm gonna be back with your mama for a bit more, but if you need me, just holler or fetch me."

"Uncle Z's outside," Mima said. "He needs to talk to you."

Boone hesitated. If he went to the porch, then he could smoke, but if Rachel woke, he wouldn't be there. It'd be easier to spend longer than he intended, for there was surely much to talk about. "Tell him to come back to the bedroom, baby girl."

He pulled the chair beside the bed and got comfortable. Ezekiel poked his head through the doorway. "Boone?"

"I'm here, come on in, just be quiet. Rachel's sleepin'."

Zeke came closer, wearing a frown. "She ain't sick or anything?"

"Naw, but she was told I had died, not Liam. She was powerful worked up when I came home."

His brother's eyes widened. "I'd think. How'd that happen?"

"Young Davy told her the boss was killed by a horse," he replied. "He didn't say a name, but she figured I'm the boss, and when I didn't come home, she thought the worst, the babies too."

"I come to tell you Katie laid out Liam, but we nailed the coffin shut. He's in no shape for folks to see, Maggie, least of all."

Boone nodded in agreement. "I reckon the coffin can stay

in the smokehouse for now. Ain't no place else and I don't figure Maggie needs it in the house, not when it's shut. What else?"

Zeke shrugged. "Nothing much happened after you left. Mattie and Moses went home with their baby, so Katie left too."

"Who's with Maggie? She ought not be left alone at a time like this."

"Jacob's with her," Ezekiel said.

"Ought to be a woman there."

"Ain't one handy," his younger brother said with a smile. "I think Mattie plans to go back and spend the night with her sister. I reckon that means Moses and the baby will be there too. Jacob said he'd light out once they got back."

Boone nodded. "I said I'd make supper before long with Mima's help, but I told Rachel I'd stay with her, too."

"Do you want Katie to come? I'll fetch her."

"Yeah, I do, Ezekiel. Thank you. Then I wouldn't have to fret over the babies. Mima's responsible, but she's still just seven years old."

Rachel stirred. "Boone?"

"I'm right here, honey."

She reached out for his hand and grasped it tight. "I was afraid it was a dream, that you weren't dead."

"It's real, honey."

"Howdy, Rachel," Ezekiel said.

She sat up. "How's Maggie?"

"She's stunned, like a bird that flew into a window," he said. "She ain't cried a lick yet. Jacob said that's 'cause it ain't really set in yet, but it will, and she will."

"I should go to her," Rachel said.

"Not today, honey," Boone told her, but his voice was gentle. "Katie's gonna come help make supper. I'll start some cornbread while waiting. I reckon the babies want to see you, and Miss Sarah Rose probably is getting hungry."

Rachel put a hand to her breasts. "I imagine so."

Boone stroked her face. "I'll fetch her."

He did as he'd said and mixed up a batch of cornbread with Mima's supervision. He didn't tell her he'd made it many times before or made ramrod rolls with it during the war. Ezekiel left to bring his wife. By the time Katie arrived, Boone had the cornbread baking in the oven. Although there was a fireplace in the main room, he'd bought Rachel a cast iron step stove for the kitchen. Katie fried potatoes, a cabbage she brought with her from the fall harvest, and bacon to complete the meal.

Rachel joined them as they gathered around the table, bringing the baby with her. Boone took his youngest daughter so she could eat first. She rewarded him with a smile and ate with one hand on his knee as if she feared he'd vanish if she wasn't touching him.

Boone ate after she did, his insides nearly caved in since he hadn't eaten all day. Comforting his wife had been more important. Jacob arrived in time to eat as well. After the meal, Rachel put the baby to bed in the cradle and announced she'd do the dishes.

"Boone, I know you want a smoke," she said. "And I'm sure you want to talk with Jacob. Katie's had a long day, and so has Ezekiel. I'll wash up with Mima's help if you'll mind the boys."

Boone settled at the table with his brother Jacob and his two sons. He rolled and fired a smoke while Jacob did the same. The domestic sounds from the kitchen were pleasant to his ear, a reminder that life continues. Rob tugged at Boone's sleeve.

"Daddy, were you dead?"

He pulled the little boy onto his lap. "No, son, it was a misunderstanding. One of the hands gave your mama news that made her think I was."

"I'm glad you ain't," the kid said and hugged his father

around the neck.

"Me too, son."

Jacob scooped up Benjamin and held him on one knee. Going on three, he could talk a little, although his words weren't always easy to understand. Now, he said, "Jay," and that meant his uncle.

"What all happened after I left?" Boone asked. "I'm glad I came home, since Rachel thought it was me that was killed. I ain't never seen her so addled."

Jacob took a long draw on his cigarette. "Katie, bless her, got Liam cleaned up as much as anybody could and dressed. Once Spider had the coffin made, Ezekiel and I wrassled him into it and nailed the lid shut. Warn't any need for folks to see Liam. Even face up, he was a mangled mess. We put the coffin in the smokehouse for now. Gotta bury him, though, before he starts to smell."

"Maggie still planning on Thanksgiving Day?"

Jacob nodded. "She wants it to be soon, she said."

"That's for the best, but she cain't change her mind once he's planted. Those hardheaded Germans will get here, I have no doubt." Boone told him. "Figure they'll want to take Maggie back with them to live in San Antonio."

His brother's eyes met his. "Maggie fears the same, but they'll never arrive in time before the funeral. Maggie wrote it all out in a letter Mac carried with him."

Boone sighed and crushed out his cigarette. "Danged if that doesn't make a conundrum."

"How so?"

"Somebody's got to look after her, keep them fed and all," he replied. "Likely that's gonna fall to me, and I'll have more than enough on my plate with Liam gone. I'll have to be ranch boss, not just the top hand now, unless one of you wants to take it up."

"Not me," Jacob said. "But I'll look after Maggie's needs. I done told her I would. That seemed to ease her mind a bit."

Boone had one question. "Why?"

"Somebody's got to do it," Jacob said. "I know what it's like to bury your other half, and besides, I've a fondness for the woman."

Boone groaned. He'd suspected something of the sort. Jacob shot him a hard look, so he put one hand over his gut. "I got wind from the cabbage," he said. "It's hard on my belly."

Which was true enough, but the idea that Jacob had an attraction to the just widowed Maggie complicated things more than a bit of flatulence. She was a pretty woman, but she likely wouldn't be in any state of mind to be courted. Decency required a widow to wait at least a year. His brother had set his sights on the least available woman around, and that concerned Boone. More troubling still, Boone recalled what Liam had confided to him last year, that marriage hadn't been all he had hoped.

"Do you ever find yourself wishing you were still footloose and fancy free, Boone?" had been Liam's question, one that Boone had answered with a resounding 'never'. Liam had then explained that he longed for his bachelor days, when he had no responsibilities and admitted he found a wife and family more convenience than necessity.

Since that confidence, Boone had told nobody. Instead, he'd watched and pondered. Although not married nearly as long, Boone had four children and Liam two. Liam acted pleasant toward his wife and family, but not affectionate. Once aware of Liam's feelings, he realized he couldn't recall the last time he'd seen Liam kiss his wife.

He had been aware that Jacob and Maggie had become friends. There had been moments when he'd worried it was more, at least on his brother's part. Jacob had loved his late wife and mourned hard, but he did seem to be sweet on Maggie Rafferty.

Boone clenched his mouth shut, though, and decided not to say anything more. What would happen would come, and all the worries in the world wouldn't change that.

"I'll go see Maggie come morning," Boone said. "We can bury Liam on Thanksgiving Day if that's what she wants. I don't figure there's gonna be much joy in feasting, although it will still happen."

"That's her plan, Boone. Deke will bring the priest and the other folks Maggie wants here for the funeral on Thursday."

Boone sighed. "I'll go see Maggie again come morning. If she doesn't stay, we're gonna need to buy Liam's share of the place. I don't fancy sharing ownership with that pack of Germans."

"I'll go with you," Jacob said. "I'm heading for my place to grab some shuteye, but I'll see you in the morning, Boone."

"I'll be here."

Jacob started for the door and then turned back with a grin. "Like the little boy said, I'm right glad you ain't dead, Boone."

Boone rubbed his belly, passed a little gas, and lit another smoke.

After that conversation, he needed it.

CHAPTER FOUR

Thanksgiving Day dawned fair but cool. Although the old saying was that blessed are the dead the rain falls on, Jacob found he was glad that the weather was fine. Maggie liked it too, said so.

"I'm glad it's a pretty day to lay Liam to rest," she told Jacob. He'd come early to help her if she needed anything done. "Though he'd work in all weathers, he was never fond of the rain or snow or cold."

Jacob found that persnickety for any class of rancher or even farmer. Back home in Kentucky, they'd never let any weather keep them from work or chores. What needed to be done had to be finished. Since coming to Texas, he'd watched his brothers go about their tasks without shirking or complaint. Still, he didn't comment. It might not please the new widow to hear what he thought. He'd liked Liam well enough, but he'd not had the history that Boone had with the man. Jacob thought Liam lacked the deep devotion that his brothers demonstrated to their families and that he had once given Sally Ann.

Maggie appeared to cope with her new status as a widow. Although he'd arrived before sunup, she had already risen, dressed, put up her hair, and made coffee. He accepted a cup, then offered to make breakfast. Since Liam died, one of them had tried to be with Maggie each day, for otherwise, she would be alone.

"I'm glad you can cook," Maggie told Jacob with a small smile.

Jacob nodded. "Ma made sure all of us, even boys, could. It's come in mighty handy, too. I ain't saying I'm a great cook, and some things are too complicated for me, but I can fry up some bacon and eggs if you'd like."

"I would," she replied with a quiet sigh. "Why, Liam couldn't so much as boil water. Oh, I suppose he did out on the trail, for he must have made coffee from time to time, or cooked something, but at home, the kitchen was mine. Can you bake biscuits?"

"I can," he replied. "They're none too pretty, but they eat all right. I've only made them on the trail and once for Boone's family. I can make some if you'd like."

"I wouldn't mind a biscuit." Maggie shared.

Jacob made a mess in preparing some, but he managed to stir, knead, cut out, and bake biscuits without burning them. As they baked, he cooked bacon in a heavy iron skillet, then fried eggs in the grease.

They sat together at the table and ate. Even though he'd prepared it, Jacob thought he served a decent enough breakfast. Maggie, who'd eaten little since Boone told her about her husband, managed to eat the eggs, a slice of bacon, and a biscuit.

"This is good," she told him. "Thank you, Jacob. You have a talent for cooking."

His face warmed with a blush. "I wouldn't say that so much, but I can keep a body from starvation."

"It's not just the food that helps," Maggie said. "You're good company. You don't ask me how I am or think I should talk all the time. You know when to be quiet and when to say a word. And you don't judge me if I'm not crying."

"I won't mind if you do, though."

"Did you weep when your wife died?"

Her question gave him pause. "I did," he replied after a moment. "But not where anyone could see."

"I haven't cried a bit," Maggie told him. "I'm sad, *ja*, but these last years, Liam's been gone so much. He sent Grace and Seamus away so they could go to school against my wishes. You might remember that my family disowned both me and Mattie after she wed Moses. I thought we'd have more children, but we never did. I've spent many hours alone, wondering what happened, why Liam didn't want to spend his time with me, not the way he used to do. We sat at this table, and most of the time, he had little to say."

"You may cry yet, you never know," Jacob said.

Maggie shrugged. "I'll mourn him, but it was almost like he's been gone longer. I got used to being without him, I suppose."

Jacob realized he had become accustomed to living without Sally Ann. He had never put it into words, but he had built a new life. His existence now revolved around his family and the ranch. It had been so long since he'd sat at the table with his wife with coffee and casual conversation, he had trouble remembering how it had been. The three girls had always been there, bouncing about, adding to the talk, or getting scolded. Breakfast with Maggie suited him, and he enjoyed it enough to long for more mornings such as this.

Remember it's the day of her husband's funeral, he reminded himself, *don't get carried away and don't risk your heart*. It was too late, though, he already had. Somewhere over the past year or two, he'd gone from wanting to offer friendship to caring about Maggie; until now, he loved her.

"We'll have a dinner after the burying, with the food that would have been for Thanksgiving," he told her now. "I reckon we'll have it here if you don't mind. There's more space. We did send word over to Laredo, and there may be some from there. The priest is coming, I know. Judge Masters, most likely, and others."

Liam had been born, baptized, and raised Catholic, although Jacob had never known him to go to church. Boone said he hadn't either.

She finished her coffee and nodded after blotting her lips with a napkin. "I don't. I've nothing else to do, not really. That will change once my parents come and bring my children. Then it will be a fight."

"It don't have to be," Jacob said. "They can't make you go back to San Antone with them."

Maggie's laugh was bitter, not bright. "They will try, though. Grace and Seamus should have been here for the funeral, but we can't wait. I'd rather they stay with me, but I doubt very much they will. Saying no to them all will be hard."

"I'll stand with you, Maggie."

"*Ja,* I know you will. Germans are hardheaded and like to fight. They will do their best to force me. You weren't here when they sent Gunther to bring Mattie back."

"No, I wasn't, but I've heard. Heard Moses wed Mattie when he could barely stand up after being so sick."

She sipped coffee. "That's true. If it comes to it, would you marry me to prevent me from being taken back against my will?"

Jacob must have heard wrong. He stuck a finger in his left ear and wiggled it.

"I don't reckon I heard you right," he said after a long pause. "You didn't say marry?"

"I did," Mattie replied. "Moses and Mattie got wed to keep Gunther Hammerschmidt from dragging her home. Maybe I shouldn't have said anything. I don't suppose you'd even want to wed anyone."

There were times to be quiet and times to be bold. He spoke up. "I'd marry you if that's what it takes to make you happy, and keep you from getting hauled off to San Antonio, Maggie. I reckon you know I've got a fondness for you. It'd be a scandal, though."

Maggie reached across the table and took his hand in hers. "You've become a friend to me, Jacob Wilson, but more than that.

I should not say such things before my husband is buried, but I could do far worse. You're a good man, Jacob."

He couldn't believe what she said. It had to be a dream. Never had he imagined that Maggie would consider becoming his wife, not under any circumstance. Until a few days ago, it had been impossible since she was married to Liam. Jacob never allowed himself to dream of such a possibility, and now Maggie talked about it as if it were not just plausible but possible.

"A widow ain't supposed to get married for at least a year."

Maggie snorted. "*Ach, Quatsch, das macht nichts!*" she told him.

Before he could part his lips to ask what that meant, Rachel and Mattie walked into the kitchen, hands filled with food.

"What nonsense doesn't matter?" Mattie asked, narrowing her eyes. Jacob watched as she took in the cozy breakfast table. "And why did you make breakfast? Rachel and I are here to cook if you need to eat. And we've brought food. Boone, Moses, and Ezekiel are on the way with more."

Maggie raised her chin and glared at her sister. With an air worthy of a queen, she said, "I didn't make breakfast – Jacob did, which was very kind of him."

A small smile flirted with Rachel's lips. "Boone wondered where you were."

"I did," his brother said as he walked into the house with his arms full. "I didn't know you were out doing acts of mercy, though."

"Acts of mercy?" Mattie said, one eyebrow lifted high.

"Yeah, as Christ commands us to do," Jacob replied. "If I recollect, that's in Matthew."

Mattie's eyes narrowed as she glared at Jacob. "It seems more like you're taking advantage of a woman just widowed," she said with heat in her tone. "What were you thinking, Jacob?

If we were in town, it'd be a disgrace."

Maggie rose. "We're not in town, though. And no one, especially not Jacob, is taking advantage of me. And if he were, it's my concern, not yours, sister."

Jacob winced. He'd meant well and hadn't intended to cause the sisters to fight. Moses stepped in behind Boone and halted as the sisters argued in German, nose to nose. Although none of them could understand, the angry tones didn't require translation.

"What's happened?" Moses asked as he arrived.

"Jacob made breakfast for Maggie," Boone said in a level voice. "I reckon he meant to help, but Mattie's thinking he's trying to take advantage of her sister, and he's not."

Rachel nodded. "If you men will bring the rest of the food, we'll see to it. Then we'll make sure Maggie's ready for the funeral. Is Father Leveillee here yet?"

That was the priest who had buried Katie's brother last year, baptized Rachel's first three children, and married Katie to Ezekiel, all on the same day.

"He's with Ezekiel," Moses said. "Are you still wanting little Sarah baptized?"

"I am," Rachel told him.

"Then we'll get it done, honey," Boone said. "Jacob, come help carry the rest of the things."

Maggie sidestepped her sister and came to Jacob. "I meant what I said."

He nodded. "We'll talk about it after Liam's buried."

She had to be speaking with a widow's grief, he thought, though he'd marry her if that's what she wanted. It couldn't be now, though; they'd have to wait a decent time.

Jacob followed Moses and Boone outside. When they were no more than ten feet away, Boone stopped. "Tell me true, Jacob, why did you make her breakfast?"

"Maggie needed to eat," he replied. "No one else was here yet."

"And that's all?"

Jacob shook his head. "You know darn well it ain't, Boone. I told you I've a fondness for her."

Boone sighed. "You did, and I saw it for myself before that. But, Jacob, you gotta go slow with it. You cain't dishonor her or make trouble. Mattie's riled up as it is."

Moses chimed in. "She'll get over it. Mattie's thinking how she'd feel if she was the one who lost a husband. Besides, she's worried what will happen when her folks come."

"I reckon they'll be a fight," Boone answered. "But let's leave that trouble for when it comes. Today we got to lay Liam to rest, and that's gonna be hard enough. Rachel's set on getting the baby baptized while the priest is here."

As soon as they had brought all the food, cooked, and determined what would be prepared in Maggie's kitchen, the men made makeshift tables and set them up outside. All morning long, a variety of people arrived from Laredo. Judge Masters was first, but there were more. Two lawyers that Liam had been acquainted with arrived, along with a couple of businessmen, the Sheriff, the owner of the livery stable, some nearby ranchers, two sheep farmers, and Mary from the Out of Luck.

The small graveyard sat on a rise not too far from the main ranch house, but out of sight. There were only three graves there: a ranch hand who had died with his boots on, including Katie's brother, Connor, and the newly dug grave for Liam. There wouldn't be a Mass, just a funeral service, so Father Leveillee stood beside the grave and the others clustered about. Between Maggie, the Wilsons, all the hands, and the visitors from town, there was a fair crowd. Boone stood with the widow on his right and his wife on his left. Mattie stood on her sister's other side, and Moses beside her. Jacob stood behind Maggie, very aware of the woman, with his niece, Jemima Ann, at his side. Boone's other children were with Katie and Ezekiel. Rachel held Sarah in her arms, and Katie had Ellie.

Boone played his guitar and sang, first a song from the Civil War, *Bonnie Blue Flag,* that Liam had loved, then two hymns, *Abide With Me* and *Nearer My God To Thee.* Mima, as she had at Connor O'Neill's funeral, sang with her daddy. Once Liam's casket was lowered into the grave, the mourners dropped clods of dirt onto it. Rob messed with some rocks, and when Mima screamed that there were spiders, Boone moved his son away, then killed the spiders that came out from under the biggest rock. Some of the hands remained to fill in the grave. Maggie rejected the judge's offer of his arm to escort her back to the house, but nodded her head toward Jacob.

Throat dry, he offered her his arm, and she took it. They walked with a slow pace back to the house, Jacob very aware that Mattie glared at him. He swore he could feel her burning gaze, but he couldn't turn down Maggie's simple request. Her small hand tucked tight into the crook of his arm, and he liked it there. Jacob wanted her, and if she wanted to wed, no matter what the reason, he would. He'd always found her lovely, but in the stark black dress, suitable for a widow, she was beautiful. The black accented her fair complexion, and the dark veil highlighted her blonde hair. He couldn't keep from smiling at her, a brief expression he hoped no one else saw, although she did. Maggie's lips curved in a brief response, then returned to a straight line.

After a moment's pause, the rest of the mourners followed them. At the house, the other three women put out the bountiful food while Maggie sat in the parlor to receive condolences. Once she'd taken the chair, Jacob moved away. He joined his brothers, along with many of the men outside, for a smoke. Boone pulled him aside.

"Have you lost your ever-lovin' mind?" he asked, his

voice conversational. "You might as well announce to everybody here you plan to court the woman."

"Boone, she wanted me to walk her back," Jacob replied. "I reckon I ought to tell you something more."

Boone's grey eyes narrowed as smoke from his cigarette wafted upward. "What in tarnation is it? I got a feelin' I ain't gonna like it."

Jacob drew a deep breath and told his brother the truth. "Maggie asked me this morning if I'd marry her if it came to that, and I'm willing."

He waited for the explosion, and it came quick.

"Jacob Wade Wilson, you cain't marry her, not this day or any time soon," Boone said. "She's not thinking straight, and you must not be neither. If she asked you that…"

"She did," Jacob admitted. "Hear me out before you start chewing on me, Boone. Getting married was your idea in the first place, the way Maggie tells it."

"Whoa!" Boone replied. "Now I know you're plumb loco. I never told you such a thing."

"Not me," Jacob told him with a deep patience he hadn't known he had. "You had Moses and Mattie step things up, get hitched before that German banker showed up on the ranch. Or that's what Maggie told me. Ain't it true?"

Boone looked like he'd been poleaxed. "That was a mite different, Jacob."

Jacob shook his head. "I don't see it was, not by much."

"Moses already had it in mind to marry Mattie," his brother stated. "He loved her and would have married her sometime anyhow. Besides, that Guttersnipe was trying to marry up with Mattie and drag her back to Laredo."

"I love Maggie," Jacob said it straight out for the first time. "And she figures her folks will want to take her back with them, and she says she ain't going, Boone. If Liam hadn't died, I'd not said a word about how I feel. I ain't even told her, but I reckon she's got an idea. She's the one who brought up the subject of marryin', not me. I do plan to court her, Boone, and if she needs me to say, 'I do,' then I will."

"Good Lord, Jacob, you cain't do that."

Jacob narrowed his eyes against the smoke that curled from their cigarettes. "I sure enough can, and I will. Ain't saying I'll do it today nor anytime soon. I know as well as you do it's respectable to wait a year. I'd wait that and more without griping. But if it comes down to stopping those Germans from dragging Maggie off against her will, I'll do what she wants."

Boone sighed and crushed out the last of his smoke under his boot. "Do you really love her, Jacob?"

"I do."

"If it's meant to be, it'll be," Boone replied. "But for the love of God, will you try to wait till it's decent?"

"Boone, I'll do my best."

"I reckon it'll all come out in the wash," his brother said, repeating something their mother often had said. "All I want to do now is get my little gal baptized so her mama's happy and go home. I'm worn out."

He looked it, Jacob thought, and he put one hand on Boone's shoulder. "I reckon we all are," he said. "I don't mean to give you trouble, Boone."

"I know," Boone replied. "None of you ever do."

His grin was small, but it was there, which reassured Jacob.

Things had changed with Liam's death. The ranch would continue, but the burden of running it would fall to Boone, a man already laden with responsibilities. Jacob resolved to help his brother more and devil him less.

But he'd still marry Maggie if she wanted, now or later.

That was certain.

CHAPTER FIVE

After the funeral dinner, the priest baptized Sarah Rose. Katie stood as godmother to the child, and to everyone's surprise, Jack McGee turned out to be Catholic, so he became godfather. Ezekiel was at his wife's side as he had been when Boone's three others were baptized. Once that sacrament was finished, most of the guests began to head out. Liam had been buried, and the meal was over, but Judge Ike Masters stopped Boone.

"All of you Wilsons will need to stay," he said. "Abe Dockins, a lawyer from Laredo, has brought Liam's last will and testament. He'll be reading it soon, and since it concerns you all and this ranch, you'd best be here."

Boone sighed. "I didn't know Liam had a will."

"Oh, he did, wrote it himself," Judge Masters said. "You might remember he once read law, back in Memphis before the war. I always thought he would have made a fair lawyer, but he chose ranching instead."

Jacob headed for the front parlor, where Maggie, clad from head to toe in black, remained. He took a seat near her, and she offered him a small smile. He would have taken her hand in his, but he knew Boone wouldn't care for it, and he didn't want to devil his brother. Boone already carried the weight of the ranch, if not the world, on his shoulders.

The lawyer donned a pair of spectacles once they had all gathered and cleared his throat.

"Mister Rafferty brought this to me more than a year ago," he told them. "He wrote it, and it's been filed, so it's legitimate. It concerns most of you here, which is why Judge Masters asked you to stay. If you don't have any questions, I'll read it, and then if you do, I'll answer them as best I can at that time."

Dockins stood, facing those gathered, and read:

I, Liam Sean Rafferty, being of sound mind and good health, do write this last will and testament for the disposal and disbursement of my property, especially my interest in the Double Deuce Ranch located between Laredo and San Antonio, Texas.

To my wife, Magdalena Baumann Rafferty, known to most as Maggie, I leave my share in the ranch but only if she remains on the property for at least one full year after my death. If she returns to her previous life in San Antonio, her quarter interest in the ranch will go to her parents, Hans and Ilse Baumann, to hold in trust for my son, Seamus Rafferty, for when he comes of age. The share of the ranch will remain Magdalena's only when she resides on the property and will remain hers, even if she should remarry. Her residence on the ranch is key. If she relocates, the ranch share reverts as previously noted above.

My share of the ranch may not be sold, not even to my partners in the enterprise, namely Boone Wilson. Moses Wilson and Ezekiel Wilson. If my wife remarries, then she can sell the ranch as she sees fit. But if she does not, at the time my son reaches maturity at the age of 21, he may sell or dispose of the land as he sees fit.

Such worldly goods as I possess, furniture, household items, and such, I leave to my wife, Magdalena.

I ask that my two children, my daughter Grace and son Seamus, continue to reside with their maternal grandparents in San Antonio and attend school there. I leave funds in the Cattleman's Bank of San Antonio to prove a dowry for my daughter and to pay for a college education for my son. Those funds will also be under the administration of the Baumanns.

I leave all livestock on the ranch to be shared jointly by the Wilson brothers, acting as the ranch. I name Boone Wilson, top hand, to become ranch boss in my place and charge him to run the operation as he sees fit. I also grant the houses that the Wilsons have on the ranch to live in for as long as they remain on the ranch.

To my wife, I leave my worldly goods, such as they are, for her to use or dispose of at her discretion.

I ask that all wages due be paid to those hands from my monies from the Cattleman's Bank of San Antonio from the ranch account and not my personal account. The bank account will be administered by Boone Wilson. For ranch purposes, he will have all say and control of the money there.

I sign this will with my own hand,
Liam Sean Rafferty
25 October 1877

A heavy silence, the kind that often portends a storm, hung in the room when the lawyer finished reading Liam's will. Jacob mulled over the main points in his mind, shaking his head. Some might say Liam had been fair – after all, he had stated the hands would be paid and that the Wilsons had homes on the ranch for as long as they lived on the property. But in every other way, Liam had outfoxed them all.

The ranch had been a four-way partnership, equal in every way, even though Liam had founded the operation. Before he'd come to Texas, his brothers had bought into the ranch, putting up their hard-earned money to become full partners. The name had changed from the Double B, which had stood for Bonnie Blue, like the flag of the former Confederacy, to the Double Deuce. As it stood now, according to the will, Maggie had inherited Liam's portion but only if she remained on the ranch for a year. If she left, as her parents were certain to advise, the ownership would be held by Maggie's in-laws until Liam's son turned 21. They would be partners in the ranch with the three Wilson brothers, and then, they would be in a partnership with Liam's son. That time was years distant for the boy could be no more than eight or nine years old.

"I don't like this nonsense," Boone said in the slow drawl he used most often when angry. "Unless Maggie stays here, her portion of the ranch, *our* ranch, will be controlled by those Germans, the ones who disowned first Maggie, then Mattie. Down the road a piece, either Liam's town-raised kid will try to take over, or we might have a shot at buying him out if he don't sell to someone else first. And that ain't for more than ten years."

"Unless Mattie remarries," Jacob said. That fact interested him, not only because he had a stake in it but because if she did, it would be the best for the Wilsons.

"Can Liam's will stand up in a court of law?" Moses asked. "He's not only keeping his part of the ranch out of our reach, but he's using Maggie's children to force her to do what he wanted. I'd rather not have the Baumanns having any say in the ranch. They're not ranchers or even country folks. And in the past, they hadn't exactly been fond of any of the Wilsons."

Ike Masters, the judge, spoke up. "I fear it can stand," he said. "You might be able to contest the part that says the current partners can't buy the other share, but it would take time and money. The one loophole is if Mrs. Rafferty remarries, then she can do as she wishes with the ranch."

Maggie stood up. "I plan to stay here. I've already said so and I mean it."

Her sister joined her. "If you stay, your children won't be with you."

"I am aware," Maggie replied with dignity. "I haven't lost my hearing nor any other faculties. I want them with me, but I've gotten as used as a mother can to them being away. I've no desire to return to our parents' home and be the poor relation, living on their charity. I won't go to San Antonio. I made up my mind about that before I ever heard this will."

"You have a year before you have to decide," Judge Masters stated.

Maggie shook her head. "I don't, if I heard correctly. I have a year to stay on the ranch before I inherit Liam's share, but if I return to San Antonio, my share goes into trust for my son, with my parents in control. I expect them to arrive within the next few weeks, so I don't have a year or months. I've got weeks if that."

"That's how I understood it," Jacob added. "I'll stand by you when they come. I reckon you know that."

"I do, Jacob, and it's much appreciated."

"We all will, Maggie," Boone told her. "If you don't want to go, there ain't no reason you must."

"Thank you, Boone. I'll rely on you and your brothers."

Mattie sighed and put her arm around her sister. "Maggie, I'll fix you a cup of tea. You're overwrought. You haven't even cried that I've seen. And you haven't eaten a thing since breakfast. I'll fix you a plate, and you can come back to the kitchen to eat. It's quieter there."

She glared at the room brimming with people, but Maggie stopped her.

"I don't want a cup of tea, and when I want to eat, I know the way to the kitchen. I need some quiet, that's all, time to think."

Mattie clicked her tongue. "Oh, sister, you don't know what you want. Come with me."

"No."

Moses came forward from the back of the room. "Mattie, darlin'," he said. "I imagine Ellie's getting hungry, and I'm ready to head out. It's been a day for all of us. Let's go home."

Mattie hesitated, and Maggie said, her voice as sharp as a kitchen knife. "Go home, please. Tomorrow I'll probably need your company."

Jacob watched as Mattie sighed, then nodded. "All right. If you need me, send for me, send one of the hands, or come to our place."

Maggie sat back down. "I will, Mathilde. I don't mean to be hateful, but –"

"I know you don't," Mattie told her and kissed her cheek. "I'll see you tomorrow."

Since they'd never make it back to Laredo before dark, the priest, the judge, and the lawyers retreated to the bunkhouse where they would stay the night. In the morning, Davy or one of the other young hands would escort them back to town. Boone gathered up his family and headed home. He looked haggard, and Jacob wondered how much sleep he'd gotten since Liam's death. Rachel's misunderstanding that he had been the one who died had been hard on him, and so had the loss of his friend. Liam's will would add to his load, and Jacob resolved that the first chance he would sit down with Boone to talk it over.

"You know where to find me should you need me," Boone said in parting.

"Get some sleep, brother," Jacob said. "You all right?"

Boone waggled one hand up and down. "*Come si, some sa,*" he said. The French phrase meaning so-so was one Jacob recalled Boone had picked up during the war. "I'm dog tired. I feel like I been rode hard and put up wet."

"What's wrong with your hand?"

Jacob noticed Boone had been rubbing the back of his hand, and there appeared to be a small welt there.

"Itches and hurts a mite," Boone said. "I smashed a couple spiders a while ago that crawled out from under a rock at the grave. Mima's afeard of them. I think one of them might have got me."

"Best make sure Rachel tends it," Jacob replied with an

odd sense of foreboding.

Boone clapped him on the back. "Ain't nothing to worry about. I just need some sleep. Come over for breakfast and we'll sort out what happens now that Liam's gone."

Ezekiel and Katie stayed a little longer, but then they too went home. Jacob was the last, and he rose, thinking Maggie might need some solitude. "I ought to light out too," he told her.

"Do you have to?" Maggie said. "I'd rather you stay, Jacob. I don't fancy being alone."

He sat back down. "I figured you might want some time to yourself. You told your sister so."

"I did," she replied. "But that's because she wanted to hover and do for me. I don't want the fuss, but you're restful to have around. You talk if I want to talk, listen when I need an ear, and you're here. That eases me more than anything."

"I can stay as long as you want," Jacob said, more than willing. "I don't want to cause a scandal, though, or trouble with your sister."

"I don't plan to tell her."

He wasn't sure if he should be glad or worried. "You cain't keep secrets like that, Maggie," he told her. "She'll get riled if you do, and I don't want to lose our friendship over some such."

"It's not her business," Maggie returned. "I don't see it as a secret, just keeping the peace."

"All right," he said, hoping it didn't explode in his face like dynamite. "I'll be here as long as you want me to be."

She smiled, and he failed to find it odd that a widow would smile at another man on the day she buried her husband. He liked it too much.

"I'm going to get out of these widow's weeds," she told him. "I'll be back. Have some coffee if you'd like."

Jacob found the pot empty, so he made fresh coffee, and it was ready by the time she returned, wearing a simple calico dress. Neither of them had eaten much earlier despite the big spread of food. They ate cold ham and some turkey along with bread spread with sweet butter, then ate some apple pie.

"I wonder if I ought to move out of this house," Maggie said as they dined. "It's much too big for me, but then where would I live? I suppose Boone's family could have it."

Jacob reached for another piece of pie. "They like their house he built just fine, and I doubt he'd want to move. It's too big for any of my other brothers as well. I reckon you'd best just stay here for now until the dust settles and we see what happens."

Despite her insistence that she would stay, he wondered if she might go home to San Antonio after all. She might not want to live with her parents, but her children were there. Of course, he'd left his daughters back in Kentucky and might never see them again, but that was different, he reasoned. He was their father, not their mother.

Maggie's face took on a stubborn expression. "I'm not leaving, not for love or money, Jacob. You're thinking I might change my mind for the children, but I won't. I love my daughter and son, but it might be best for them to stay. They've been there long enough; they have become town folk now and might chafe at the ranch."

"I was," he admitted.

"Didn't you leave your children behind when you came to Texas?"

"I did but...."

"There's not any but, Jacob. You left them where they would grow and prosper, didn't you, in the place you thought best for them?"

"That's true, but I came to my family, my brothers."

"And left your mother and another brother behind?"

"I did. It was best at the time."

"I've two more sisters besides Mattie," she told him.

"Minna and Lena, and a younger brother, Freddy. Their lives are in San Antonio. I've been gone so long that any closeness we once had is long gone, I fear. They're all so much younger, and they have no idea what it's like to live on a ranch. Your family is more like my family now than they are."

He had to ask. "Am I like family?"

Maggie smiled. "No. It's probably not right to say this now, on the day of Liam's funeral, but I admire you. Jacob Wilson. The more Liam became distant, the more I dreamed of what it would be like if I'd been unmarried when I met you. I would have liked it if you could have courted me."

That should have shocked him, but instead it pleased him. "Maggie, I've felt the same way."

"If it comes to the fact I must wed to stay here, you're willing to marry?" she asked. "And it will be a real marriage, not something false?"

Before he answered, Jacob thought of all the things Boone had said. Although they had disagreed, he valued his oldest brother's opinion and thought his view had merit. "I am," he said. "Though I'd rather we take our time, Maggie. My ma used to say, 'marry in haste, repent in leisure,' and though I don't think I'd repent ever, I think it best if we can take our own time about it."

She nodded, but since he thought she appeared more than a little sad, he added, "But if it needs to be, yes, I'll wed you, Maggie, even if it's tomorrow."

Her smile returned. "Then that's good," she said. "I'd prefer you court me also. We're friends and have been for a good while, but the path to becoming husband and wife is different."

"It is, and we'll find it, Maggie."

"Yes, we will."

Jacob lingered until dusk, then headed back to the small cabin. It seemed lonelier than ever now, and although he was tired, he didn't sleep for a long time. He sat, lost in his thoughts, smoking the occasional cigarette and staring into the fire. As he contemplated his future, he said a farewell in his mind and heart to Sally Ann. A part of him would always love her, and he would not forget her, but Maggie was the future, not the past, and he thought his heart was large enough to have room for them both.

In the morning, he rose at dawn from habit. When the sun was up, Jacob headed for Boone's house, remembering the invitation for breakfast. He wondered just how Boone intended to sort out the ranch now. His brother would be the main boss and deserved it, he thought. Jacob resisted the temptation to visit Maggie first but resolved that later he would go by to see how she fared. If it wasn't late fall, near winter, he would have picked some wildflowers for her. The next time he headed into town, he'd buy her some small gift as a token of his affection – if he wasn't married to her first. He would also buy a wedding ring to have ready just in case.

When he had almost reached Boone's house, Mima came flying out the front door and took off with a run in his direction. It was cold enough that her breath came out as frost, and she didn't notice him until he caught her.

"Where you goin' in such a rush, baby girl?" he asked, using Boone's pet name for the child.

"I was comin' to fetch you, Uncle Jay," she cried, and he noticed for the first time that she'd been crying. "Daddy's sick and Mama said to fetch you, Mo-Mo, and Z too."

His guts clenched tight. "Boone's sick?"

The little girl nodded. "He got sick last night, and he's no better this morning, maybe worse."

"You need to get back in the house," Jacob said. "I'll go see what's wrong. You ought not be out in this cold."

Mima slipped her hand into his, and they walked back to the house. Jacob entered to find Rachel nursing the baby in the rocking chair. She wore a worried frown, which eased a fraction when she saw him.

"Jacob, I'm glad you're here. Boone's sick in bed. If you want to go back, go ahead."

"What's the matter with him?" Jacob asked.

"It seems like a spider bite," she told him.

He nodded and headed back to the bedroom to see his brother, worried. Boone was never sick.

CHAPTER SIX

In all the long years since the war, Boone seldom dreamed about it. Most of the time, he didn't think about it either. Easier not to remember, although he had served with Liam as well as both Mac and Deacon Lee. When he did dream about those battles, it usually came during a time of stress. Liam's death probably prompted the dream he had the night following his old friend's funeral.

It had been September, and the night before the battle, it had rained. They'd slept in the mud, soaked to the skin and uncomfortable, but in the morning, the sun returned, and the day turned humid. Boone was dirtier than he could ever remember being, and although he didn't admit it to anyone except himself, he wished he had stayed in Kentucky. But he'd joined up when the call came, not because he believed in the Confederate States of America or wanted to preserve slavery but to protect his home, his family, his country. States' rights mattered to him, and young as he was, he didn't think a bunch of addlepated fools up in Washington, DC, should decide what happened in the South, especially in Kentucky.

But he was no quitter, and when he could, he wrote home to his widowed Ma and the children, all younger. He'd made friends too, the kind made under the worst circumstances, in conditions that bonded men for life. Liam Rafferty, son of Irish immigrants or maybe a grandson, had read law up to Memphis before the war, but now he was near a brother. So was Deacon Lee and a young Scotsman they all called Mac.

Lee had taken his Army north into Maryland, farther north than Boone had ever been, to show the Federal troops that they could and would advance. Their company sergeant, the one they all called Pop because he was older, was there, silent in his support as always.

There had been a few skirmishes the night before, but at dawn the battle began. As they fought to hold their positions close to Antietam Creek, the fight spilled out into a cornfield. The Yanks overran them, and the fighting grew bloody on both sides. Boone would never forget the smoke from the cannons or the roar as they fired repeatedly. The shouts and cries of men from both sides had echoed in his ears. The stench of blood and death hung over the field, and when a Union sharpshooter took aim at Liam, Boone moved with speed to block the shot. Liam had been winged but not seriously, but Boone took a bullet in his left thigh.

The battle had raged for a good twelve hours, and it was a long time before his friends could carry him to a field hospital. Boone would likely have bled to death had Deke not made a tourniquet with his belt. By the time Lee retreated, thousands of men lay dead in the cornfield and scattered across the hills. Although there had been no obvious winner, President Abe Lincoln called it a victory for the North. Sharpsburg had been remembered as the bloodiest day of the war, even when it was all over and Lee surrendered at Appomattox.

He'd lived through Sharpsburg, and except for being shot in the chest at Laredo, in retribution for a crazy sheriff thinking Boone had killed his brother at Sharpsburg, he'd never been as sick with fever and pain as he had been there.

Boone woke with a start, surprised he lay in his own bed with Rachel beside him. He'd expected to wake in the field hospital or worse, hidden in the hills while his friends did their best to tend his wound as the battle raged. As he became aware, however, his hand ached, throbbing deep into the flesh. Last night, it had hurt a bit and itched, but he'd thought little about it, so tired that he fell asleep as soon as he stretched out.

Now he didn't feel good, not at all. In the dim light, he lifted his hand and moaned because it sent pain radiating from it. He couldn't see it well enough to determine what might be wrong, but his slight cry woke his wife.

"Boone? What's the matter?"

"I'm feelin' a mite puny."

Rachel sat up and put her hand on his brow. "Boone, you're feverish."

"I'm sick," he said. "I'm aching all over, and I'm hot. My hand hurts the worst."

His belly was uneasy too, and when he tried to sit up, the room spun in circles like a do-si-do at a dance.

The bed shifted as she rose and struck a match to light the lamp.

"Did you do something to your hand? Let me see it."

Boone held it up and winced. It hurt, but it also looked terrible. There was a bright red patch of skin surrounding a raised blister. His hand appeared puffy, as if it were swollen. For a moment, he was perplexed, then he remembered killing the spiders.

"A spider might have got me," he told her. "A fiddleback."

Her gaze narrowed. "When?"

"At Liam's funeral," he said. "Rob turned over a rock, and there were spiders underneath. Mima's afraid, so I killed them, but I reckon one of them bit me. Jacob said I ought to let you tend it."

"Why didn't you?" she asked. "Why did you tell your brother and not me?"

"I don't rightly know," he replied with a sigh. "I was worn out and didn't think about it, honey."

"You should have. Fiddleback spiders have poison," Rachel said. "I could have poulticed it or something. I don't know much about spider bites, but I've heard they can be bad, Boone."

"Let's hope not," he said, although he could tell it was so. Fever baked hard into his bones, and he hadn't felt so ill in years.

"I'll go make some willow bark tea," Rachel said. "You stay in bed, Boone."

It remained dark outside, but he thought it must be near morning. Mima came into the room, sleepy-eyed in her flannel nightgown. "Daddy's what's wrong?"

"I don't feel so good," he told her, but he did his best to sound reassuring. "I'll be fine, though, I reckon."

She narrowed her eyes in a way that enhanced her resemblance to his mother and put the back of her hand against his forehead. "You've got a fever. I'll go fetch some water and bathe your poor head."

Sometimes he forgot she was just seven. She often acted far older than her years. Before he could say anything, she had a basin of water and a soft rag. Mima wiped his face and neck. He savored the coolness, and if he closed his eyes, he could almost think it was his mother, the other Jemima, tending him.

Boone got down the willow bark, although he thought sure he'd puke. As daylight banished the dark, Mima refused to return to bed.

"I want to take care of my daddy," she told Rachel.

Rachel had the child wash the spider bite with lye soap and warm water. The harsh lye stung his skin, and even Mima's light touch brought pain. After it'd been cleansed, Rachel brought a spare pillow where his hand could rest. Between that and the willow bark tea, Boone drifted back to sleep but woke past daylight. He tried to sit up, and dizziness struck. Before he could try again, a chill hit him with force, and he shivered. As soon as she noticed, Rachel covered him with a quilt.

"I doubt I could feel much worse and still be on this side of this grass," he said after the chill eased.

Rachel kissed his lips, then said in a gentle voice. "You were much sicker in Laredo, and you thought you were dying then."

"Everyone thought so," he reminded her. "I likely would have except for you."

Boone managed to wallow up and prop up on pillows. "Reckon I could get coffee?"

She smiled. "I've got a pot on the stove."

Some of the cold lingered from the chill, and he thought it might help. He sipped it slow, but his guts didn't like it much. "Best fetch a bucket," he told Rachel.

"Why?"

"I'm gonna puke," he said and did.

Rachel folded her arms across her chest. "Mima," she said. "Go fetch your uncles. I need their help. I'm going to need your aunties, too."

Boone thought he might have slept again, for when he woke, Jacob sat beside the bed in a chair tipped back against the wall.

"Heard you were poorly," Jacob said. "I met Mima on the way to fetch me."

"I don't feel so good, that's true," Boone said. "Reckon I did get bit by one of those spiders."

"That hand looks plumb awful," Jacob observed. "You don't look much better, Boone."

"I'll do," he said, but it was more bravado than brag. "I don't want Rachel or Mima taking on over this."

"Might be a bit late for that. Mima was on her way to fetch all of us, so I came back with her. I reckon I'll go after Moses and Zeke directly. Rachel wants Katie and Mattie to come as well. She thinks they might have more doctoring know-how than she does."

"That could be," Boone said. "I reckon I can use all the help I can get."

Rachel fussed over him and wanted him to eat. Although he was hungry, he wouldn't, afraid he'd sick it back up. He also turned down more willow bark tea.

"It's bitter," he said and made a face. "I don't know how

much it helps anyhow."

"It'll ease some of the pain from your hand," his wife said. "And might help with the fever. I can put some honey in it to help with the taste or make some sage tea if you'd rather."

Boone laid one hand over his belly. "Mebbe in a bit, honey. Where's Mima?"

"Watching the little ones," Rachel said. "She's most unhappy with me that I won't let her come tend you."

He managed a small grin. "It eases me when she does, and that's a fact. When you can spare her, maybe she can put another wet cloth on my head, maybe sing to me a little."

"I can spare her if that's what you want," Rachel told him.

"I'd like it fine."

Mima bathed his face and neck again with cool water, then sat beside the bed and sang to him in a pretty voice. Everyone told Boone he sang sweet, and likely he did, but right then, his young daughter's voice soothed him like no other. She gave him back the songs he'd sung all her life, everything from ballads to hymns to Irish tunes. If he hadn't felt so rotten, he would have joined her. Instead, although he hurt no less and felt no better, Boone slept.

When he woke, the room brimmed full. All three of his brothers were there, which aggravated him because somebody ought to be working. Zeke's bride, Katie, and Moses' wife, Mattie, were also there. Rachel hovered in the bedroom door, and Mima hadn't left his side.

Mattie stood at the bedside, checking his hand. Although she used an easy touch, it hurt, which had probably been what awakened him. "It's a spider bite, there's no doubt," she announced. "I'll get a potato poultice on it, and it should draw out some of the poison."

Katie peered down at it. "Aye, that would be wise," she said. "Did ye soak in it salt water at all?"

Rachel shook her head. "I never thought about it. If he had told me when he came home, I might've."

"Nay matter, we can do it after the potato poultice," Katie said. "Is it sore, Boone?"

Glad someone had finally spoken to him, he nodded. "It pains me a fair bit."

She put the back of her hand against his cheek and winced. "Ye're fevered, too."

"He's had a few chills as well," Rachel told them. "He's refused any more willow bark tea, though. Do either of you know any other fever cures?"

"Coneflower tea works almost as well," Mattie said. "I think there's still a good bit near the garden. Would you drink it if I brewed it, Boone? I could sweeten it with honey."

"I can try," he said.

Moses glared at him. "He'll drink it if I gotta pour it down his throat."

Boone's voice dropped lower. "You can try, Mosey."

"And I'll get it done in the state you're in," Moses replied. "That fever needs to come down, Boone."

"Ye can put sliced onions on his feet as well," Katie said. When the others stared at her, she added, "'Twill draw the fever. I've seen it work in Ireland. I see Mima's been bathing him with water, that's grand, and he needs to drink as well."

Boone began to feel more like a dish being prepared than a sick man in bed. Mattie sliced an unpeeled potato and placed it on the bite, then bound it in place with a strip of cloth. She promised to place a fresh slice in an hour's time. Katie removed his socks, placed thick onion slices against the bottoms of his feet, then pulled the socks on again.

He would have protested, but another chill struck, and he shivered for a good half hour before it abated. Rachel put another quilt on him, and Mima clung to his uninjured left hand. Her small face wore a worried expression.

"He'll be fine in a few days' time, *leannán*," Katie told her.

"Do you promise?"

Katie made the sign of the cross and kissed her thumb. "I do, on the holy cross of our Lord," she said.

"From your mouth to God's ear," Boone said, his voice soft.

He couldn't see his hand, and it felt a little different, but the womenfolk vowed the potato poultice had helped, so a fresh slice was bound in place.

"You need to eat something, Boone," Rachel told him.

"Nay, 'tis starve a fever," Katie said.

Rachel met her sister-in-law's gaze without blinking. "He might have died years ago in Laredo if I hadn't fed him with a worse fever than this one," she replied. "If he can keep some food down, it will give him strength."

Jacob frowned. "You puked?"

Boone nodded. "Earlier, yeah."

Rachel offered everything from biscuits with sausage gravy to refried beans to oatmeal, but Boone turned them all down. He hated vomiting and the way his guts rolled; he surely would if he ate. He did manage to drink a little of the coneflower tea sweetened with honey. Mima folded a wet rag and made a compress for his head, which lasted till the fever heat dried it out. She replaced it then, her gray eyes serious and sober as she watched over him.

He managed to sleep a little and woke to someone knocking on the door. Boone groaned and sat up, startling his oldest daughter. "Who's here?"

Jacob put all four legs of his chair on the floor. "I'll find out."

He returned with a smile. "It's Maggie," he said. "She had one of the hands bring her over in the wagon. She made some potato soup for you, Boone, if you think you can eat a little. She killed and plucked a chicken, too, so maybe someone can make you dumplings tomorrow. I put it in the cold box out on the porch."

Boone had fashioned a cold box in one corner of the front porch to keep perishables. It worked fine in cold or cool weather, but not in spring or summer. Then, anything to be kept had to be stored in the springhouse near the main ranch house.

He hadn't eaten since after Liam's funeral the day before and he was hungry. Potato soup sounded tasty. "I might could manage a bit of the soup."

"Rachel's got it heating on the stove – got a bit cold on the way over," Jacob said. "One of the gals will bring a bowl in for you. How's your hand?"

The last time they removed the potato poultice, Katie had placed it in a bowl with warm water and salt. Boone lifted it, noting that the skin had wrinkled from the long soak. "Sore but not as painful," he said, surprised.

Jacob touched two fingers to his brother's forehead. "You're still fevered, though."

It seemed as if everyone from the smallest to the oldest had checked him for fever. "Don't none of you got anything better to do than see if I'm feverish?" he asked, knowing he sounded as petulant as a child.

"Cain't help but worry," Jacob answered. "You ain't never sick, Boone. I haven't seen you abed since I came to Texas."

Boone snorted, almost amused. "I don't take sick often, that's true," he said. "Ask the kid, though, how bad I was after I got shot at the saloon in Laredo. And when Mima was small, both Rachel and me had the grippe right bad."

"Last time I recall that horse, Devil's Mischief tossed and stomped you a bit before you went off to the war – you couldn't have been more than maybe 16, and I was 14 or so."

"Auntie Katie said he'll be fine," Mima said. "She promised."

"And she's right," Boone said. "Baby girl, you ought not worry about your old daddy."

She shook her head. "You worry 'bout me, so I get to worry 'bout you."

Jacob laughed, and after a moment, so did Boone, just a little. "Out of the mouths of babes," Jacob said. "Sometimes I vow she not only looks like Ma but sounds like her too."

Boone nodded. "She does. I wish Ma would come. The older I get, the more I do believe I miss her."

Rachel entered, carrying a small bowl of soup and a spoon. "Boone, will you try to eat a little? You're going to get weaker if you don't."

"I will, honey," he said. "I'm darn puny enough now."

Jacob helped Rachel raise Boone higher against the pillows, but with one afflicted hand, he had trouble holding the bowl. Boone figured he could feed himself, but it proved more difficult than he expected. Rachel took over the spoon, but when the boys kicked up a ruckus, she handed it to Jemima Ann.

"Help your daddy," she told the girl.

Boone balanced the bowl in his lap and Mima fed him, one spoon at a time. She was very meticulous and didn't drip any soup on the covers or on him. He managed to almost finish the small portion and earned a smile from Mima.

"Do you want more?" she asked.

"Best not," he said. "It's mighty tasty, though. If Maggie wants to come back here, I'll tell her so."

Jacob stood. "I'll bring her, then I wouldn't mind a bowl of that myself."

Maggie appeared, dressed in black. "Boone, how are you feeling?"

"Sicker than a horse," he said. "Weaker than a newborn

calf, but that soup you made nearabout, revived me. It's good. Thank you for making it."

Her fair skin blushed a faint pink. "*Bitte,*" she said, giving him the German response. "You've always been good to me, Boone, so when I heard, I made soup. I brought a chicken, too, so tomorrow Rachel can make chicken and dumplings for you."

"I appreciate it, Maggie."

"I see you have a good young nurse," she said and winked at Mima. "I'll leave you in her capable hands. I'll see if Rachel needs help. Katie and my sister are here, also."

Boone nodded. He was weary, and he wanted to let the fine soup settle in his stomach, so he closed his eyes. Once he slept, only his daughter remained, faithful at his side.

CHAPTER SEVEN

The women were huddled together in the kitchen, talking in low voices. From the way worry knotted Rachel's forehead, Jacob figured they discussed Boone's condition. He remained concerned, so he joined them.

"How's Boone doing? Is he in a bad way?" he asked.

Rachel, Katie, Maggie, and Mattie turned toward him.

"I don't know," Rachel said. A single tear slid down her cheek, and that worried Jacob more than anything.

Katie, who had trained with the Sisters of Charity in Galveston, spoke up. "He's right sick and that's a fact," she told them. "'Tis the venom from the spider making him so. The poultices and soaking it in salt water will leech some of it out of his body, but he'll be ill for another few days. Once the venom, that poison, is gone, he'll improve. I promised wee Mima that Boone would be fine, and I meant it. He'll be weak, no doubt, for a bit, but he'll recover, Jacob."

He hadn't realized he was holding his breath until he let it out. Katie's words encouraged him. He'd been more bothered than he had wanted to admit or say aloud. "Thank God."

Rachel wiped away the tear and tried to smile. "I'll take your word for it," she said. "I'm glad, so glad. A few days ago, I thought it was Boone that had been killed by the horse, but it wasn't. Now he's sick."

She looked weary, and Jacob realized she'd probably had little sleep. "Who's minding the little ones?"

"Moses and Ezekiel," she replied. "Did you want to eat? There's the soup that Maggie made and cornbread, too."

"I would, thanks," he told her. He hadn't eaten yet today,

and with surprise, he realized it was late afternoon, near evening. No wonder he was hungry.

Jacob carried his supper to the table in the front room and joined his brothers. Ezekiel rocked Rob and sang to him, although his voice was nowhere as clear or true as Boone's. Sarah Rose slept in the cradle, and Moses held his daughter Ellie on one knee and Boone's youngest boy, Benjamin, up against his left shoulder. Both children slept.

"Did Mima eat?" Zeke asked, and when Jacob shook his head, added, "She ought to, then, get some sleep too. She ain't but seven years old."

Maggie joined them with her own bowl of soup. "I sent Rachel to bring her out. They both need to eat something and get some rest. If they won't leave Boone's side, is there still a trundle under the bed?"

"I believe so," Moses said. "One of us needs to sit with Boone, though, while they sleep. I can do it – he sat with me when I near died of pneumonia."

"I'll stay with him for a bit," Maggie told him. "I've no one to go home to anyway. You can take over after me if you'd like. I thought I might stay until midnight, but I can be here longer if I'm needed."

Rachel and her oldest daughter ate, then Rachel fed the baby. It took a lot of persuasion, but Jacob convinced them to rest. They slept in the girls' bedroom. "We'll be near if Boone needs us," Rachel said. Mima had fallen asleep at the table, and Ezekiel carried her to bed.

He and Katie remained to watch over the other children, but Moses and Mattie, after confirming that Maggie would sit up with Boone, took their daughter and went home.

"Send Jacob or Zeke for me when you're ready for me to take your place," Moses said. "I'll be right over."

"I will," Maggie promised. She turned to Jacob. "Are you

staying, then?"

"I thought I would," he told her. "As long as you don't mind."

She gave him a smile. "I don't, Jacob. I'd like it if you'd stay."

He carried a second chair to Boone's bedroom, then sat in it, tilted back against the wall.

Although he did want to stay for his brother, Jacob admitted he also remained to spend time with Maggie. Boone might have softened a little on his position about her after he'd said he loved the woman, but Mattie's outrage hadn't changed. During the night at a sickbed, with a house filled with people, there shouldn't be any talk.

Boone woke and asked for water. After he'd drank most of a cup, he said, "Where's Rachel?"

"Asleep," Maggie said. "Both her and little Jemima. Would you like a little something to eat? I do believe there's some potato soup left."

He shook his head. "I ain't feelin' good at all, so maybe after a bit, not now."

Jacob rose and clapped a workworn hand on Boone's brow. "He's burning up."

"Fevers rise at night," Maggie said. She fixed a compress for his brother's forehead. Then she coaxed Boone to drink some of the coneflower tea blended with honey.

Then she tried a bread and milk poultice on the spider bite. Jacob studied the bite and thought it might look a wee bit improved. Maybe the different poultice would help.

"What about garlic?" he asked. He remembered a folk cure used back in Kentucky.

"For what?"

"I've seen Ma peel and slice garlic, then put it on wounds," Jacob told her. "It works wonders. I had a bad cut on my hand once, and the garlic drew out most of the infection."

"It's worth a try," she said. "It will smell, though."

He laughed. "Cain't be no worse than the onions Katie put on his feet."

Maggie made a face. "I'm taking those off. They do stink, and I don't know if they helped in the least."

"I can do that."

While she rustled up some garlic in the kitchen, Jacob removed Boone's socks and the reeking onions. Then he washed his brother's feet with lye soap to remove some of the stench. He dug out a fresh pair of socks and wrangled them onto Boone's feet.

Boone stirred at that. "What in tarnation are you doing?"

"Changing your socks."

"Did my feet smell that bad?"

The flash of humor pleased Jacob, and he laughed. "Naw, but the onion Katie put on 'em did."

"I swear I smell garlic," Boone said.

"You do," Maggie said as she entered the room. "Jacob thought we should try some garlic on that spider bite."

He expected Boone to object, but he didn't.

"If it works, do it," he said. "Hand's paining me some again, and I'm right weary of being sick."

Maggie bound the hand after laying the fresh garlic on the bite. "I made some valerian tea as well," she said. "I sweetened it with both honey and sugar. It'll help you sleep if you can get it down."

"I'll try."

Boone remained restless for the next half hour, but then either the tea or fatigue brought him sleep. Through the long night, Maggie tended Boone, placing fresh compresses on his forehead. Jacob helped when he could. He repositioned his brother so that he wasn't propped against pillows, figuring he'd sleep better lying down. They talked, at first, about Boone and his condition, but then about other things.

He talked about the Mark Twain book he'd been reading, a little at a time. Always a little hesitant to share his love of books, he'd found many people scoffed at a farmer or a ranch hand who claimed to read, but Maggie's face brightened.

"Oh, which one?" she asked. "Was it *Tom Sawyer?* I read it last year."

Jacob hadn't read that one yet. "No, this one was about his travels in the West," he told her. "*Roughing It.*"

"I read a bit of that one," Maggie said. "Liam had it, but since the farthest I've traveled was from San Antonio here, I'll confess I didn't enjoy it much. The country seemed too wild and too big after town. We had just been wed and I expected romance, not a grueling trip."

"It can be a hard trip, but that's some pretty country."

"I found it so, afterward. Living on the ranch, I came to appreciate the land and the beauty of it. That proved to be a good thing, since Liam often left for San Antonio or Laredo for long weeks or more. When Grace was little, I swear, he was gone more than he was here. There were no other women on the ranch, not then, and I got very lonesome."

Jacob bit his tongue so he wouldn't make a rude comment. If he ever married Mattie – or any good woman – he sure wouldn't leave her alone on a ranch for long periods of time.

"I bet you were glad when Boone brought Rachel."

She smiled. "Oh, I was, and then my parents sent Mattie to be a help with Grace the summer that Seamus was born. They regretted it almost as soon as they sent her, but she fell in love with Moses. Now there's four women on the ranch. Did you like the book?"

"I do, so far," he answered. "I ain't finished it yet. I've done my share of traveling, from Kentucky here and trailing cattle, but

Twain rode about different country, so I'm intrigued. I doubt I'll
ever see that part of the west, so it's good to read about it."

"Do you wish you could?"

He hesitated, then spoke the truth. "Naw, I'm rooted right
here, I reckon. I wouldn't want to leave my brothers behind. It's
good to have some family around. What's that other book about,
the one about someone named Tom?"

"*The Adventures of Tom Sawyer*," Maggie cried. "Oh, it's a
fun book to read, all about a rascal of a boy named Tom Sawyer,
an orphan living with his Aunt Polly in a town on the Missouri
River. He gets into plenty of trouble and scrapes. I laughed a lot
reading it, and I think you'd like it, Jacob. You can borrow it if
you like."

"I likely will once I finish *Roughing It.*"

In between, they tended Boone, whose fever climbed and
who suffered several rounds of chills. He shivered hard when
a chill struck, and Jacob prayed for each round to end. After a
chill, Boone slept for a bit, worn out from the havoc wreaked on
his body. He woke once, asked for some scrambled eggs, and
when Maggie went to the kitchen, Katie roused and made them
for Boone.

He ate most of them and complained he might puke, but
didn't.

After midnight, Jacob and Maggie talked about poetry
they loved. He recited from memory one of his favorites, "The
Village Blacksmith".

"I liked it because it was about something real, something
I knew," he told her. "So I learned it by memory at school. Later,
after Sally Ann passed, I thought often of these lines,

He needs must think of her once more,
How in the grave she lies;
And with his hard, rough hand he wipes
A tear out of his eyes.

Maggie sighed. "Do you mourn her still, Jacob?

"I always will, but it ain't the same now," he replied. "I won't lie – I'm sorry she died, but I have a different life now. I miss my gals, but then they're near growed up now. They wouldn't be the same little girls I knew, not anymore. I'm happy enough here in Texas, Maggie, and I reckon I'd be content with you."

She reached over and took his hand in hers. Her smaller hand fit into his, and he savored the feel of her flesh against his. Maybe, he thought, she understands about my daughters. Maybe she feels the same about her children. He almost told her that he loved her, but he held back.

"Maggie, I'll wed you if need be to keep your family from snatching you off to San Antone," he said. "But if you're still willing, I'll marry you in a year, when the time has passed enough to be decent."

Her lips lifted into a smile. "I'll marry you whenever it's time," she told him. "It's not just about all the business with my parents. I do care for you, Jacob."

She lifted his hand toward her mouth and kissed it once, her lips soft and tender against his skin. A rush of tenderness filled him. It had been so long since a woman touched him with romantic affection. He bent and delivered a soft kiss to her hand that still held his. Jacob might have done more, maybe kissed her on the mouth. They faced each other, and he leaned toward her when Moses entered the bedroom without knocking. He halted. His eyes widened and his mouth drooped.

"I came to see if Maggie needed me to take her place with Boone," he said after a long moment. "You're surely not canoodling, are you?"

"Well, we ain't *now*," Jacob replied.

"Don't you think it might be a mite soon? She buried her husband day before yesterday." There was no condemnation, just curiosity in his tone.

Maggie released Jacob's hand. "I might if I were a fine society widow up in San Antonio," she said. "But I'm not. I don't suppose anyone told you or that anyone else knows this but Boone, but if my family tries to take me back home, I asked Jacob if he would marry me to stop it. I got the idea from you and Mattie."

Moses stared at her, then took the chair Jacob vacated and sat.

"I reckon that was different. She wasn't just widowed, and we'd been courtin'."

"I've been smitten with her for some time," Jacob said. "Though I never thought anything would come of it, not when Liam was alive. Even if the Baumanns don't drag her back to San Antone, I mean to marry her in a decent time."

Moses sighed. "My wife already thinks you're trying to take advantage of the new widow. I don't think I'll tell her this just yet."

"I'd say that's wise," Jacob replied.

"Besides all the courtin', how's Boone?"

Jacob stood with his arms folded against his chest and shrugged. "He ain't no better but he's not worse, either. Still got fever, and he's had several hard chills so far during the night. I think the poultices Maggie's put on are helping, though. Katie vows he'll be fine in the long run."

Moses scrubbed his face with both hands. "I purely hope so. It's worrisome 'cause he seldom gets sick. Maggie, do you plan to stay or go home?"

"I'll stay," his sister-in-law told him. "I've nothing else pressing. Jacob should try to sleep, though. You look so weary."

"I'm dog tired," Jacob admitted. "In a few hours, I'll have been up for twenty-four. I feel almost as worn out as if I'd been ridin' drag on a drive."

"If you want to go home for a spell, I'll stay," Moses said.

His small cabin lacked appeal. By now, he figured the fire had gone out, and it would be cold as well as lonesome. Jacob didn't want to be away from Maggie or Boone.

"I'll stay, though I might sleep." He eyed the trundle bed with interest and reached down to remove his boots. "I reckon I can stretch out right there."

The dull headache he'd had for hours increased, and he kneaded his forehead. Sleep would help that, he figured.

"Don't you feel well?" Maggie asked.

"Just got a bit of a headache, that's all. It ain't nothing sleep won't cure."

Moses sighed. "I hope so, Jacob. I've wondered if there ain't something more plaguing Boone than just that spider bite. What if he's caught some other sickness?"

It was November, the season for many illnesses, so Moses made a fair point, but it wasn't something Jacob wanted to contemplate. Listing them in his mind sent terror rushing through his body. Yellow fever, cholera, typhoid fever, typhus, smallpox, diphtheria, measles, and scarlet fever headed the list, followed by lesser fevers like the grippe.

"I surely hope not," Jacob said. If so, they were all in danger of catching the disease.

"It's doubtful," Maggie told them. "Katie swears he'll start recovering as soon as the poison has worked through his body. It's but the second day. He should be improved by Sunday or Monday. If not, then we'll consider the possibility."

"Fair enough," Moses said.

Jacob nodded in agreement, then stretched out on the trundle bed.

"Wake me if you have need of me," he said.

He wasn't sure he could sleep, but he did because the next he knew, it was daylight, and someone had covered him with a quilt. His headache was gone, and the aroma of coffee brought him fully awake. Jacob rolled over and sat up.

Both Moses and Maggie were gone. Rachel sat beside her husband with Jemima Ann at her side. She smiled at him. "Would you like some coffee, Jacob? Mima can fetch you a cup."

"I would, thanks," he said. "How's Boone?"

"I'm still on this side of the grass," his brother said, in a surly tone. "And I had coffee and ain't puked it back up yet."

Jacob grinned and stood up, then came over to the side of the bed in his stocking feet. If Boone could be cross, he was likely on the mend. "I reckon that's right good, Boone."

"He's still feverish," Rachel said. "He took a chill a bit ago, but Jacob, look at the spider bite!"

He leaned closer as she unwrapped it, concerned it might have worsened. Instead, the redness had receded, and the area around it appeared to be less swollen. "I'll be! Is it still paining you?"

"Not as much," Boone said. A faint grin flirted with his lips. "I still feel terrible, but it's a start, I reckon."

His niece brought her uncle Jay a cup of coffee, and Jacob accepted it with thanks. He sipped the brew with pleasure. "I'd say so."

Still very pale, Boone sat back against several pillows. Rachel rose and kissed him. Boone put his uninjured hand on her back and then caressed her face. "I love you, honey."

That got him another kiss and a big smile. Mima took his hand and held it.

"I'll get you something to eat," Rachel said. "What do you think you can eat, Boone?"

"I don't rightly know, but I'm a bit hungry. Don't want to rile my belly, though."

Rachel tucked her hands beneath the edges of her apron. "I can fix you some milk toast," she said. He made a face and shook his head. "Beef tea? Maggie brought a chicken yesterday, but I doubt you're able to eat chicken and dumplings. But I could make some broth. Or I could make milk gravy."

"I don't reckon there'd be sausage with that gravy."

She tilted her head. "There could be, although I'm not sure you could stomach it, Boone."

"He had a scrambled egg last night," Jacob offered.

"Milk gravy will do," Boone said. "I don't need the meat, but a biscuit under it might not go amiss."

He ate most of a single biscuit covered with gravy. Jacob had the same, but with some sausage. Then he put on his boots and made ready to leave.

"Where you goin'?" Boone asked.

"I got chores to do," Jacob answered. "I'll see if the hands can do most of them, but somebody's got to run this ranch. I reckon it's me till you get back on your feet, Boone. I'll be back later."

Boone nodded. "Awright, I'll be here."

For the first time since Jacob learned Boone had taken ill, he felt confident that he would be. He left with a lightness in his step and a merry tune on his lips.

CHAPTER EIGHT

By Monday morning, three full days after he'd taken sick, Boone had improved. Jacob handled the daily workings of the ranch in the meantime. The hands had done their part, and most hadn't even required instruction. Jack McGee and the older hands had made sure the basic chores were done. Jacob had been sleeping in his small cabin, and when he headed over early that morning, he had gone straight to Boone's bedroom. Rachel sat beside the bed, and when he entered, she stretched out her hand to him. She had tears in her eyes.

"What's wrong?" he asked as he crossed the room.

"Not a thing," she replied. "Boone's fever broke, Jacob."

He grinned. "Thank the Lord."

"He's sleeping now," she told him. "I expect he'll do plenty of that for a few days as he recovers. I'm going to make chicken and dumplings for him in a bit."

"He'll like that fine. Do my brothers know?"

Rachel shook her head. "You're the first, you and Mima. I'd appreciate it if you go tell them."

The little girl and her brothers were asleep on the trundle bed. Until then, Jacob hadn't noticed the cradle had been moved into the corner of the room. Sarah Rose was tucked into it.

"I will," Jacob said. "Rachel, I'm glad. I've been awful worried."

She smiled at him. "So was I."

"Boone'll want coffee when he wakes," he told her. "I'll make some before I head out. I'll fix breakfast too, if you like."

"I would," Rachel said. "Thank you."

"*De nada*," he replied, using one of the Spanish phrases

he'd picked up.

Cornbread was easier than biscuits, so Jacob stirred up a pan and baked it while he fried bacon and scrambled some eggs. He made the coffee strong, the way his brother preferred, and by the time the food was ready, the children were up. He fed them first, then took a plate to Rachel.

"If there's coffee, I'd like some," Boone said, awake and sitting up against the pillows.

"I'll bring you a cup," Jacob said. "Though I fear my skills as a waiter are somewhat lacking. There's breakfast made if you feel up to eating."

Boone drank the coffee with pleasure, then managed to eat some scrambled eggs and a piece of cornbread. "Best go fetch the others," he said when he'd finished. "I reckon they should know I'm stayin' on this side of the grass."

Jacob headed for the dog trot cabin. Ezekiel sat on the steps, smoking, and stood when he approached.

"Must be news since it's early yet," he said. The sun was up but barely. "I surely hope it's good, not bad."

"It is," Jacob said, sinking down beside Zeke. "Boone's fever broke. He sent me to fetch you and Moses."

Ezekiel's grin, absent in recent days, emerged, and he whooped. "Hallelujah! I never thought a spider bite could make a body so sick."

"Me neither."

"I'll go tell Katie, then head over."

"I need to let Moses know."

Mattie opened the door to his knock, but when he told her why he'd come, she smiled.

"Moses will be happy to hear that," she said. "Come in, Jacob. I've got biscuits baking if you're hungry."

"I appreciate, but I already ate," he said.

Moses emerged from the bedroom. "I'll be happy to hear

what?"

"Boone's fever broke," Jacob told him. "He wants you and Ezekiel to come over."

Moses wore a happy expression. "I'll go directly."

"I'll go, too," Mattie said.

"I'd best go tell the hands," Jacob said. "I gotta make sure they're takin' care of chores and such."

He headed for the bunkhouse because he figured the men who worked on the ranch would want to know the glad tidings, but his real destination was the main ranch house. Jacob wanted to let Maggie know, and he longed to see her. Their interrupted moment when she'd told him she cared and kissed his hand had been pleasing. He'd returned the kiss and might have given her a proper one if Moses hadn't arrived.

Jacob found Maggie in the kitchen, washing clothes using a scrub board. He entered without knocking, removing his hat to show respect. She glanced up and offered a smile.

"Good morning, Jacob," she said, "You've a cheerful look this morning. How's Boone?"

"His fever broke," he said.

She put down her washboard and embraced him with exuberant delight. "That's wonderful!"

Her head rested on his chest, and he held her close, her sweet curves against his body. Jacob inhaled her aroma of soap from the wash and lavender from the powder she used. Maggie fit in his arms, and he savored the moment. When she stepped back, he missed her, although she was no more than a few feet away. *Maybe I should've kissed her while I had the chance,* he thought.

"It's sweet news," Jacob said. "Maggie, I reckon there's a thing I ought to say to you..."

"I'd rather you kissed me proper," she replied, and shocked him. Before he could gather his addled wits enough to answer, she put her wet hands on his shoulders and drew him close. Before he could say boo, Maggie stood on her tiptoes and placed her lips on his mouth. Jacob tried to resist and do the right thing, but the moment her mouth touched his, he was lost. He pulled her to him and kissed her, sweet and tender.

"*Gott in Himmel,*" Maggie exclaimed when he released her.

"Is that in a good way or bad?" he asked, worried he might have crossed a line by kissing her.

"*Sehr gut,*" she replied. "I told you I like you, Jacob Wilson, but I fear that's not true."

His heart grew heavy, and he sighed. "It ain't?"

Maggie shook her head. "No, it's not. Jacob, I do believe I have a fondness for you, more than a friend would have."

Her words made no sense for a moment, then he stared at her. "How can that be?" he asked, his mind reeling. "Maggie, I'm smitten with you and that's no secret."

Jacob loved her, but he wasn't sure if this was the time to admit it.

"You're wondering how I can say those words, and my husband just buried?"

Thankful she'd returned to speaking English, not German, he nodded.

She placed both her hands over her heart. "I'm not altogether sure myself," she answered. "But it's how I feel, no mistake about it."

"I always heard you wed Liam out of love."

Maggie shrugged. "I think I loved the notion of leaving San Antonio as much as I did Liam," she told him. "I saw how Boone looks at Rachel, how he treats her as if she's a treasure. I watched my sister fall in love with Moses. I saw how he pined for her when she went back to town, and I've seen Ezekiel with Katie. I never had any of that with Liam, Jacob, not in all the years, not after two babies. But I think I could have it with you."

His scarred old heart paused beating, then went wild,

hammering in his chest until he thought he might die from it. Jacob had fallen for Maggie over time, his admiration growing into love, but he'd never thought he could ever tell her how he felt. With Liam dead, not quite a week, he wouldn't have said as much as he did if she hadn't suggested marriage to keep her on the ranch. But with what she told him now, everything changed.

"We might could," he said, his voice husky with emotion and soft. "But we'll be a scandal if we wed so soon after your husband died."

"I don't care," Maggie said with a toss of her head. "Unless my family tries to force me back to San Antonio, we'll wait until it's decent, Jacob. But we'll know, and for now, that's enough."

It would have been enough to satisfy Jacob for the rest of his life, but now, he craved more. He had become a patient man, though, and he would wait. "Oh, Maggie, sweetheart…"

She held up one hand. "Hush! Someone's coming."

Maggie picked up her washboard and began scrubbing a calico dress. Jacob hoped the heat he sensed on his cheeks faded fast. Moses and Mattie walked into the kitchen, then stopped short. Moses' lips curved into a smirk, but Mattie put her hands on her hips.

"What's this?"

"I'm doing the wash," Maggie said, unruffled. "Jacob came to tell me the good news about Boone."

Mattie glanced from her sister to Jacob. Maggie's hands were covered in suds up to her wrists, and Jacob leaned against the wall, several feet away. "It's grand," Mattie said, apparently mollified.

Jacob straightened his posture. "I reckon I'd better make tracks over there before Boone wonders what's keeping me."

"We're headed there now," Moses told him. "We can walk together."

Jacob nodded. "Where's little Ellie?"

"Katie's keeping her," Mattie said. "I doubt I'll stay long unless Rachel needs my help. I'd forgotten it's wash day. I've laundry to do myself."

"Bring it over if you want," Maggie told her. "Rachel's too. I've little else to do."

Jacob's eyes met hers, and she gave a slight nod. He would be back, later, he vowed.

Boone was out of bed, sitting in the rocker with Benjamin in his lap, when Jacob returned with Moses and Mattie. Although he wore both a shirt and pants, Rachel had tucked a blanket around Boone's shoulders.

"I didn't expect to find you out of bed," Jacob said.

"I don't reckon it'll last long," Boone told him. "I'm puny as a sickly calf and weary. The little ones, though, liked seeing me get up for a bit, so I did."

"Where's Ezekiel?"

"Took Mima to ride her pony," he said. "Poor little gal begged, and she deserves it. He'll be back directly."

Though weak and still ashen, Boone asked about the ranch, gathering details about what had been done while he was on the sick list. Jack Webb came by to offer get-well wishes and ask about a horse that developed a limp. Mattie gathered up the family's dirty laundry and bundled it with hers. She headed off to her sister's house with the load.

"I'll help her and then return later," she said, leaving her husband with a kiss.

Jacob watched, thinking about what Maggie had said. He pondered it more while he bounced Benjamin on one knee. Rachel touched Boone each time she entered the room, her hands lingering to caress his shoulders or rake through his hair. She planted kisses on his face often, and the looks she sent his way were nothing short of adoration. By the same token, Boone caught Rachel's hand or stroked her cheek many times. When Zeke returned with Mima, the child was full of chatter about riding Bluebell, but she also rushed to kiss her daddy's cheek. Jacob couldn't remember ever seeing such casual affection between Liam and his children.

After he'd had a bit of bean soup Rachel had concocted, Boone rose on his own power. He stood, shaky, until Jacob and Moses flanked him.

"I reckon I'll lay down a spell," he said. "Got to get some strength so I can eat some chicken and dumplins this evening."

When Jacob took Boone's arm to steady him, his brother tried to pull away. "Let me help," Jacob told him. "You don't want to end up on the floor or relapse, do you?"

"Naw," Boone said with the ghost of a grin. "I'd rather not."

By the time he sprawled on the bed, sweat beaded on his face. Rachel had followed, and she tucked the blankets around him. "Sleep as long as you can, Boone," she told him. "I'm not going anywhere, and neither are the chicken and dumplings."

Jacob took the boys, five-year-old Robert and Benjamin, who would turn three come January, for a ramble around the ranch. It wasn't quite as cold as it had been, and the sun was shining. Both boys had been cooped up for too long, so he let them stretch their legs and run a little. They sat on the bench outside his small cabin for a bit and cloud watched. It was an entertainment Ma had used during their childhood, so Jacob asked them to decide what the clouds resembled.

"I reckon that one looks like a fish," he told them, and they laughed.

"That one over yonder looks to me like a yearling colt," Robert, very much his father's son, said and pointed. "And that one is like a bull."

Late in the afternoon, they wandered back toward Boone's house and met Mattie on the way, carrying the clean, dry laundry.

Maggie was with her. Jacob offered to carry the clothing, folded into a pair of baskets.

"Thank you," Mattie told him. She and Maggie took the boy's hands.

At the house, the rich aroma of chicken and dumplings filled the air along with the fragrance of fresh baked bread. Katie, clad in an apron, stuck her head out of the kitchen to greet them. Ezekiel faced Mima over a checkerboard, and both were intent on the game. Moses and Rachel were both absent.

"He's with Boone," Ezekiel said, anticipating Jacob's question. "So is Rachel. Mac is back from San Antonio, and he's in there, too."

Jacob's stomach clenched. "Did he bring word from Maggie's folks?"

Zeke shrugged. "I don't know. I been teaching Mima how to play checkers and she's right good at it. She keeps on like this; you or Boone can teach her chess in a few years. I don't have the mind for it, myself."

"I reckon I'll go find out the news," Jacob said.

He could hear Boone's raised voice before he reached the bedroom.

"What in tarnation do they intend to do, Mac?"

"Aye, weel, I dinna ken," Mac replied in his deep burr. Jacob realized he'd never know the man's name, nothing but Mac, and made a vow to remedy that. "They took the news hard and said Maggie – they called her 'Magdalena' should come home. Nothing 'twas said about whether they would come to fetch her. I didn't tarry, man."

"I figured," Boone said. "Takes six or seven days to get to San Antonio, and you're back in less than a week. You must have ridden hard, like the devil was chasing your tail."

Mac grinned. "Aye, I did. I've no use for the towns, never did."

"Did her folks send a letter or any word?" Rachel asked.

He produced a sealed paper. "Aye."

Jacob stood in the bedroom doorway. "I'll fetch Maggie back so she can read it."

Boone nodded. "Yeah, we all need to hear what it says so we can be ready if the Baumanns come after her."

Maggie came, her sister at her heels. She sat down in one of the chairs and opened the letter with such care that a body would have thought it contained a rattlesnake. She skimmed it, then read it aloud.

Dear Daughter,

We received your letter about the death of your husband and shared the sad tidings with your two children. We were not able to make the journey to the ranch for the funeral, nor do your children, Grace and Seamus, wish to return. They are settled here in San Antonio and happy attending the German English school as you once did. Seamus prefers to be called James, and both are using our name, Baumann, at this time. They are learning, among other things, geography, algebra, and history. Both now speak German as well. I urge you to get some of the ranch hands to bring you home as soon as you may travel. If that is not possible, write to inform us, and we will hire someone to bring you home. There is nothing left for you on that desolate property in the back country. I will respect your wish that Gunther Hammerschmidt not come fetch you, although he was widowed last year and would make a suitable second husband for you in San Antonio. Mutter has aired your old bedroom and made it ready for your arrival. I am certain that your Irish husband left you nothing worth remaining for on the ranch. We will look for your arrival, and if you should need a situation to earn money for your keep, I know of two families that seek a governess for their children.

Your father, Hans Baumann

Maggie put down the letter and shook her head. She wore

a curious expression, and Jacob couldn't tell if she was on the verge of tears or laughter. Mattie lifted the letter and read it, then said, "Oh, Sister!"

"If by that you mean I should give in to their demand and go home, then no," Maggie said.

"It might be best," Mattie replied. "I don't quite know."

"Would you go back if something happened to Moses?" Maggie asked. "If they changed Ellie into Elsa or Elfriede and she went by Baumann instead of Wilson?"

Mattie's face turned crimson. "Well, no, I wouldn't, Maggie, but…"

"There are no buts," she cried. "I'd rather be here than governess to some little German hellions or God forbid, marry Gunther. You didn't want that fool – do you think I would?"

Rachel stood. "Maybe you'd best take the discussion to the other room," she said with a glance at Boone. "Boone's recovering. He needs quiet."

"I reckon I'm fine," Boone said in a slow drawl. "I need to hear what's gonna happen as much as anyone. Maggie's inheriting Liam's share of the ranch, a quarter of it. If she goes home, then her folks get ahold of it until her son grows up. I do believe that's very much my business. It would disturb me more not to know. Sit back down, honey."

Maggie stood as Rachel took a seat. "Boone, I meant what I said before – I'm staying on the ranch. Even if you threw me off for some reason, I'd go to Laredo, not San Antonio. I'd ask Mary at the Out of Luck for a job before I'd spend the rest of my days minding someone else's children."

"Magdalena!" Mattie cried. "You wouldn't."

"I wouldn't be a saloon girl, no," Maggie said. "I think I might be a bit old for it. I can cook, though, and I could prepare meals or something else."

"Maggie, you've a home on this ranch as long as I'm here,"

Boone said. "That would be true even if Liam didn't leave a will or his share to you. It don't sound like your folks are sending anyone to fetch you yet, so let's leave it lay for now. I'd like to enjoy a bowl of chicken with dumplings with the family – which to my way of thinking, includes you."

Jacob did his best to hide a smile. The woman had spunk, he thought, and he liked it. If no one planned to come after her, he'd wait a reasonable time to marry Maggie, but marry her he would.

"Then let's go eat," Jacob said. "Boone, I'll lend a hand if you need one."

His brother shot him a look that said much more than words, but all he spoke was, "I'd be obliged, Jacob."

CHAPTER NINE

They marked one week after Liam's untimely death, then two. While Boone had been ill, December had arrived. His recuperation was a slow process, but he gained strength daily. He managed to get Jacob aside to ask a favor.

"I married Rachel eight years ago last Thursday," he said. "I meant to get her a present of some kind or another. I'd ride to Laredo myself, but I fear it's a mite soon to make the trip. Would you be willing to go and see if you can find a pretty locket or at least a string of beads or something?"

Jacob had wanted to head for town to get a little courting gift for Maggie, so he agreed.

"I can go on Saturday. I doubt any of us will go back before Christmas, so you might make a list, Boone. I think Ezekiel would like to go along with me."

"Long as he doesn't get in any fisticuffs or scrapes," Boone replied. "I don't reckon he will now, he's married and all, gonna be a daddy."

"He won't, and if he does, I'd get him out of it," Jacob said.

"See if there's a letter come from Ma, too," Boone added. "It's been a while since we've heard, and I'm hoping all is well back in Kentucky."

"I will, Boone. I reckon it is."

On Saturday, December 14, Jacob and Zeke headed out early in the wagon. In Laredo, they nearly filled the wagon bed with supplies for the ranch, Christmas plunder, and a few gifts. Jacob found a heart-shaped locket he thought Boone would like for Rachel, and he bought some beads for Maggie. He'd slip them to her on the sly, he thought, so no one would get any wrong ideas. They bought some peppermint stick candies for the little ones, a few toys and such, and a length of a pretty calico that would become a dress for Mima. He splurged on some fresh oranges for Christmas and a few books, including a copy of *Alice in Wonderland,* especially for little Jemima Ann.

They ate, not at the Out of Luck Saloon, but at the café, then headed back home. There had been no letters waiting from Ma or anyone else. It was almost sundown by the time they reached the ranch, and dark before they had the wagon unloaded. Before they could eat the beef and frijoles Rachel had prepared, they unhitched and stabled the horses once the wagon was parked.

Jacob left the Christmas things at his little cabin. Boone met him there, and he gave him the locket. "I hope you like it," he said.

Boone let it dangle from his fingers and nodded. "It's right pretty. I think Rachel will like it. Did you have any trouble?"

"Naw, none. And no letters either."

The grin on Boone's lips faded. "I hoped there would be."

"Me, too."

"Head on over for supper, Jacob. There's plenty. All of us are comin' and after we eat, Mima wants to sing some Christmas carols."

Rachel served the tender beef over mounds of mashed potatoes with a rich brown gravy. The frijoles refritos, another favorite of Boone's that she'd learned to make, were served on the side. Jacob savored the meal and watched as his brothers, with their wives and children, made merry. After they ate, Boone got his guitar and played a few chords. Mima clapped her hands with delight. "Sing a Christmas song, Daddy."

"It's still nearabout two weeks until Christmas," he told her with a grin. "Ain't it awful early?"

She shook her head, and her tandem braids swung from side to side.

"I will, baby girl, but first I got to sing a song for your mama," he said. "A few days ago was the anniversary of when we wed. I didn't forget, honey. I reckon you figured I did, but that wasn't the case. I was waiting for something."

Rachel met his gaze and smiled. "What was that?"

Boone dangled the heart-shaped locket from his hand. "A gift for you," he told her. "You got my heart. I thought it wouldn't hurt anything for you to have one to wear to show that."

She took it from him and fumbled until she had it clasped about her neck. Then she cupped it in her hand. "It's beautiful, Boone, thank you."

"I love you, honey," he said. "I'd marry you again if I could. You might recollect when I first sang this old ballad to you, changing the name to Rachel."

In his sweet, true voice, Boone sang an ancient Irish song, *Eileen Aroon.* He changed the woman's name to Rachel every time, and there were tears on Rachel's face by the time he finished. She rose, and despite the guitar in his hands, she leaned close and kissed him full on the mouth. "I remember and I love you, Boone Wilson."

Jacob smiled and wondered if there might be another child in about nine months or so after this night. He didn't ponder the possibility long because he joined in singing with the others as Boone and Mima led them in a rousing chorus of *Jingle Bells.* Then they sang many others, everything from *Joy To The World* to *O Come All Ye Faithful.* Rachel and Katie sang that one in Latin. When Boone began to strum the notes for *Silent Night,* Mattie held up one hand.

"Oh, we can't sing that one, not without my sister," she cried. "We sing it in German, together."

Jacob nodded. Maggie had been the one person missing, but he didn't dare ask after her. She wasn't family, not quite yet, but he'd wished all evening that she had been present.

Boone nodded. "Fair enough. We got time before Christmas to sing it. I'll sing one more, one I learned during the war. It's called *Deck The Halls.*"

Before the song ended, they were all joining in the fa-la-la-la-la-la-la-la refrain.

"That's it for now," Boone said and set the guitar aside. Rachel picked it up and carried it to the corner, where it sat. "I'm near give out, and it's past these children's bedtime."

"It's past yours, too," Rachel said. "You're still recovering from that nasty spider bite."

He nodded, and Jacob thought his brother looked weary. "I know it better than anyone, honey. Thought tomorrow afternoon we might sing a few hymns if anyone's willing to join in the singing."

Mima and Rob clapped their hands. "Yes, oh, yes, please."

Moses spoke up. "Come eat dinner with us first, then. Rachel shouldn't have to do all the work."

Once the good nights and farewells were said, Jacob walked back to the small cabin. He didn't wait for anyone to walk partway with him. Instead, he enjoyed the crisp night air and the stars that decorated the wide sky above. Hands in his pockets, not minding the chill wind, he took his time walking back. The beads he'd bought for Maggie were in his pocket, but he decided he'd best not visit her this late. She might well be awake, but if anyone, family, or ranch hands, noticed, it would be a disgrace.

On Sunday, after a fine meal at Mattie and Moses' place, they returned to Boone's more spacious quarters. After the singing, Boone told them a piece of news Jacob hadn't expected.

"I thought now that we own the ranch, us and Maggie, we might build a little church," he said. "Wouldn't hurt to have a house of worship on the property. I don't figure we can have a preacher or a priest, least not all the time, but it would come in handy. I don't plan to start on it till spring, maybe, but it's an idea."

Ezekiel, once the wildest of all the Wilson brothers, nodded. "I like it, Boone. It'd be a place to having weddings, baptizing, and such."

"It would," Moses said. "I'm glad you thought of that, Boone."

"Man thinks about a lot of things when he's laid up," Boone replied. "The other thing I reckoned I'd best mention is this – I know from the letter they sent back it don't sound like Maggie's folks plan to come to fetch her, but I think we should be aware they might show up anyhow. We need to be ready. I don't want any fight, but I don't want trouble neither."

Mattie frowned. "Do you really think they might come to the ranch?"

"I do or send someone. It's been near three weeks since Liam passed, and since the ranch ain't sent her home, I fear they might try to fetch Maggie home."

"What do you plan to do if that happens?" Mattie asked. "It's my folks as well."

Boone's genial expression faded. "I'm aware, Mattie," he said. "Like I said, I don't want any trouble. Your sister says she's staying, and I respect that. I'm ranch boss now, so it's my concern what happens here. I'd rather not get blindsided."

"We'll be on the lookout," Jacob said. He didn't want any difficulty either, but if they came, he'd be marrying Maggie sooner. That part of it he liked fine. "You can tell all the hands, too."

"I already did," Boone said.

As the week continued, the men continued the daily work of the ranch. Winter was the lighter season for chores, but there remained much to do. The two dairy cows had to be milked, and the rest of the stock had to be watered. Despite the cold temperatures, there remained plenty of grass to graze in the pastures, but sometimes a bit of hay was needed, too. That required shifting the stock every few days. Horses needed to be shod and exercised. Saddles and tack were repaired. Shoveling out the horse barns was a never-ending task. Maintenance on the barbed wire fences had to be done as well.

On Wednesday, the young ranch hand Davy, who had misinformed Rachel about who died, came riding up to Boone's house around nine in the morning. Normally, Boone would be out on the ranch, hard at work, but since the spider bite, he'd been starting early, then returning home for a late breakfast and a bit of a rest. Jacob had joined him to eat and sat smoking on the front porch. When Davy galloped up and reined in the animal, he came to his feet.

"What is it?" He did a quick mental tally. Moses and Ezekiel were at the corrals, working some of the horses. He prayed nothing had gone amiss with either one.

"Wagon's coming," Davy said, gasping for breath. He'd ridden hard to get there. "I'd say it may be as much as an hour out, but it's heading here. Ain't nowhere else it could be going."

Boone emerged from the house and heard Davy. "I'd best get saddled up," he said. "If it's those Germans, it's likely to get a mite unpleasant. Go tell my brothers to meet us at the main ranch house, pronto."

"Do you think it's them?" Jacob asked as he crushed out his smoke.

"I have no idea," Boone said. "But I'd rather we be ready than not."

He returned inside and came back with his gun belt buckled in place for the first time since he'd been ill. He wore his overcoat as well. "Are you packing iron?"

Jacob pulled back his duster to reveal his pistol. "I am."

"I told Rachel to keep the little ones inside until we find out what's going on," Boone said. "Let's get the horses and ride over there. I plan to meet this wagon, whoever may be driving it."

At Maggie's house, Boone knocked, then entered without waiting.

Maggie was kneading bread dough at the table and glanced up with alarm.

"Boone, what's the matter?"

"Maybe something, maybe nothing," he told her. "The hands spotted a wagon heading this direction, so I reckoned we'd best be here when it arrives."

She paled. "Do you suppose it's my parents?"

"I don't know," Boone replied. "I hope it ain't."

Jacob didn't say it aloud, but he hoped it was, for then he'd marry Mattie as soon as they could get a judge or preacher to the ranch. He'd take her to Laredo if necessary.

Maggie attacked the bread dough with vengeance in her eyes. "I hope not either."

Moses and Zeke rode up and then tied their mounts beside the others at the hitching rack. By then, the wagon was visible as it approached across the open country. The four brothers stood together, smoking but saying little. As it became closer, Moses squinted.

"I swear that looks like Phineas Dawson's rig," he said. "Might be him driving the team. I cain't see for sure yet."

Boone shaded his eyes with one hand. "Might be. I reckon we'll find out soon. I wouldn't think Phin would take on the job of dragging Maggie back to town, but it could be."

Ezekiel stared. "Who's that sitting beside Phin on the wagon seat?" he asked. "Don't look like one of the Germans. They're mostly fair and blond – that man is dark."

Jacob narrowed his gaze. "He is, dark as Garrett," he told them. "Even got the moustache like Garrett. Favors him a good bit."

As the most recent Wilson arrival in Texas, Jacob had seen Garrett more recently than any of the others. Still, after he spoke, he noticed Moses take a closer gander.

Boone took a few steps forward. "If it is – and I ain't saying it is – Garrett, then what's become of Ma?"

"Sure, and she's in the wagon," Katie said from behind them. Jacob turned to see Ezekiel's wife with Mima in tow. Boone scowled at her.

"I told Rachel to keep those little ones home till we see what we're facing," he said. "You had no call to bring Jemima Ann up here, Katie. Mima, you'd best go home."

His daughter shook her head. Jacob saw she was wearing her best dress, one more thing likely to make Boone angry. "I came to see my Granny," she said.

"Baby girl, don't talk nonsense," Boone replied. "Far as I know, your granny's still in Kentucky."

As he spoke, the man who sat beside Phineas doffed his hat, then waved it in wide circles as he shouted, "Hello, the house!"

Jacob would have known that voice anywhere, gruff and a little gravely. He pulled off his hat and returned the salute. "Boone," he said, and grasped his brother's shoulder. "Boone, it *is* Garrett."

From where they waited, they watched their brother Garrett come to his feet as the wagon rolled to a stop. He wore a big grin, and so did Phin. Jacob's lips stretched into a wide smile. Moses and Ezekiel started forward, calling to their brother, but Boone stood still.

"If Garrett's come," he said in a low voice. "Where's Ma? He surely wouldn't come and leave her alone back home."

Jacob's guts twisted into a knot. No letters had come lately from Kentucky. Their mother wasn't young, and so many things could happen to a person. He stepped closer to Boone, who stood ramrod straight. Then he recalled what Katie had said, "she's in the wagon," and most of his worry eased.

Garrett leapt from the wagon seat, and his brothers circled him. They pounded each other on the back, they sparred a little, and then they hugged. Jacob grabbed him around the neck. Garrett was the next brother after Jacob.

"It's been too long," he said as he gripped Garrett. "Where's Ma?"

"I'm right here, Jacob Wade Wilson," Jemima Wilson said. She had more gray hair than when he'd last seen her, and her face a few more lines, but little else had changed. Jacob rushed forward, and she embraced him. Then she hugged Zeke and Moses.

Boone hadn't moved. He stood and stared for a long moment. His gaze fell on his mother, and raw emotion poured into his face. He'd been gone from home the longest, and Jacob's heart broke a little when he saw a single tear slide down his brother's cheek.

"Ma," Boone said in a cracked voice. "Oh, Ma. I feared I'd never see you again in this life."

The senior Jemima Wilson took her oldest boy in her arms and folded him close. Tough, grown-up Boone put his head down on his mama's shoulder, and Jacob would swear he shed more tears.

"I feared the same, Boone," Ma said. "That's why I come to Texas, to my boys. You look some peaked. Are you well?"

Mima joined her daddy. "He got bit by a spider," she said. "Made him awful sick, but he's on the mend now. Granny, I'm named for you. I'm Jemima Ann, and I'm seven years old."

Without letting go of Boone, Ma pulled the little girl into their embrace and held her close in a three-way hug.

"I'm right pleased to meet you, little gal," she told Mima. "My heart hungered after you. You've got your daddy's eyes."

Mima laughed. "Daddy and the uncles say I favor you, Granny."

"Then I reckon you do," her grandmother said. "Why, you don't even have a coat on, honey child. Boone, is this your house?"

Jacob didn't think he'd seen his brother with such a huge grin in years.

"Naw, this is the main ranch house. Mine's not far, Ma. Rachel, my wife, she won't even know you're here yet."

Jack Mc Gee stepped forward. "I'll go tell her, Boone, if you want."

"I'd be much obliged," Boone said. "Where's Otis?"

The old cook spoke up. "Right here, boss."

"Got any beef my wife can cook for supper to welcome my Ma and brother?"

Spider Webb chuckled. "In need of a fatted calf?"

Boone laughed. "Something of the sort. Beef steaks would do."

"I'll fetch some over directly."

Maggie emerged from the house with a shawl wrapped around her shoulders. Jacob had noticed she had watched from the window. By now, she would know the new arrivals weren't her folks or anyone they sent, but she might not realize who they were.

"It's my Ma and my brother Garrett," Jacob said after he met her. "They came from Kentucky."

"That's wonderful," she cried. "Would they like to get out of the cold?"

"They might."

Jacob opened his mouth to ask, then closed it as Boone turned from Ma to Garrett, who now stood alone.

"It's been a long time, brother," Garrett said. "I reckon I was no more than 16 when you came home after the war and not yet 17 when you left again."

Boone nodded. "I would've been 21, nearabout."

Garrett laughed. "You acted like a father to us after ours died, Boone, and I've not forgotten that. We had our good times too, swimming in the creeks, going huntin' and fishin' and such. I wasn't but ten when Pa passed."

"I was fifteen," Boone said. "I thought I was a man grown."

"You were to me," Garrett said. "I missed you after you'd gone to Texas, Boone. We all did. Is there a place for me on this ranch?"

Boone grinned. "I can always use a good hand and a hard worker. I've no doubt you're both. And a brother is always welcome. I've missed you as well, often wondered how you fared."

The two embraced with affection. Jacob, watching, realized that love within a family never dies. Ties made early in life remained, he thought, and were still strong.

Mima left her granny's side as the brothers broke apart, smiling and talking over each other in their excitement.

"I'm Mima," she said. "I'm pleased to meet you, Gee-haw!"

Boone guffawed. "Garrett, this is my oldest baby girl, Jemima Ann Wilson, but we call her 'Mima'."

Garrett bowed. "Likewise, little lady, but why call me that?"

Moses joined the conversation. "She's got names for all her uncles," he told Garrett. "I'm Mo-Mo, Ezekiel is Z, and Jacob is Jay. I reckon you get to be Gee-haw!"

They laughed since the nickname referred to horse commands, gee for right and haw for left.

"That does beat all," Garrett said. "But I'll take it."

"Welcome to Texas, brother," Boone said. "I'm right glad you're here."

CHAPTER TEN

The day was fair, but the wind had a bite, so Boone accepted Maggie's invitation to come inside. That would give Rachel time to process the news. She'd want to straighten up the house a bit, he figured, and probably change into one of her better dresses. Besides, Boone needed some coffee, which Maggie provided, and he welcomed the chance to sit down for a bit. Maggie handed out snickerdoodle cookies and offered milk to Mima, who turned it down in favor of coffee.

"I see she's your daughter, Boone," Garrett said. "Taking coffee over milk."

"She's fond of it," he replied with a grin. "Her mama makes her drink milk every day, though. Rachel was a schoolteacher before she married me."

Ma helped herself to another cookie. "I feel as if I know her from your letters, Boone. Ezekiel, was that your wife who was here? Where did she go?"

"It was," Zeke said. "That was my Katie. She went to fetch Mattie, Moses' wife, and their Ellie."

Jacob gave a lazy smile. "Mattie is sister to Maggie," he said. He'd introduced Maggie as Liam's widow a few minutes earlier.

Phineas Dawson had joined the Wilsons at the table and spoke up for the first time.

"Miz Wilson, where do you want me to unload your trunk and such? I'll likely make a start back to San Antone 'fore long. Got letters to deliver first. My family's gonna want me home for Christmas, and that's in a week, so I'd best make tracks."

"I don't rightly know yet, Mr. Dawson," Ma said. "Boone?"

His brain still hadn't wrapped around the fact that his mother had arrived along with his brother. He hadn't thought ahead far enough to consider who might stay where. His growing family filled his house, but he could tuck Garrett into the boys' room or Ma in with Mima. Before he could offer a solution, his brother did.

"Garrett could stay with us for a bit," Moses said. "We've got the spare bed."

"There's room at the little cabin," Jacob stated. "Ma or Garrett could stay with me, though, if they both do, we'd need another bed."

"Your mother's welcome to stay here," Maggie added. "I've got the space."

Jack McGee, who had returned, added his two cents' worth. "There's room aplenty in the bunkhouse, too, should your brother want to sleep there."

"Appears you have some choices, Ma," Boone said. "You're welcome to come in with us as well if you wouldn't mind a passel of kids underfoot."

"I can bunk in with Moses to start," Garrett said. "If his bride doesn't mind."

"I doubt she will," Moses said.

Jemima Wilson looked around the table at her sons and smiled. "I'd be happy anywhere, but I think I'll stay at this small cabin with Jacob for now. He's likely the loneliest of you all. I can cook, should I want there."

"Ma, you can eat with us," Boone told her. "Or with any of your sons. Besides, we often eat together anyway."

She nodded. "I'd like that fine, but there's times when a woman might want to keep a hand in cooking too."

Without bothering to knock, Robert burst into the house, his hair as brown as Boone's, and halted when he saw the two strangers.

"Mama sent me," he said.

Boone beckoned the boy to him. "Ma, Garrett, this is my oldest son, Robert. We call him Rob most of the time. Son, this is your Granny and your uncle Garrett."

Garrett nodded at the child. "Your sister here has named me Gee-haw," he said with a smile beneath his wide moustache. "I'll answer to it."

Ma opened her arms. "Come here, Robert. You're named, I reckon, for their daddy and my husband. It's a fine name."

Rob came to her with slow steps, eyes wide. His grandmother pulled him into a hug, and he wrapped his arms around her. She set him on her knee and studied his face. "He favors your daddy some through the eyes," she pronounced. "Looks more like Garrett here than the rest of you."

"That makes him the most handsome," Garrett said, and they all laughed.

"What did your mama say to tell us?" Boone asked.

"She said come to the house whenever you're ready. Ol' Mister Webb brought some beef steaks, and she said she'll have a fine supper for everyone. At dinner time, she said tell you it'll be just 'taters and frijoles."

Ma planted a kiss on the back of Rob's neck. "I don't know what a free-hole-a might be, but it'll eat just fine."

"Best beans you've ever had," Ezekiel said.

"I'm gonna take that trunk over to Jake's place," Phin said. "Garrett, you'd best get your gear out of the wagon."

"If you don't mind, maybe you could drop Ma off at the house," Boone said.

Ma shook her head. "There's no need. I can walk, and these children can lead the way."

"Ma..."

"I'm glad of the chance to stretch my legs a bit," she told him. "I rode that wagon for a week to get here, and the train before that. I ain't feeble just yet, Boone."

The fact that she was still feisty as ever pleased him, and he chuckled. "Ma, I've missed you awful bad," he said. "I'm glad you're here."

"I told you I'd come."

"You did. Why didn't you write and say you were headin' this way? I got worried we hadn't had any letters lately."

She smiled. "I figured we'd get here before a letter might. Come on, Mima and Rob. Take Granny over to your house. I want to see your brother and sister and meet your mama."

"I'll be there directly, Ma," Boone said.

"I'll go fetch Mattie and Ellie," Moses said. "I'll walk if you want to borrow my horse, Garrett."

"If you do, we'll take a short ride around the ranch," Boone told him. "Show you the lay of the land."

Garrett nodded. "Phineas, will you drop my gear at Jacob's? I'll fetch it later."

"Licorice is a good mount," Moses told him.

Ezekiel promised to bring Katie over by supper time, if not before. "Right now, though, I'm going huntin'," he told them.

"We got plenty of meat," Boone said.

"We don't have turkey, though, and I recollect Ma's right fond of it. I thought I'd shoot a couple birds for tomorrow's dinner."

Ma clapped her hands together with delight. "I would enjoy that, Ezekiel."

With two more adult mouths to feed, Boone had no protest.

Within the next half hour, everyone, including Boone, was prepared to leave except Jacob. Boone sent a backwards glance at his brother and pointed his finger at him.

"Come ride with us," he said.

Jacob glanced at Mattie, then nodded. "I reckon I can."

Once they had mounted, Boone turned to Jacob. "I'm

beginning to think you'd best go visit the Out of Luck and get a girl, Jacob, before you lose what sense you got left and we end up having a shotgun wedding."

"I still have all my faculties, Boone, and I ain't going to anything that might result in that," Jacob said. His voice held an edge of anger. "You know better than that."

"I wish I did," Boone said. "You're addlepated. If I don't know better, I'd vow and swear Maggie bewitched you."

Garrett dug in his pocket for baccy and rolled a smoke. "Jacob's got courting trouble?"

"I don't," Jacob replied, but at the same time Boone said, "He does, and that's a fact."

"Do tell," Garrett said. "If I'm going to be known as Gee-haw, I reckon you ought to share the family gossip."

After a dozen or so years apart, there had been a layer of awkwardness at first, but as they talked, it melted away as if it had never existed. "Jacob here is smitten with Liam's widow, Maggie," Boone said.

Garrett whistled. "And how long has the man been dead?"

"About three weeks," Boone said.

"Fast work," Garrett said and laughed.

"It wasn't so quick as all that," Jacob interrupted as the horses walked forward. "I've had a fondness for Maggie for some time. It was just I never thought anything would come of it, her being married and all."

"Then Liam died," Boone said.

He rode between his two brothers, enjoying ribbing Jacob about Maggie. Although he'd objected since Liam had scarcely been buried, Boone did see that Jacob cared for the woman. To his amazement, he'd seen that Maggie returned that affection.

"Tell him about her family," Jacob added.

"Liam sent Maggie's two children off to San Antonio for school and to live with her folks, hard-headed German folk.

Liam's will gave her his share of the ranch – if she stays on it for at least a year. If not, it goes to her parents to hold in trust for their boy. She's not of a mind to leave the ranch, and so she proposed marriage to Jacob here. Got the idea from Mattie, her sister, because she married Moses to stay. It was a mite different, though, since they'd courted and she'd come back here against their wishes to nurse him with the pneumonia."

"I said I'd wed her if it came to that," Jacob stated. "And even if it don't, we still plan to wed a little down the road."

"I don't doubt that one bit," Boone said. Although he might not be quite ready to give his blessing, he saw that it would happen, so he might as well offer his support.

"I wish you well with it," Garrett said. "I'm still a bachelor and likely to remain one."

Famous last words, Boone thought, but didn't say it. Seemed like every time one of the Wilson brothers came to Texas, the next thing anyone knew, they found a bride. "C'mon, let's get these horses moving, and I'll show you the ranch."

First, Boone rode past their houses, the dog trot cabins where Zeke and Moses lived, the small cabin Jacob called home that Garrett would share, and his house. Then he took them on a loop around the ranch, not the entire perimeter but a fair portion of it, pointing out highlights like the bunkhouse, the corrals and barns, and some of the stock.

"How many acres?" Garrett asked. Back home in Kentucky, they'd had 250 acres, part planted in tobacco and the rest for raising horses.

"10,000, give or take," Boone said.

Garrett's eyes enlarged. "And you own it? You must be a rich man, Boone."

"Not hardly," he told his brother. "I don't own it – Ezekiel, Moses, and me each have one of four shares. Liam had the other, but now that he's gone, Maggie owns the rest. Ranch brings in enough to keep it going and pay wages, not much more."

They'd reached the pond and reined in their horses.

"Pretty place," Garrett said. "Got any fish in it?"

"Not really," Boone said. "Fishing is better over to the Rio Grande at Laredo."

Garrett rolled a fresh cigarette and lit it. "Can Maggie sell her portion of the ranch?"

"She can if she remarries, according to Liam's will. Why?"

"I reckon I'd like to buy her out if that's possible."

He said it in a casual voice, but Boone turned to look at him. So did Jacob.

"It would take a fair amount."

Boone reminded himself this wasn't the 16-year-old kid brother he remembered but a grown man.

"I reckon I have enough," Garrett told him. "I sold all the Morgans so we could come to Texas, and Ma sold the homeplace. Between me and Ma, we got a good bit. Put a chunk of it in the Cattleman's Bank up at San Antonio."

"That's where we've got the ranch account."

Garrett nodded. "Yeah, that's what Phin Dawson told me. It's why I chose it."

Boone considered it. He hadn't expected that his mother would come to Texas. She had said she would for so long, he had about decided it was nothing but a dream. But here she was, and his other brother too. Since Garrett sold the Morgan horses and Ma sold the homeplace, they were here to stay.

"If the chance comes up and she's willing to sell her share to you, I'd be over the moon," Boone said. "It'd be a Wilson ranch all around. Maybe we could get Jacob to have a piece of it, too."

"I'd like that," Jacob said. "I got some saved for that purpose, though I doubt it's near as much as Garrett has. Might change the name again after that."

"What's wrong with Double Deuce?" Boone asked. "It

started out the Double B under Liam for Bonnie Blue, like the flag, then when we bought in, we called it Double Deuce. Deuce is two, and double deuce is four. That's how many of us are or were partners."

"There would be more than four of us, but it's just a name," Garrett said. "I can still count, Boone."

Boone grinned and fired his own smoke. "Well, so can I. Let's go look at the barbed wire, then eat some dinner. The womenfolk will be wondering what took so long."

The table was set and laden with food. Besides the refried beans Rachel had promised, there were cornmeal waffles. Boone hadn't had one since he last left Kentucky, so he knew Ma had made those. The waffles paired well with the beans, but there were no potatoes.

His mother sat in the rocking chair with Sarah Rose on her shoulder and Benjamin in her lap. Mima stood with one hand on the rocker while Rob played with his horses on the floor. Zeke and Moses were there along with their wives. Moses had little Ellie tucked into his arms.

"You have sweet children, Boone," Ma said as he entered. "Smart as whips, too. This little fella favors you, son."

"I've said so since the day he was born," Moses said with a grin.

"Moses brought him," Boone said. "I was out riding the range with Liam. I'm hungry. Where's the 'taters, Rachel?"

"I'm keeping them for supper," she told him. "Your Ma made cornmeal waffles."

"That'll be a treat. Ain't had them like she makes them in years."

The meal was simple but delicious. Boone relished every bite, but more than the food, he savored his family, his mother and brother Garrett, most of all. Ma fit into his daily life like a foot into a shoe, he thought. He watched her with his wife and with his little ones, pleased that they blended, all one family. His heart swelled with joy, and even while eating, he couldn't stop grinning. With fourteen people ranging from Ma's age down to the baby gathered around his table, he thought he'd bust his buttons with pride.

"I don't hardly recollect the last time I was at the same table with Ma and all my brothers," Boone said. "Likely after I came back from the war."

He'd been young and shattered after four long, hard years as a soldier. Home hadn't proved to be the refuge he had hoped. It had changed little, but he had, and he had left, trying to find the pieces of himself he'd lost.

"I'd say that's right, son," Ma replied. "And that's been what, twelve, no, thirteen years. It was too long. You left, then Ezekiel took off following you, then Moses, then Jacob. My heart has ached for all of you. It's been lonesome these last years with only Garrett. Your letters kept me going, but it was hard, reading about the grandchildren I feared I might never know. Times you were hurt, Boone, or any of you sick, I thought I'd lose my mind worrying."

"We're all here, though, in one piece and alive," he told her.

She shook her head. "I thought I'd lost you when that Liam wrote after you were shot, but then, praise God, you lived. Then I feared you'd hang, and Moses came to see you didn't. I doubt much you've written every time one of you took sick or got hurt."

Boone scraped up the last bite of frijoles on his plate. "I did write you about Moses being so bad sick, Ma. I thought he was a goner."

"You did," she said. "But Rachel here tells me that Ezekiel got stabbed and beaten some time back in Laredo and that you came near having Jacob's hand amputated. I heard about horses throwing folks and such. Then little Mima told me about this spider bite. Let me see your hand, Boone."

Obedient as a child, he stretched out his left hand. The spider bite had healed a great deal, but there remained an irritated spot the size of a quarter. Around it, his skin remained reddish, and it was still a little sore. Ma leaned down and studied it. "It's not looking too bad. Once I get unpacked, I'll make some comfrey paste and put on it. If you leave it on, it should heal fine."

He nodded. "Alright, this evening. I gotta go put up Sprat, though, and see about re-shoeing some of the horses with Jacob's help."

Rachel paused, clearing the table, and laid her hands on his shoulders.

"Boone, you look weary," she said. "Stay and rest a spell. You didn't this morning."

"I'm good," he told her, although he wasn't. Fatigue hung over him as heavy as a wool blanket on a July morning. His body ached, and his hand twinged. A slight headache warned that he needed a respite. He'd ridden over a good portion of the ranch, the most he'd done since he was laid up. A dull headache signaled he needed to slow down and sleep if he could.

"You're not," Rachel said with affection. She knew him better than anyone. "Go lay down, Boone, so you can enjoy supper. Mima wants to sing with you afterward so Ma can hear what a pretty voice she has."

Her fingers kneaded his taut shoulders as she spoke, and he surrendered as his muscles relaxed.

"I will, then, honey. If Benjamin needs a nap, he can lay down with me, I reckon."

"He does, that's for certain," Rachel replied. "Take him, Boone. I'll come check on both of you after I clean the kitchen."

"God gave me hands," Ma said. "I can do that if you need to tend to Boone. Besides, there's Katie and Mattie here to help."

Boone hid a grin. His mother and wife had a mutual regard. If they hadn't, Rachel wouldn't have called her 'Ma' but Mrs. Wilson, and Ma wouldn't have offered to help if she didn't approve of his bride. "Let them do it all, Ma," he said. "Let Jacob take you over to his cabin so you can get settled. You might use a rest yourself. You came a long way."

"I would like to see the place," Ma replied. "I could use a bit of a wash, and I'd like to change out of this dress I've worn for a week."

Jacob came to his feet. "Then let's head over. Phineas should have brought your trunk over there. Boone, we'll be back in time for supper."

"I'll be here," he said.

Boone lifted his youngest boy out of his mother's lap and headed for his bed. Stretching out his tired body appealed, and although Benjamin wiggled for the first ten minutes, it wasn't long until they both slept.

CHAPTER ELEVEN

Jacob tended to be neat. He didn't toss his clothing or gear on the floor and did his best to keep his small place clean. When he'd left that morning, he had no idea that his mother and brother would arrive or that he'd be sharing his home with Ma. He might not admit it, but since Ezekiel married and moved, he had been more than a little lonely. He'd married young and spent the better part of his adult life with Sally Ann until she died after giving birth to a child he'd buried with her. Garrett would be welcome too, he thought, as he opened the door and let Ma walk into his living space. There was room enough, though it might be a little close, but if he opted to stay at Moses' for now, that worked too.

"Here it is," he said as he followed her into the single room. "Home sweet home."

Ma walked across to the fireplace, stopped, then nodded. "It's right nice," she commented. "Ain't big but it's enough for two of us, or three should Garrett wear out his welcome."

He laughed. They'd often thought in tandem and hadn't lost the knack. "He might. I don't know if anyone mentioned it or if I should say, but Mattie's in the family way."

"Rachel told me and Katie, too, she said."

"You'll have plenty of grandbabies here," he said. She'd left behind three in Kentucky, his daughters, and he ached to ask how they fared. After his wife's death, Sally Ann's folks had taken them home. It had been the right thing to do, and he knew it. He'd been grieving hard, and on his best day, Jacob floundered with taking care of young ones. If he'd had boys, he might have managed, but girls were a mystery. He'd become a better uncle than he'd ever been a father.

Ma removed her bonnet and walked over to her trunk. She opened it, and the sweet tang of lemon verbena wafted into the cabin. "You're likely wondering what news about your gals," she said. "They're well, Jacob. They've thrived at their grandparents. Faith, Hope, and Charity are as pretty as their mama when she was young. When they heard I was coming to Texas for good, they each wrote you a letter."

She handed him a stack of papers, tied with a ribbon. Jacob took them, but he couldn't read them now. He would need to be alone for that, so he put them on the mantle.

"I'll fetch your water," he said. "You said you'd like a wash."

"Thank you," Ma said. "I'll find the dress I want while you're gone."

Jacob returned with a fresh bucket and then left so she could have privacy.

"I'll be back directly," he told her. "I'd best see to something on the ranch."

Ma's eyes twinkled, and she smiled. "Might that be a fetching young widow woman?"

He felt the heat on his cheeks and nodded. Never had been able to pull the wool over Ma's eyes, not much. She had a touch of what Katie called being fey as well. Ma knew things no one told her and always had.

"I reckon it might be," he told her.

"She's a comely woman," Ma said. "She seems to be as taken with you as you are with her. How long has she been widowed?"

Boone would tell her if he didn't. "Not quite a month."

Ma's eyebrows shot upward. "That's not long at all."

"I've admired her for a long time," Jacob told her. "I never thought we could be more than friends till Liam died. I still wouldn't be thinking about courting nor marriage, but she asked me if I'd wed her if her folks tried to take her back to San Antonio."

Ma wore a perplexed expression. "And if they don't, you won't get married?"

"We'll wed," Jacob said. "But if they don't, we'll wait a decent time first."

Jemima nodded. "Maggie's husband was Liam, that Boone served with in the war, and that started this ranch, is that right?"

"It is."

"Was he not a good husband for her to be willing to marry again so soon?"

"That's Maggie's to say, not mine," Jacob told his mother. "He changed, Ma, even in the two years or so I've been here. He did send her children away, and he's the one who wrote the will that complicates what the rest of us can do with the ranch."

"Do you believe she's sure in her mind and heart?" Ma asked.

Jacob didn't flinch under the questions. Ma had a way of being direct.

"I do," he said.

Jemima Wilson met his gaze without blinking. "Then I wish you well of her, Jacob. You're much too young to spend the rest of your days alone. You might even have more children."

He laughed. He'd like nothing better. "Maybe so."

Jacob kissed his mother's cheek and picked up his hat. "I don't reckon I'll be long. I just want to see how she's faring with all this. She's left lonesome a good part of the time."

"Ask her to come to supper at Boone's," Ma told him. "Your brother will have more than enough and isn't she sister to Moses' wife?"

"Yeah, she is, and I will," Jacob replied.

He took the shortest route across the ranch to the main house. When Jacob mounted the steps to the back door, he heard

Maggie weeping. He burst inside without bothering to knock. She sat at the table with her face cradled in her arms as she sobbed.

"Maggie, sugar," he said. "What's wrong?"

At the sound of his voice, she stilled. Maggie raised her blotchy face to him.

"Oh, Jacob, thank goodness you're here. I prayed you would come, I did."

He sat down across from her and reached for her hand. "Tell me why you're crying."

"My family sent a letter," she told him and handed him a sheet of paper. "They hired someone to deliver it all the way from town. You can read it. They've disowned me. As far as they're concerned, I'm dead to them. They told Grace and Seamus that I'm as dead as Liam."

Her voice broke as she spoke, and tears rained down her cheeks. Jacob rose, then knelt beside her chair. "Maggie, I'm so sorry," he told her. "That's wicked of them. I'll understand if you change your mind. If you want to go to San Antonio, I'll take you myself."

Maggie shook her head. "I don't. I wouldn't go now, not for love or money. It's too late, anyway. It's done. If I went, they would turn me away from the door. I don't understand it, not one bit. They were strict in raising us and prideful, thinking Germans are better than anyone else, but I would never have dreamed they would do something like this, not ever."

"I reckon not," he said. Jacob couldn't begin to understand. Love bound his family together. Not one of them would ever disown another, no matter what happened. "Surely they don't mean it."

"Oh, they do," she said. "Read it, Jacob, and you'll see."

He returned to a chair and read the letter. He had trouble with the fancy handwriting, but he managed to read it, his outrage and anger growing with each word that he read. If he had been a cussing man, he would have turned the air blue with the foulest oaths. The words he read were cruel and cold. Jacob wondered how such people could have produced daughters who were kind and good.

"Our grandparents would be so sad," Maggie said. "Oma and Opa were very different than our parents. Opa would have wanted to beat them with his cane, I'm sure. Mattie and I are the oldest children, so we spent more time with them. Oma liked to say they raised us, which always made my parents angry, but it's true."

That answered his unspoken question and settled the uneasy feeling it'd brought.

Jacob read the letter one more time, in disbelief that any parent could write such a spiteful letter to any child.

Mrs. Magdalena Bauman Rafferty:
Since you have chosen to remain on that ranch in the company of rough individuals and to not return to your home here in San Antonio, we have no choice but to disown you. You will not have any reason to return here, nor any possessions, nor money, when the day comes that we pass from this life. We will consider you as dead to us from this day forward. We have formal plans to adopt your two children, Grace and Seamus, as our own. Attorneys have told us there will be no problem to do so. Since you failed to return to your family, it will be considered abandonment by the letter of the law. Grace wishes to become Greta, and Seamus will be called James. They will no longer use the name of Rafferty but Bauman.

The will written by your late husband will stand, however. We received a copy of it since we are mentioned and had it read by our attorney. If you do not remain on that ranch for twelve months, one year's time, you will forfeit all interest in it, and we will hold it in trust for James when he comes of age. If you stay for that year or if you remarry, then all rights to the ranch remain with you.

No matter what you decide about your residency on the ranch, do not contact us or your children. We will not speak your name. Photographs of you will be destroyed, as will any possessions you might have remaining in this house.

We regret that we once sent Mathilde to the ranch and believe it is through you that she defied us by returning to pursue one of those Wilson brothers who now own the ranch. In our opinion, those men are no better than outlaws. They are of the lowest tier of society. We have sent a letter inviting her to return with her one child, Eleanor, and should she not come, she will also be disowned.

You have made your bed, Magdalena, now lie in it.

Unless we have reason to oversee the ranch for James, we will not write to you again, and should you come to our door, you will be turned away. You are dead to us and to your children. We have told them that you, as well as their father, Liam Rafferty, have died.

Hans and Ilse Bauman

San Antonio, Texas

He handed it back to her. Maggie glanced at it, then crumpled it into a ball and tossed it on the floor. A half-sob caught in her throat, but she swallowed it. Then she stood.

"You asked if I would change my mind about staying," she said, her voice shaking as if she had an ague. "If you wonder if I feel different about you or about us, I don't. I do want to marry you. I just hope you still feel the same."

"I do," he said. "Maggie, there ain't a thing that could change how I feel. I'm powerful sorry they wrote this to you, but when I tell a woman I love her, it's for always."

She gazed at him with tearful eyes, and he pulled her into his arms. Jacob didn't kiss her; he just held her close, offering the comfort of his body. For the first few moments, she stood rigid, but then she relaxed against him with a long sigh. She laid her head against his shoulder, and he rubbed her back.

"Guess that settles any notion your folks would come to the wedding," Jacob said. He was serious, but she laughed a little.

"It does," Maggie replied. "I'm so glad you're here, Jacob."

"I came to ask you to come over to Boone's for supper with the rest of us," he told her. "I hated to think of you up here alone. If you don't want to come, I can bide here with you."

"Oh, no, you can't," she cried. "I won't keep you from your family. Why your mother and brother just arrived! I shouldn't intrude."

"Ma told me to ask you," Jacob said. "You're Mattie's sister, so you're family too."

The thought seemed to ease her, and she smiled. "You're right," she said. "And they'll be my family after we marry, the only family I'll have. I'll go, thank you."

"I'll wait and walk you there when it's time."

Before she could wash her face or change her dress, Moses and Mattie arrived. Like he had done, they came into the house without knocking. Mattie had been weeping, too. Both stopped when they saw Jacob seated at the table across from Maggie. The crumpled letter had been retrieved from the floor and lay between them.

"I see I'm not the only one who received a letter," Mattie said. "Sister, this is awful."

"It is."

"I'm sure they don't mean it, though," Mattie told her sister. "If we go to San Antonio, I believe they'll relent."

Jacob exchanged a doubtful glance with his brother but said nothing.

"They won't," Maggie replied. "It's what Gunther wanted, what he said when he came here to try to get you to go back. Even if they would, I won't forgive them for this. They told my children that I'm dead. That's ten times worse than disowning me and threatening to disown you. Do you plan to take Ellie and go to San Antonio?"

Mattie paled. "You know I don't!"

"Then we must think of ourselves as orphans," Maggie said.

"Aren't you upset about this?"

"I've cried my tears," Maggie replied. "Now I'm going to go wash my face, change into a dress that isn't black, and go with Jacob to Boone's for supper. I'd suggest you do the same."

There was a heavy moment of silence until Moses spoke. "That's what I intend to do. Cain't let this rob us of all joy. Mattie and Maggie, it ain't like your folks were around much anyway or made much effort to keep in touch."

"Well, they do live in San Antonio," Mattie said, sounding upset.

"And Ma's been in Kentucky all this long time, but we all managed to write," Moses said. "I ain't gonna fight with you over this, Mattie. I told you so, and I mean it. It's a terrible thing, that's true, but if we let it tear us apart, then they get what they want. I don't begin to understand this, but I love you and this baby. You're in the family way, so you're likely to get riled up. But if you don't want to be here, I'll carry you over to San Antone myself."

Jacob held his breath. Moses had ventured his heart with his words, and if Mattie asked to go, it would devastate him. All the color drained from Mattie's face, and she sank into a chair.

"Moses, I do want to be here, with you."

"Then ain't nothing to worry over," he said. "Or take on about. Let's head on over to Boone's, then. Ma's got Ellie there by now. I'm hankering after seeing my little gal after all this mess."

"I can hitch up a wagon and team if you'd rather ride," Jacob said.

Maggie smiled at him. "I think that would be a grand thing."

"Then whilst you're getting ready, I'll do that and be back."

Moses sighed. "I'll go with you, Jacob."

They donned their hats, and Jacob put his coat back on. Moses hadn't bothered to take his off. Outside, the sun shone, but the wind remained cool. Neither spoke until they were three yards from the house.

"What kind of people would do such a thing to their daughters?" Jacob asked.

"Yellow-bellied, lowdown, sorry excuses for human beings," Moses replied. "I guess you ain't never met them?"

"Never had any reason to meet them."

"I have," Moses said. "They sent Mattie here to help Maggie when she was going to have Seamus. Then they summoned her back after they got wind we were courtin'. They had a German banker they wanted Mattie to marry..."

"Hammerschmidt," Jacob said. "It was his men that jumped me in San Antonio when I was coming here. I've heard Boone mention him, never says his first name the same twice."

Moses laughed. "That's the one. Real piece of work, that man. Her family tried to get Mattie to marry the banker, but she wouldn't. I got to pining after her and went to town to court her. They treated me like I was dirt on the bottom of their boot, nearabout the rudest folks I ever met. Her father tried to be fair at first, but it didn't last long. I come back to the ranch without her and without much hope. Then, after I got so sick with pneumonia, somehow she had a feeling I needed her, so she talked Phin Dawson into bringing her. If she hadn't come, I reckon I would've died – Boone thinks the same. Anyhow, they sent Hammerschmidt to fetch her, had the word out they were engaged, but thanks to Boone, we pulled a fast one and were already married. He threatened then that her family would consider her dead if she didn't come back, so he's had a hand in this."

"Now I get what Maggie was talking about," Jacob said.

"Yeah, that's the story of our weddin'," Moses laughed. "Those Germans were hot about it then, tried this on before. After Ellie was born, I thought they might come around, but they never did."

"Sounds like no great loss," Jacob observed.

Moses shrugged. "It's their folks, though, good or bad, I reckon. It's got to be hard for them."

"I can't imagine," Jacob said. "Wouldn't never happen in our family."

"It wouldn't, that's a fact."

They hitched a pair of draft horses to the best wagon and took it over to the main ranch house. Both sisters emerged, wearing coats and wool scarves. Jacob climbed down from the seat and handed Mattie up to sit beside Moses. Then he assisted Maggie into the back, where a low bench along one side provided seating.

In the wagon, she held onto his hand. Jacob tucked it into his coat pocket with a smile. She leaned against him, and he did his best to shield her from the wind. If her sister noticed, she said nothing, but then she was likely preoccupied with the family situation. Besides, Mattie faced the other direction.

"Are you warm enough?" he asked Maggie, who nodded.

"Thank you, Jacob," she told him.

"For what?"

Her smile emerged. "Coming to my house today when I needed you," she said. "Comforting me, inviting me to supper with the family, and for caring for me. Without you, I'd be in despair, and I might've been tempted to go back to San Antonio."

"Would you have, though?"

Maggie tilted her head as she considered it. "No, I don't believe I would."

"Sugar, I'm glad of it," he told her.

When they reached Boone's house, his brother came onto the porch, a smoke jutted into the corner of his lip. "I heard the wagon," he said. "Wondered what's the occasion."

Moses set the wagon brake, reached the ground, and lifted his wife down as if she were a porcelain doll. "I reckon you don't know this yet, but Dawson brought Mattie and Maggie letters from their folks, disowning them. They've told Maggie's children that she's dead, all because she didn't hightail it back to their house and obey. Those Germans asked Mattie to bring Ellie and come back or she's disowned, too."

"What in tarnation?" Boone said. His grin faded away like the last light of sunset. "That's lowdown and dirty."

"It is," Moses said. "Both sisters are mighty upset over it, too. So, we brought them over in the wagon. It didn't seem good to leave Maggie alone after such news."

"Naw, it wouldn't be. I'm glad you brought her along. Where is she?"

Jacob took the cue to act. He helped Maggie down from the wagon bed and stood beside her. "We're right here."

Boone stared at them, Jacob standing there with Maggie's small hand tucked into the crook of his arm. Emotion flickered in his eyes, gray as storm clouds, and Jacob braced himself, afraid he'd made Boone furious.

"I see that," Boone said. His lips twitched as if he fought a smile. "Come on in, you're both welcome. Rachel's got supper ready to put on the table, and Ma's been asking where you were."

Jacob's belly had been coiled tighter than a spring, but now, it eased, and he grinned as he led Maggie into the house.

CHAPTER TWELVE

The five brothers ate first, along with their mother. Although the table was large, it wasn't big enough to seat fifteen at one time, so they ate in shifts. If it had been Jacob's choice, he would have let the women dine before the men, but that wasn't the custom. The tender beefsteaks, crisp fried potatoes, hominy, leather britches beans, and light bread were delicious. He savored them, but his focus remained on Maggie. With the other women, she alternated between the main room and the kitchen. She rocked her niece, Ellie, for a while, and Jacob recalled the girl had turned one somewhere around the time Liam managed to get himself killed by the loco horse. He wondered, watching Maggie, if she mourned her lost children, but decided he wouldn't ask. He knew well the pain of someone probing emotional wounds. Deep in thought, he missed some of the conversation."Jacob, what do you think?" Ezekiel asked."About what?"Zeke hooted. "I could tell you wasn't paying any mind to what we're talking about," he said. "I asked if y'all wanted to eat turkey tomorrow or save them till Christmas Day. It ain't but a week."

"I didn't even know you got a turkey."

"I got three," Ezekiel said. "They're hanging up outside over to our place, high enough no critters can reach. I shot 'em for Ma, recollecting how well she likes the meat, but I'm good either way."

"We butchered a hog not all that long ago," Boone told them. "We can eat ham, I reckon. Might butcher another sow if we need it. Got one penned that we been feedin' corn, fattening it up."

"We could eat roast pork on New Year's, maybe," Garrett

said. "Then salt down the rest of it or save some to cure bacon."

"We go through an almighty lot of bacon," Boone replied. "That'd be best."

"Ma? Would you like turkey tomorrow?"

Ma smiled. "I'd relish it, son."

"Then we'll have turkey. What's left might run us a day or two until closer to Christmas."

Once all of them had eaten, Boone got his guitar, and Mima joined him. Everyone found a seat. Although there weren't quite enough chairs, they managed to use upturned buckets or boxes or sprawl on the floor.

The first few songs Boone sang with his daughter were the old tunes Ma had once sung to them. They sang the one about the red fox that Katie also loved, and she added her voice to theirs. After another two, they switched to Christmas carols. By the time they finished, the hour was late, and all the children except for Mima were fast asleep.

Boone carried the boys to bed while Rachel took the baby to the cradle.

Jacob stood and stretched. "We've got the wagon here, so if any of you want a ride, I'll take you home in style this once."

Both Moses and Ezekiel accepted the offer so their wives, both with child, wouldn't have to walk. Ma agreed too and climbed up without aid onto the wagon seat beside Jacob. At the last moment, after he'd taken the reins in hand, Boone joined them.

"I thought I'd go along for the ride," Boone said. "Then I'll help you unhitch the horses and put away the wagon."

"Fair enough," Jacob said, although he figured Boone had a reason. His oldest brother appeared tired, and he'd been yawning for better than an hour. "I don't mind the company."

First stop was the dog trot cabin, where the two couples left the wagon, Moses carrying his daughter. Then they took Ma to Jacob's small cabin. Boone helped her down.

"Do you want me to come fix the fire?" he asked.

She shook her head. "Banked it before I left," she told him. Then she kissed his cheek. "I'll see you tomorrow, Boone. Feels good to be able to say that again."

Boone offered a slight grin. "It had been too long, Ma."

She nodded. "I'll see you directly, Jacob."

"I won't be long."

Maggie remained, and Boone offered her a hand up to sit between them on the wagon seat.

"Thank you," she told him.

He swung up beside her. "I reckon you both wonder why I came along."

"I was curious," Jacob said. "I figured you got something to say."

Boone gave a little laugh. "I do. Do you want to hear it now or wait till we're at Maggie's?"

She drew her coat closer against the cold. "Let's talk at the house. It's warmer."

They left her at her house, then stabled the horses and dealt with the wagon.

"Ain't Rachel gonna be looking out for you?" Jacob asked as they hoofed it back from the barns.

"I told her what I'm thinking," he said. "She won't wait up."

His tone was genial, but Jacob wondered if Boone planned to lay down the law about courting Maggie. "If this is about…"

"You know it is," Boone said. "But I think you'll like what I have to tell you."

Maggie had fresh coffee brewed, so they gathered around her table. She poured each of them a cup and said, "Well, let's have it, Boone."

"First, I'm sorry about what's happened with your folks

and your children," Boone said. "It ain't right, not by any stretch. It's made me take a different look, though, at this thing between the two of you. Ain't no secret I've not been happy about the notion of a wedding, but it doesn't appear that's going to be necessary right now."

Jacob parted his lips to speak, and Boone held up one hand. "Let me get this said, then if you want to argue, you can. I can see it's not just some fool notion of Jacob's, that both of you seem fond. If he's smitten, then so are you. It ain't my business on what that might say about your late husband, so I won't mention it. If you two want to court, then I'm in favor."

Maggie smiled. "I'm pleased to hear that, Boone."

"Keep listening a bit longer," he told her. "It's too soon for you to wed, not when Liam's not yet a month in the ground. A year's considered the decent time, but I ain't worried about that. I don't want no scandal, though, or gossip. We're a fair piece from town on the ranch, but word travels, and it wouldn't take much for the tale to be told in Laredo, even up to San Antonio. You've known each other a spell, but you ain't courted. My notion is that you court her, Jacob, for a bit and see how that goes. If it's good between you, which I figure it will be, maybe a wedding this spring, before the trail drive might be in order. Or you can wait till late summer or even fall. In the meantime, though, it don't seem proper for Maggie to live alone in this house and for Jacob to come calling. I ain't got time or inclination to be a chaperone."

"Boone..." Jacob interrupted.

"I'm near finished," Boone said. "Here's my notion. Maggie, your sister's in the family way. You're likely to be lonely rattling around this place. I thought maybe Mattie and Moses might move in with you for now. You'd have company, and Mattie would have the same. If they're here, then no one can wag their tongues should Jacob come calling. Jacob, half the dog trot cabin is big enough for you, Garrett, and Ma to share."

"True," Jacob said, mulling over Boone's idea. "What about the small cabin? Surely you don't mean to let it sit empty."

"No, I don't. I thought Deacon Lee could bring his wife to live there. He's bellyached plenty about her living in Laredo and him here on the ranch. He's always wantin' to take off for town to see her, and I figure they'd like to take up housekeeping together, as it should be for man and wife. What do you think?"

Boone's idea astonished Jacob. The little cabin fit him like a well-made shirt, and he'd never thought about moving to other quarters. Although it would do for him and Ma, the two-room cabin space beside Ezekiel's appealed. Ma would like it, he thought, because it was closer to her other children. Garrett wouldn't have to impose on Moses and Mattie. If Maggie no longer lived alone, his presence in the main ranch house would be welcome, not suspect.

"You're a wise man, Boone," he said, after a few moments. "When you'd have time to come up with this?"

"I mulled it over while eating supper," Boone replied. "It works, don't it?"

"It does," Jacob said. "Maggie, what do you think?"

"Liam was often slow to come home," she said. "But he did park his boots beside the bed every night if he wasn't trailing cattle or riding the ranch. It's been lonely since he's gone. I would enjoy the company if Mattie and Moses are willing."

"I'll ask them come morning," Boone said. "If they are, we'll get things moved on Saturday, as long as the weather holds. If that's settled, then I'm heading home. I'm ready to lay down my weary head. Let's go, Jacob."

Jacob hesitated. "I'll be right behind you, Boone. I'd like to bid Maggie good night."

Boone rolled his eyes but nodded. "I'll wait on the porch, so don't take too long."

Jacob rose when Boone closed the door behind him, but

stood still. Then he offered his hand to Maggie, who took it. He raised her to her feet, and without a word, he kissed her. He kept it slow and sweet, then he held her close.

"You've had a day," he said. "But I like Boone's notion. Even more, I like being able to court you."

She lifted one hand and stroked his cheek. "I am looking forward to courting, Jacob," she told him. "I'll dream about a spring wedding."

He touched her hair and nodded. "Sweet dreams, then, sugar."

As the two brothers strolled through the December night, Jacob asked Boone, "What changed your mind about me courtin' Maggie?"

"I can tell that you love her," Boone replied. "It's a dirty trick her folks did, telling her children she's dead. I had a taste of that myself, by pure accident, not long ago, and there was no reason to hurt them or her that way. I reckon folks may think this is to keep hold of the ranch, and I cain't deny that's a small part. More than that, though, I see the way you look at each other. I have a good wife, one I love more than anything, and I'd like you to have that again, Jacob."

His brother's simple words moved him, and Jacob stopped. He hugged Boone.

"I reckon we don't say it near enough, but I love you, brother," he said.

"Likewise," Boone replied, sounded a bit embarrassed or maybe emotional. "I love you and all the family. Ain't one of us would ever do what Maggie's folks are doing. It's done my heart good to have Ma here and Garrett. I meant to go home, back to Kentucky, but then I married Rachel, and she was with child. There're times I felt awful bad about that. I know Ma figured I'd be back, the rest of you too, but one by one, you came here, and now this is home."

"They say home is where the heart is, don't they?" Jacob said. "That's right, and we're here."

They went their separate ways, Boone to his house, Jacob to the small cabin.

On Saturday, it took several wagons, the family, and most of the ranch hands, but the move was completed by supper time. Maggie fed everyone a hearty stew with beef, onions, potatoes, and carrots that she called *Marsch*. Mattie made biscuits, and Katie brought a dried apple cake. Everything hadn't yet been put to rights, but no one minded. Although Boone announced that, other than necessary chores, there would be no work expected on Sunday, Maggie and her sister vowed they would get things put away in their places.

"And we want to get a *Tannenbaum*," Mattie said, eyes sparkling. "Ellie was too young to notice last year, but I want her to have one. We won't bring it inside or decorate until Christmas Eve, but it's our tradition."

Jacob listened with a smile. If the sisters wanted a Christmas tree, he'd bring them one. He knew where to find a fair-sized red cedar tree, one not too big or tall to bring indoors. It remained small enough to have a pretty shape, wider at the base and growing to a point at the top. He hadn't grown up with a Christmas tree, but the custom that began with German immigrants had become more popular.

"I'll fetch you one," he said. "I got one spotted."

"Thank you, Jacob," Mattie said. Her gratitude gave him a warm glow near his heart, but it was Maggie's smile that meant the most.

"We'll have plenty to do come Monday," Boone said. "I'll need every one of you to give a hand with that. I'm worn plumb out, so I think we'll head for the house. Good night, all of you."

"Aren't we going to sing tonight, Daddy?" Mima asked.

"Naw, baby girl. I gotta get some shut-eye, and so do you.

Might sing a few hymns tomorrow if anyone's willing to listen."

"I believe we're cooking our dinners on our own," Rachel said. "I'd like to keep it simple because we'll be cooking for Christmas soon."

Ma nodded. "I'll fix something for Jacob and Garrett, but any of you is always welcome at my table. Boone, you'd best come by tomorrow morning. I never got around to doctoring your hand. It looks a bit sore. Is it?"

"I knocked it against the wagon, got it hurting a little. Took the scab off but it's fine, I reckon."

"I'll have the comfrey ready," his mother told him. "I'm 'bout ready to head home as well. I'd like to get settled in the new place."

Jacob would like the same. "I'll take you, Ma. Boone ain't the only one weary."

He longed for his bed even though it now stood in a different place. They'd brought both beds from the smaller cabin, and Moses left one so there would be enough. Deacon Lee had headed for Laredo with a wagon to bring his wife and their household plunder. He said they had a bed they'd bring, grinning ear to ear once he found out his wife would be living on the ranch.

Ma baked biscuits on Sunday morning and fried up some bacon. She made coffee and borrowed some sweet butter from Katie. Jacob had just begun to eat when Boone arrived and entered without knocking. By the stiff way that Boone moved, Jacob figured his back trouble had returned.

"The biscuits are still hot, son," Ma said. "Get a plate, Boone, and eat."

"I will, thanks," he said as he sank into a chair.

"Back troubling you again?" Jacob asked.

"A mite," Boone said. "It'll pass, I reckon. I doubt all the lifting and toting did it much good."

"I brought some magic oil liniment," Ma told him. "If you want some, I'm happy to share."

"Rachel makes some kind of cream," he said. "It eases it some. When it's bad, she makes a mustard plaster."

Ma nodded. "If you want to try it, just say so. I'll apply it if you want, since you probably can't reach your own back."

Jacob filled his mouth with a biscuit to hide his grin. Ma spoke as if Boone were still a boy.

"Maybe," Boone said. "I did want you to doctor this spider bite with comfrey, though. It's one reason I came."

After breakfast, Ma took a good, hard look at the spider bite. She washed it off with some witch hazel, then mixed up a comfrey paste and spread it over the spot.

"It appears to be healing, Boone," she said. "I'd mind it, though, so it doesn't get riled up or go bad. Does it hurt?"

He shrugged. "Twinge or two, nothing more."

"Sit here till that dries hard," Ma directed him. "I don't suppose anyone holds church here on the ranch?"

Her question conjured up memories of attending church back home in Kentucky. The old log church had been there long before any of them were born, Jacob recalled. Most Sunday mornings, the place had been full. The songs were powerful, and the preaching often focused on the possibility of damnation. He'd never known Ma to miss a service unless one of them was sick, so he wasn't surprised she asked.

"No, never have," Boone said. "But I've decided we should build a little church here. Then we could meet there on Sundays, and it'd be a place for weddings, funerals, and baptisms."

Ma nodded. "Weddings and funerals, I see that, but baptisms? Ain't there a creek or pond handy?"

Boone drew a deep breath. "Rachel and Katie are both Catholic, Ma. They like the little ones sprinkled and blessed by a priest. So far, we've had to do that at the main ranch house, but I thought a church would be a better spot."

Jacob waited to see how Ma reacted. He'd never known her to be judgmental about religion, and when she replied, she wasn't now.

"It would, and I like the idea, Boone. You might could use it as a schoolhouse, too."

"Sure, that's a good notion, Ma. Mima and Rob can read and write, but before long, we'll have a lot of little ones needing to learn their letters. I hadn't thought that far ahead."

Garrett spoke up. "Sounds like a fine notion. I reckon the nearest church or school is off to San Antonio."

"Laredo's closer but not near close enough for either one," Jacob told him. "You can get there and back in a day if you start early. That's where we get any supplies we don't have here. We've already been to get some things for Christmas, but I'd be happy to take you to see the place whenever you want."

"I'd like that," Garrett said. "My traveling legs could use a rest first, but I'd be game by New Year's or so."

Mentioning Christmas reminded Jacob he'd promised to go fetch a tree. Although he'd enjoy a day of rest after moving two households, he should go soon. Tomorrow, Boone had plenty of chores planned.

"I think I'll head out soon to get that tree for Mattie," he said. "Garrett, you want to come?"

"We riding or takin' a wagon?"

"Wagon, I reckon 'cause we gotta haul the tree."

"Then let's go," Garrett said. "I'd like to see more of this ranch."

It was a good mile, maybe two, to reach the stand of cedar trees Jacob had seen. At the time, he'd never thought of Christmas trees, but found them pretty with their evergreen color against the fall landscape. He chose the straightest, most attractive one. Together, he and Garrett sawed it down, then shook it to remove any bugs or mites. They loaded it into the wagon and took it back to the ranch.

He said it was for Mattie, and that was true. But Jacob fetched the tree back to see it bring a smile to Maggie's lips. Even better than a cedar tree would have been some mistletoe, but he figured he might get a kiss without it.

CHAPTER THIRTEEN

Despite the fact that it was two days until Christmas, Monday on the ranch proved long and busy. Boone had warned them there would be many chores, and he hadn't exaggerated. For Jacob and Ezekiel, there were still a few horses in the remuda that needed to be shod. Two cows were about to calve, and one of them delivered twins. Hay needed to be put out for the cattle, and there were repairs needed on the barns. Moses spent some time repairing and shoring up some of the corrals. Garrett worked hard, proving he hadn't gone soft in the years apart. After the recent chilly days, the sun came out. Temperatures rose until it almost felt like a spring day, not December.

At the end of the day, Ma served up a rich burgoo, a classic Kentucky stew. She used venison that Ezekiel had shot days earlier and hung in the smokehouse along with some prairie chicken, squirrel, onions, carrots, dried lima beans, corn, and potatoes. She prepared it at Boone's and served it there, although she refused to use the stove. Her sons and their families came and went, enjoying the treat along with several pans of crackling bread.

"Ma, that really hits the spot," Jacob told her. "I ain't had burgoo since I left home."

"I never make it exactly the same," Ma replied. "I use whatever meat I got, vegetables too."

"Why's it called burgoo?" Mima asked.

"I don't know, child," her grandmother said. "Some say it comes from saying bird stew fast, others say it's just a name someone came up with. I know how to make it, and never cared why it's named what it is. Do you like it?"

The little girl nodded. "I do."

"It's good eating in the winter. I thought the weather would stay cold," Ma said. "It's near as warm as springtime out there. Is that how winter is here?"

"Sometimes," Boone said as he dived into his second bowl. "It worries me, though, because I've seen it like this right before some bad weather hits, snow or ice, and such."

Ezekiel glanced up from his supper. "I learned that the hard way."

"How's that?"

"Three years ago this month, there come a day like this. I had the fool notion to head off to town while the weather was good. Moses, he had a cold already and wouldn't go. I did, but a big snow come up out of nowhere and my horse threw me. Wasn't hurt, but I took shelter as best I could. I likely would've frozen to death, but Moses come after me. He brought me back safe, but that's when he took sick so bad with the pneumonia. If he'd died, it'd been my fault sure as shoutin'."

Jacob hadn't heard the full story, but it made sense now. He'd known for some time that Zeke blamed himself for Moses getting so sick, but he never understood why.

"That ain't true," Moses said. "I've told you that plenty of times. I would've taken sick anyhow."

"Anyhow," Boone interrupted before the brothers quarreled. "What matters right now is that it's fixin' to get colder and probably bad. We'd best prepare as much as we can, make sure the animals got hay and such. If it does snow, it likely won't last long, but we gotta stay warm and safe. I don't know that I can stand anyone gettin' sick or nothing."

Christmas Eve morning dawned fair, but by noon, heavy clouds raced in from the west and temperatures dropped. The wind kicked up and blew hard as the clouds grew darker, and light sleet began to fall. All the women were at the main ranch house baking cookies and other favorites for the holiday. The two hams from the last pig slaughtered would be the centerpiece of the feast. In addition to baking, Mattie and some of the children were decorating the tree Jacob had delivered. It stood in the parlor window, the powerful cedar fragrance spreading through the rooms and mingling with the sweet smell of cinnamon and molasses.

Boone made certain every home on the ranch, including the bunkhouse, had plenty of wood on hand. Each of the brothers had a job. Moses brought staples like flour, milk, butter, and such to everyone. Ezekiel delivered meat from the smokehouse to Spider so that the hands would have a holiday meal even if the snow stacked high. Jacob tended the horses, then the rest of the livestock to ensure they had access to hay and water. The water would freeze eventually, and it would be necessary to break the ice so the animals could drink. Garrett worked with Boone after being outfitted with winter cowboy gear. His garments brought from Kentucky came close, but he needed gloves, a heavier coat, and a wool hat to wear beneath his broad-brimmed one.

The hands were out rounding up as many of the cattle as they could, driving them back to the corrals and barns so they wouldn't be lost or freeze to death in the weather. Jacob tracked down Deacon Lee to find out if he had enough supplies laid in at the small cabin. Deke had brought his wife from Laredo the day before and settled into the place. His bride, Abigail, was town-raised so Jacob wondered if she would be prepared for the weather.

By mid-afternoon, the snow fell fast and heavily. So Jacob retrieved the trinkets and such he'd bought in town for Christmas. He toted it over to the ranch house and turned it over to Moses, who found a hiding place where it could be kept till morning. The lot included some papers of pins, some lace, and spools of thread for the women. Boone fetched all the quilts, blankets, and pillows from his house, along with some of his family's warmer garments. Last, Jacob brought his few books to share along with a checkerboard.

Jacob was the last to come inside, and when he did, he paused to stamp snow from his boots at the back door. Maggie met him there.

"I was starting to worry," she told him. "Everyone else is here. I feared you got lost or frozen."

He shook his head. "Naw, just taking care of some things."

She touched his hand and shivered. "Jacob! You're like ice. Come get warm before you catch a chill."

Both the kitchen and parlor were comfortable after the Arctic blast outside. Jacob joined Boone and Moses at the kitchen table. Maggie brought him a cup of coffee. He held it between his hands, savoring the heat, then drank it.

"I was about to head out to find you," Boone, always the worrier, said. "I'm glad you made it in. I thought maybe you'd run into trouble."

The coffee helped, but it took most of the remaining day before Jacob wasn't cold. The family gathered in either the parlor or the kitchen. After a time, he headed to the parlor to say his howdys.

"Jay! Come see the Christmas tree," Mima cried as she ran to meet him. "It's the prettiest thing."

The cedar tree had been decked out with homemade ornaments ranging from paper cutouts, homemade snowflakes, dried flowers and berries, and some ribbons. Popcorn strings were wrapped around the tree to add a festive flair.

"It's nice," Jacob said. He'd heard of trees with candles, but there were none, and he was glad. No candles meant no chance for fire. There weren't any places left to sit, so he sank down into a corner, the same as Garrett and Ezekiel. Moses and Boone remained at the table adjacent to the kitchen. He could smell the tang of their cigarettes and wished he had one. Fatigue took over before he could rise, though, and he fell asleep leaning against the wall. He woke, stiff with a crick in his neck, and rose. Jacob stretched and groaned a little. Garrett laughed from where he leaned in the doorway.

"Ain't the most comfortable place," he said. "I woke in the same shape."

"I shouldn't have slept," Jacob replied. "I didn't mean to, just to rest."

"You were cold and worn out," Ma said from her seat. She had Boone's two oldest cuddled against her like bookends. "I reckon you needed it."

"Could be. Did I sleep clear through supper?"

Garrett laughed, and the others joined him. "It ain't but four o'clock," he told him. "You didn't sleep all that long."

Jacob scrubbed his face with both hands. "I thought it was night with the lamps lit and all."

"That's because of the snow. It's dark outside, and snow's still coming down hard."

"What is for supper anyhow?"

"I believe Maggie and Mattie said they would make pancakes and bacon," Ma said. "The big feast will be tomorrow."

His stomach rumbled, and Jacob realized he hadn't eaten since early morning. "Sounds tasty. When will we eat?"

"Boone wants to talk at us first," Garrett told him. "Might as well come out to the table where he's took up residence. While you wait for food, there's plenty of coffee."

The blended smell of coffee and tobacco hung over the table where Boone sat, along with Ezekiel and Moses. He and Garrett took a seat. Without waiting to be asked, Maggie poured them both coffee and brought it to the table. Jacob sipped, grateful.

"What's the story?" he asked Boone. "Garrett said you needed to tell us something."

"I do," Boone said. "For one, it's shaping up to be as bad a snowstorm as I've ever seen in these parts, worse than the one where Moses went to fetch Ezekiel back. I reckon in a few days it will warm up enough to melt, but in the meantime, it's serious business. We got most of the stock in, so that's a good thing, and I reckon they'll manage. Come tomorrow, or the next day, we likely ought to bust the ice so they can drink and make sure they have hay. Tonight, though, I'm thinking the five of us ought to head over to sleep either at one of the cabins or my house."

Jacob muffled a groan. "Aw, Boone, we'll near freeze gettin' there. Why would we want to do that? Cain't we sleep here?"

"In case you ain't noticed, there's sixteen people crammed into this house," Boone said. "We'll be bunking on the floor if we stay here, and it's airish for that. I figure Maggie and Mattie can sleep in the bed, and Ellie in her bed. Ma can sleep in the children's room with Mima, Benjamin, and Robert. Our little one can sleep in the cradle Ellie's outgrown. Katie and Rachel can share the bed upstairs. That don't leave much of any place for us to stretch out."

Moses frowned. "I'd rather not leave Mattie, not in the shape she's in, during this snow."

Ezekiel nodded his head in agreement. "I don't want to leave Katie, neither."

"I know that. I ain't happy about being away from my family myself," Boone told them. "I'm being practical, that's all."

"Your house or any of the cabins will be cold as a witch's heart by now," Garrett said. "I don't know, but that it's best to stay here, rather than brave the weather."

Rachel came into the room, carrying Sarah Rose. Her expression changed when she heard what Boone said, and she spoke up. "Boone, I'd rather you not leave us here and go to the house. I'll worry myself sick if you do. I wouldn't know if you made it there or if you were wandering in the snow. If anything happened, we'd have no way to send for you."

From the shocked look on Boone's face, he hadn't considered any of those things.

"I reckon that's so," Boone said, his voice low and slow. Always the one to fret and worry, Jacob could see he hadn't considered any of those possibilities. "Maybe we should stay put, then, honey."

"You'll be warm enough if you sleep in the parlor," Rachel stated. "If you keep the stove stoked, it won't be bad even on the floor. I'll sleep there beside you if you want."

"I want you tucked up in bed, warm and snug," he replied. He appealed to his brothers. "What do you think? Stay or go?"

"Stay," Jacob said. He'd rather not be that far away from Maggie should she need him.

Ezekiel, Moses, and Garrett agreed, so Boone sighed. "Awright, then, we'll stay here," he said. "I wadn't lookin' forward to marching through the snow. Back during the war, we kept to winter camp most of the time, but we got caught out in it more than once. I like to froze to death."

It was never far from Jacob's mind that his oldest brother had endured hardships beyond his imagination during the war. Times like now, he thought, Boone had to be about the bravest man he'd ever known. It took some sand to live through a war, but Boone had done it. No wonder when he'd come home, he'd been in a dark mindset, Jacob thought, or that he seldom spoke about the experience.

"Ain't no need for any of us to freeze now," Jacob said.

"Or be hungry," Maggie said with a bright smile. "I'll get started cooking."

The delicious scent of frying bacon wafted through the house, and there was laughter as the women prepared stacks of pancakes. There was plenty of sweet butter and syrup. The table seated six, so they ate in three shifts. Jacob ate two rounds of pancakes with bacon. Afterward, full as tick, he returned to the parlor and found a seat.

"Will you read to me, Jay?" Mima asked. She had her book of fairy tales tucked beneath one arm.

He patted the settee beside him. "Sure, I will. Where's Rob? I reckon he'd like to hear a story too."

"I don't know," she replied, her grey eyes gone dark. "I ain't seen him for a bit."

A vague alarm tickled Jacob's spine, and he closed the book. "I reckon we'd best go find him," he told her. "There's not many places he can be."

"He might be hiding."

"Could be," he said. "Let's track him down."

First, they peered behind each piece of furniture in the parlor, then he opened the front door to peer out. He saw no sign of Rob, so they walked into the kitchen. Boone and the rest of his brothers were playing blackjack with an old deck of cards they had found. Jacob looked under the table and through the kitchen, opening the cupboards and cabinets. Rob wasn't in any of them, and the womenfolk, including Ma, were busy. Rachel washed dishes, and the others were preparing food for Christmas Day. Several trays of molasses cookies were ready for the oven. Chattering and laughing, none of them paid any mind as he and Mima passed through the room.

Jacob glanced at the narrow stairs that led up to the smallest bedroom under the eaves.

"Would Rob go up there?" he asked Mima, who shrugged.

"I don't know. He might."

"Run up and see," he told her. "I'll go check the bedrooms."

The boy had to be in one of those three places, he figured. As he searched the children's rooms without finding him, Mima returned to report that her brother wasn't upstairs either. After kneeling to check beneath the beds, Jacob rose. His knees and back ached.

"Well, he's got to be in Moses and Mattie's room," he said aloud, praying it was true.

A thorough examination found nothing, not a bit of dust or the boy. Jacob sighed. His vague alarm had become a major concern. The house had been built with two front doors, and when he crossed the room to check it, he found it slightly ajar.

"Mima, you don't reckon Robert would go outside, do you?"

"He might," she said. "He's been watching it snow all day, saying he'd like to play outside in it, but Mama said no."

Jacob, heart beating like a drum in a Fourth of July parade, jerked open the door. Snow fell and swirled, cutting visibility to almost zero. When he glanced down at the porch, he drew a hard breath and held it. Small footprints, fast filling in with snow, could be seen. He gazed into the darkness to find they continued into the yard.

"Get your daddy, now," he cried. "Go, Jemima Ann, and hurry."

He thought he'd keel over and die in the eternity before Boone exploded into the room.

"What's the matter?" he asked. "Mima come to fetch me, half-crying and wringing her hands. It's got Rachel plumb riled up."

"We couldn't find Rob," Jacob told him. "We looked everywhere in the house, but Boone, I think he went outside."

Boone paled, and a frown line divided his forehead. "Surely not."

"Come see the footprints before the snow covers them," Jacob said. "Boone, we gotta go get him before he freezes to death."

Hatless and coatless, Boone stepped onto the porch and

shouted, "Rob! Robert John Wilson!"

The wind whistled beneath the eaves, but no answer came. Boone shouted again, then turned around with such speed he almost toppled Jacob. "Get your coat and gear," he hollered. "I'll tell the others."

"I want to go!" Mima said.

Jacob paused in his rush to get his things. "You cain't, baby girl," he told her. "You gotta stay with your mama and granny and aunties."

He picked her up, big as she was at seven, and deposited her in the kitchen, which had erupted into chaos. Rachel sobbed into a corner of her apron. Ma stood like a statue, her face set in hard, grim lines. Maggie and Mattie hugged each other, speaking in soft German. Katie, her hair like a flame, clutched Ezekiel's arm as he wrestled into his coat.

"Ye've got to find him," she cried. "He's gone home, I fear, to get his horses to play, but he'll be lost in the snow. If ye don't find him soon, I fear for his life."

Zeke shook off her hand. "What are you sayin', woman? Are you telling me it's too late already?"

"Nay, never," Katie said, her voice cracking with emotion. "But it won't be long, that's what I'm tellin' you. Ye must hurry."

Jacob stomped across the room, his boots loud on the hardwood floor. Before he grabbed his coat, hat, and winter clothing, he stopped. The woman had witchy ways, no doubt of it.

"What have you seen?" he asked her in a whisper. "Tell me."

"'Tis too terrible to say," she whimpered.

"Tell me before he's a goner."

She leaned in close, her breath warm against his ear. "I saw him curled up asleep in the snow, Jacob, but if ye don't find him quick, he'll sleep forever."

Boone rubbed Rachel's back as she wept. "Hush, honey," he told her. "I'll find him, and we'll get him warm. Don't fret."

"Get that boy home, Boone," Ma told him. "Or I'll put on a coat and go myself."

"You'll stay here," he replied in the no-nonsense tone he used with the hands. "I don't want to be lookin' for you next, Ma. I said I'll fetch him home, and I will."

Boone bolted through the door without another word. Jacob and the rest of the brothers followed him, moving as fast as they dared. The wind sliced through them like a sharp knife from hell, and snow blew into their faces. Jacob raised his bandana to protect his face and plunged out, calling the boy's name, all too aware that Rob probably wouldn't hear any of them over the rush of the wind.

CHAPTER FOURTEEN

The cold hit Boone hard, like a bullet at close range. When he'd been shot in the chest at the Out of Luck, it had carried the same intense reaction. He drew his coat closer and trudged through the snow, wanting to run but forcing himself to walk. It was treacherous underfoot, and if he hurried, he would likely fall and maybe hurt himself. That would hinder finding his boy, so he kept a reasonable pace. His brothers, all four of them, fanned out around him. Their voices cried out into the fierce gale and were swept away.

There were so many places for a boy to go on a ranch, too many hidey-holes Rob might seek. As he struggled through the bitter snow, Boone reflected on the child. He had always been of a quieter nature than Jemima Ann, content to play with his horses or other toys. Rob had a steadiness about him that Boone had always thought would serve him well as a man.

Although he did his best to make time for his little ones, Boone worried now that he'd neglected his children too often. He'd come late after a long day in the saddle many times. Although he'd always rocked the children and sang to them, he most often lacked the time to get down and play horses with his boy.

Back when Rob was born, Boone still trailed cattle every spring, so the boy had been a few months old when he had headed out. Now he wished he'd quit the trail sooner, spent more time with his family. He planned to start teaching the boy to ride in the coming year and looked forward to the day he could teach him to be a good ranch hand. The way Rob loved his toy horses, he'd figured he would be a natural. He'd imagined the day he would teach him to shoot, and as the oldest, Boone had figured Rob would be the one to inherit his Griswold pistol one day.

Now, his guts were knotted hard, and his belly hurt as he traipsed onward. They checked the garden patch, bare after the autumn harvest, then the closest barn. He veered toward the dog trot cabins, hoping he wouldn't get lost on the way, but both were empty.

"I'm headin' to my house," he yelled, hoping his brothers could hear him over the wind. "If you find him, fire a shot. Surely I can hear that despite the weather."

Jacob joined him. "I'll go with you. Zeke and Moses are headin' to the bunkhouse to see if he might be there. Garrett said he'll check the other barn."

Boone nodded, unable to speak around the knot of tears in his throat. Fear choked him and seized the breath in his lungs. They were checking the structures, but he worried Rob might have wandered out toward the pastures or the pond. If they didn't find him soon, he would likely die, and Boone thought if he did, he might lay down and die too.

He couldn't, though. Rachel depended on him, and so did all his children. He did his best to shake down the terror and focus. As he neared his house, barely visible through the driving snow, he thought he glimpsed a small figure curled up on the porch. Boone started forward, tripped, and went to his knees in the deep snow. Jacob must have seen too, for he sprinted forward.

"It's Rob, Boone," he yelled, making his voice echo over the sound of the storm. "He's alive but cold."

"Let's get him home," Boone said. Relief made his head spin, and he thought for a moment he might fall into a faint. "We gotta make tracks, though."

"Maybe we should take him inside and get a fire going first," Jacob suggested.

Boone had already considered, then rejected that idea.

"Cain't. Rachel will be waitin' and I gotta let her know he's found."

He pulled his pistol and fired three times.

"If you got more blankets in there, let's wrap him up then," Jacob said.

They swaddled the boy like a baby, wrapped so tight in two blankets he couldn't move. His eyes had been closed, and Boone figured he'd been asleep. That was a right scary notion for he knew that folks who froze to death often drifted into sleep, then died.

"Daddy," Rob cried. "Daddy, I'm cold."

"I reckon so, son," Boone said. "We're taking you back to the ranch house to get warm."

"I want my horses!"

Jacob took the boy out of Boone's arms. "Go grab 'em," he said. "The kid risked his life for them. I'll carry him, Boone."

Boone protested, but Jacob refused to listen. "You just got over that spider bite. I don't want to see you take a relapse or get down sick. I'll head back, you follow right behind me, but for the love of God, Boone, don't get lost in the snow."

"All right," Boone said. He entered his home, grabbed the toys, and followed Jacob's wake. They still had to make it back and get warm again. Then they had to worry whether any of them had frostbite or would take sick from the cold.

The return journey seemed to take twice as long. Maybe it was his imagination, but the snow fell harder and thicker. The wind blew with more strength. More than once, the snow dragged Boone to his knees, and he rejoiced that Jacob carried Rob. He would have dropped him in the snow.

Halfway back, the others caught up with them.

"Is the boy all right?" Garrett asked.

"Howdy Gee-haw," Rob replied, showing more animation than he had.

They all laughed, even Boone.

"I'd take that as a yeah," Moses said.

Rachel peered out the door with a shawl over her head. She gasped when she saw Jacob toting a blanket-wrapped burden until Rob wiggled his head out.

"Mama, I'm home."

She reached for him, tears on her cheeks, then her eyes rolled back in her head, and she collapsed in a faint. Boone pushed forward and caught her before he hit the floor. He scooped her up into his arms and staggered as he carried her into the parlor. He laid her on the settee.

"C'mon, honey," he said. "I brought Rob home like I promised."

"It's the shock," Mattie said, coming into the room. "Let's get that child into dry clothes and warm."

Moses took his nephew from Jacob, who moved by the stove, warming his hands. "We all need to change."

"If you don't mind wearing Liam's things," Maggie said. "There's plenty to go around."

Boone would wear the devil's shirt if necessary. He grasped Rachel's hands, and she roused. "Your hands are like ice," she said. "Boone, you'd best get warmed up. Where's Robert?"

"Mattie took him to change clothes. Are you well, honey? You scared me when you swooned."

"'Twas the shock and the joy," Katie said. "I've tea and coffee made."

Rachel sat up. "I am, Boone. Go get into something dry, please."

By the time they had all put on dry clothing, their own or Liam's, Ezekiel had stoked the parlor stove. Heat radiated from it. Boone sipped coffee; dog tired but possessed with quiet joy. Rachel sat beside him with their son on her lap and Mima beside them. Ma had Benjamin and Sarah Rose slept in the cradle that her cousin Ellie had outgrown. Boone put an arm around Rachel and snugged her close. She tucked into the curve of his arm and leaned against his shoulder. Holding her close with his family at hand was a balm for his soul. He'd feared the worst but had brought his son home, safe and apparently sound.

"How's he doin'?" he asked his wife.

"He's warm and dry, fast asleep," she answered.

"Do you think he'll take sick over this?" That was his remaining concern.

"I doubt it," Rachel said. "How do you feel, Boone?"

"I'm grand," he said and meant it. When he stood, his back would give him trouble, but he wasn't cold, and his belly had eased soon as they got Robert inside. Sleep would take care of his fatigue. He didn't want these moments of contentment to end, but his daughter stirred.

"Daddy?"

"What is it, baby girl?"

"We ought to go to bed," she told him. "It's awful late and tomorrow's Christmas."

Her words brought a smile. "Think Santy Claus will be coming?"

Boone couldn't see her, but he could imagine the look in her grey eyes. "Daddy, there ain't no such thing and you know it."

He laughed. Ma hadn't raised her boys with any nonsense about St. Nick, and he hadn't filled his children's heads with it either. Rachel had mentioned it, and there were always a few little gifts. He figured if the young ones wanted to believe they came from an old man who traveled around handing out presents, they could. Mima, though, was a sensible child.

"Santy or not, it's past time for your children to put to bed," Ma said from a chair across the room. Until she spoke, Boone had forgotten she was there. "You need some sleep, yourself, Boone."

He would rather not move, but she was right. "I do, Ma, and that's a fact. Rachel, honey, you want to take Rob to bed. Mima, you should go with them."

"I'll take this one," Ma said, rising with Benjamin in his arms. "There's room enough in the children's bedroom for Rachel to sleep too. I doubt she wants to be parted from little Robert. It's likely warmer than upstairs anyhow. Besides, Ezekiel and Katie went to bed some time ago."

"What about Mattie and Maggie?"

"They're abed as well."

Once all his children were tucked into bed, his mother and wife beside them, Boone considered having one more cup of coffee, then decided against it. He returned to the parlor where he found Jacob putting the gifts beneath the tree. He turned around when he heard Boone's footsteps.

"You caught me," Jacob said with a grin. "Good thing it wasn't the babies."

Boone laughed. "Mima knows different, but it might have disillusioned Rob or Benjamin. Where's Moses and Garrett?"

"Fast asleep on the kitchen floor, not far from the stove. They're wrapped in blankets and quilts, too. I'm fixing to get some sleep as soon as I'm done with this."

"Might as well bunk in here," Boone said. He really didn't want to be alone, not after the emotional turmoil.

"I reckoned I would. You can take the settee, though. I'll make do with one of these parlor chairs or curl up on the floor myself. I've slept far worse."

"I've done the same. I don't feel right taking the best spot, though."

"You earned it, brother," Jacob said. "I'm right glad we found your boy before it was too late. I was some worried."

"I was near out of my mind," Boone replied. "I'll grab a blanket and bed down, then. I'm worn plumb out."

He tugged off his boots, one at a time, and stretched out. Boone thought he probably wouldn't sleep because he remained keyed up after the search for Rob, but he was out as soon as he used a blanket.

His sleep was fitful and troubled. Dreams tormented him. Images of searching for his son with a different and dire outcome haunted him. Boone woke shivering, although the parlor remained warm, and sat up. For a few moments, he couldn't remember if the nightmares were accurate, but then he recalled Jacob toting Rob home. He exhaled a slow breath and reached for his boots. From the kitchen, the sound of his children laughing was a blessing.

Boone rubbed his eyes, still sleepy, and headed for the kitchen. He craved coffee and some grub, then he'd look for a razor so he could shave. He hated whiskers and would remove them after he ate.

Although the table sat six, they'd managed to sit ten, using a few upturned boxes, a stool, and other furniture. Although Ma sat at the table, the other women bustled around the kitchen, some eating standing up with a plate in their hands. Boone accepted a cup and drank it with pleasure. He ate a biscuit served with some sausage, then begged the loan of a razor.

By the time he finished, the children clamored to open presents, so they all crowded into the parlor. The oranges were a hit, along with the peppermint sticks. Mima screeched with delight when she unwrapped the Lewis Carroll book and a primer, something she'd long wanted. There was a set of alphabet blocks for Rob and Benjamin to share. Although Rob knew his letters and could read, he stacked them and spelled out a few simple words. The first was 'horse'. The calico dress goods were welcomed, and there would be enough left after making a dress for Jemima Ann to make aprons for all the women. A toy cow pleased Rob, and Boone expected there would soon be new games that used the boy's horses.

Jacob handed out papers of pins and spools of thread for the ladies. They each received an orange, too, and some candy.

"I didn't know you'd be here, Ma," Boone said. "Nor Garrett, so there's no gifts. There's tobacco we'll share, but we're light on gifts for the men, but that's no problem."

"Being here with all my sons in one place is the only gift I need," Ma said. "Christmas ain't all about presents anyway. Let's hear the Christmas story out of the Bible, then we've got dinner to fix."

"I got a present for Mama and Daddy first," Mima said, grinning.

"All right, baby girl, let's have it."

Boone wondered if she'd made something for them, maybe a handkerchief or such. She'd taken to sewing at six with surprising enjoyment and skill. Instead, the little girl lifted her baby sister to the floor and took her hand.

"Show them, Rosey-Posey," she said.

The small girl, later to walk than her older siblings had been, toddled a few steps, clinging to Mima's hand. Mima let go, and she continued for a step or two, then stopped. Her perplexed look made them all laugh, but Boone had tears in his eyes to see his youngest take her first steps. He hadn't been there for the boys, just Jemima Ann.

He scooped up Sarah Rose and hugged her. "Good work, little gal."

With those words, he gave her a nickname.

Then Boone read the familiar passage from Luke.

Outside, the snow had stopped, and the sun shone. Everything he could see had a white mantle of snow. By the light of day, he saw how the snow had drifted in many places. He figured they should break ice for the stock and do a few chores, but Deacon Lee and Mac knocked at the door in the late morning.

"Merry Christmas," Deke said as Boone let him inside.

"Aye, happy Christmas ta ye all," Mac added.

"We come to tell you we've already done what chores had to be taken care of today," Deke said. "And busted the ice off the water so the livestock could drink. We put out hay as well. It's our gift to you, Boone. You're a fine top hand and now the main boss."

Their gesture touched Boone's heart. "I try to be," he said. "Thank you, and the same to you. I appreciate it more than you know – had to go out looking for my boy in the snow last night. He'd wandered out, trying to go fetch his toys from the house."

"Is he well?" Deacon Lee asked.

"He is, thanks for asking," Boone said. "Come, have some coffee or a bite to eat. Dinner ain't ready, but there's plenty of cookies and such, probably some biscuits and sausage left too."

First, they said no, but then they did come in long enough to have coffee, eat biscuits with butter and honey, and get warm. Then they departed after Deke shared a bit of news.

"My wife's in the family way," he told Boone with a wide grin. "Cain't tell you how proud I am or glad you gave us a home here on the ranch. I would have near died if she'd still been in town in this shape."

Boone slapped him on the back. "That's wonderful news, Deke. Rachel and the other gals will be happy to help her out. Once the snow melts, you bring her to eat at my house so they can get to know each other."

"I will, Boone. I gotta go, she's making a Christmas dinner at the cabin for me, and Cookie's got a feast planned for the hands at the bunkhouse."

The Wilsons' Christmas meal was as close to a banquet as anything Boone had ever had. There was plenty of ham, frijoles, sweet potatoes, Irish potatoes mashed to creamy perfection, gravy, fresh-baked light bread, corn, pickles, a huge beef roast, and Boone's favorite dish, chicken and dumplings. For dessert, there were pumpkin and apple pies. There were molasses cookies, sugar cookies, and snickerdoodles. Katie made an Irish apple cake, and Ma contributed a stack cake.

After they'd eaten and once the kitchen had been put to rights, they gathered to sing Christmas carols. Boone and Mima sang as the others joined in, but after several carols, Ma took the lead. They sang through the evening. If anyone got hungry, there was an abundance of food remaining.

By the morning after Christmas, temperatures rose and the thaw began. Melting snow dripped and sounded like rain throughout the day. Mud replaced the deep snow, but everyone made it back to their own houses. Boone got his family settled, then took off to help with the never-ending chores.

He returned late, mud-covered, and wet through. Rachel fussed at him.

"You'll catch a chill, Boone," she said.

"I need to eat, then I'll clean up and change," he told her.

A coughing fit seized him, and she sighed. She brought him hot coffee and a plate of frijoles. She warmed up some of the chicken and dumplings they had carried home, too.

"I don't like the sound of that cough," she said. Her hand clapped across his forehead, and he knew she checked for fever.

"I'm alright," he told her. "It's Rob I'm still worried about."

"He's fine."

Robert never became sick from his excursion into the snow, not as much as a cold, but Boone came down with a heavy cold. He accepted it with good cheer and refused to take to his bed, no matter how much Rachel fussed. As he buckled on his pistol, preparing to walk out the door, Rachel fussed.

"I wish you'd stay home, Boone. I don't want you getting worse or having pneumonia like Moses did," she told him.

"I ain't," Boone said. "I'll suffer through this snot-nose

and gladly. I'd rather me be sick than Rob. I'll manage and be glad. I'd rather not have had to face burying our boy. It could've been that, Rachel. If he'd been out much longer, it would have."

In his mind's eye, he could see that small grave in the ranch cemetery, tucked beside Katie's brother Connor or Liam. The image would haunt him for a long time because he knew it had come very close. They'd found Rob asleep, and if it'd been another half hour, he wouldn't have awakened. Although he knew it wasn't his fault, somehow Boone blamed himself for not keeping track of his children. He should have made certain the doors leading outside were locked tight.

Her expression shifted. She stood on her toes and kissed him. "It didn't, though. I love you, Boone Wilson. Will you at least try to come home early so you can rest?"

"Yeah," he told her. "I'll try, but it won't likely happen. Will you rub my back this evening, maybe rub that stuff you make on it?"

"You know I will," she replied. "Is your back paining you?"

"It's more of a bother than the cold. I reckon I'm gettin' to be an old man."

"Never," Rachel said.

He laughed and headed out for a day's work, his heart and mind with Rachel and his family.

If he could spare the time to stay, he would have.

CHAPTER FIFTEEN

On New Year's Day, they ate roast pork from the sow they butchered after Christmas along with seasoned black-eyed peas for luck. Between the unanticipated arrival of his mother and brother, Garrett, and the holiday season, life on the ranch had been turned upside down. Jacob craved a return to routine. He'd enjoyed celebrating Christmas with all his family for the first time in years, all except the scare young Rob gave them when he ventured out into the snowstorm. Jacob wanted to settle into life, sharing a cabin with Garrett, and get serious in his courtship of Maggie Rafferty. Before he could do either, he had to teach Garrett how to be a cowboy.

Back home, Garrett had worked with the Morgan horses they had raised, but he'd also been a tobacco farmer. No crops were raised on the Double Deuce, just hay for the livestock and the large garden that the women tended. Jacob did his best to help his brother adjust to being a ranch hand. Garrett could ride any horse and tame the wildest one, but when it came to cattle, he was green as a fifteen-year-old. Other than a milk cow, he'd never been around cattle. His attempts to drive them from one pen to the field would have been amusing if it hadn't been so pitiful. He lacked any roping skills, and when Boone attempted to teach him, he became frustrated.

"He'll get the hang of it, Boone," Jacob told him. "And if he don't, he can work with the horses. He knows how to do that. It's where you started me out. I doubt I was a whole lot better than Garrett. Besides, give him time. He's not been here two weeks yet."

Boone pushed back his hat and sighed. "I reckon you're

right. Seems longer."

He started to say more, but started coughing. When he'd finished, Jacob looked at him with some concern. "You all right?"

"I'm better than I was," Boone answered. "I'm nearabout over this cold."

"You'd best take care of yourself, so you don't get sicker."

"You sound like Rachel now."

"Your wife's a wise woman, Boone."

After the snow, the weather had warmed up into the 40s, even 50s by day, dropping to the thirties by night. It was a welcome reprieve after the bitter cold, but after the brief break for Christmas and the snow, they worked long hours in the saddle.

On the first Friday in 1879, Jacob caught Boone as he headed home.

"Garrett's been wanting to see the sights of Laredo," he told him. "Reckon you can spare both of us tomorrow to go?"

Boone took off his hat and ran one hand over his hair. "I reckon so. If I didn't have so much going, I'd go too."

"I wish you would," Jacob said. "I doubt much Zeke or Moses will, not with their wives in the shape that they're in."

"True enough, and someone needs to be here on the Double Deuce," Boone said. "I just hope they both have their babies before time to trail cattle. Neither will want to go, and I can't blame them for that. We'll need more hands, though, if that's how it falls out."

"You could come," Jacob suggested.

"Not I," Boone said. "I cain't leave my wife and children for months, or I would. Besides, I'm the ranch boss now, not just top hand. It's best if I'm here, I reckon."

"Yeah, I reckon so."

They stood within spitting distance of Boone's front porch. The door opened, and Rachel stepped outside. "I thought I heard you," she said with a smile. "Supper's ready to put on the table."

"I'm comin', honey."

Jacob saw the look that passed between them, a wordless declaration of love. Rachel's face, when she gazed at her husband, lit like a full moon. Boone looked back with as tender a look as he ever wore. *I want that,* Jacob thought, *I want that with Maggie.*

Although he'd loved his Sally Ann, it had never been that intense between them. Married young, still in their teens, he had cared for her as much as he knew how. They'd built a life together, raised three daughters, and been content until she died after a difficult childbirth. Maggie brought out something he hadn't known he possessed, a gentle yet powerful love. He had done his best to protect Sally Ann and be a good provider, but he'd lay down his life for Maggie without hesitation.

"I'll let you go eat," Jacob said. "I'll tell Garrett we're good to head to town come morning."

Boone nodded, then surprised Jacob. "I might go. If so, I'll be over before sunup. If not, I ain't goin'."

"Fair enough," Jacob told him.

The first light of dawn barely showed on the horizon when Jacob and Garrett rose. Ma was awake before either of them. She served up bacon and biscuits despite the early hour.

"I'm eager to see this place," Garrett said as he munched through his second biscuit. "Since we're here to stay, I'd like to get familiar. Is it fair-sized?"

Jacob laughed. "It is. A good bit larger than Hazard back home, but nowhere near the size of San Antonio or some of the other places you must have passed through on the train."

"Hazard ain't much more than a wide spot in the road," Garrett said. "We had to get over to Louisville to get the train."

"How'd you manage that?"

"Hitched up the last two horses, then sold them and the wagon when we got there.

"Laredo's booming these days," Boone said as he entered.

He paused to snatch a slice of bacon from Jacob's plate. "It's more like three towns in one, you got your American folks, Mexicans on both sides of the Rio Grande, and the Army at Fort McIntosh. Too big for me, other than to visit or get goods."

"Good morning to you, son," Ma said. "Want some coffee?"

Boone kissed her cheek. "I wouldn't mind a cup."

"Does this mean you're going to town too?" Jacob asked.

"It surely does," Boone told him. "Rachel said there's a few things she would like, and I doubt any of us will make tracks there again till early spring. I'd rather be there, too, for your first visit, Garrett. Ain't a bad place, but we've had some poor luck there."

Moses strolled into the cabin. "True enough, Boone. I reckon being shot and thought to die would top the list, followed by near being hanged for a murder you didn't do. Then the kid got himself beat near to death and stabbed. Don't suppose nothing like that will happen today, though."

"You goin'? Boone asked.

"Naw, I figured I'd stay here. Might check fences. Some might be down after the snow."

"There's a letter Katie hoped you might take to her aunt," Ma said, indicating where it sat on the mantle with a nod.

"We'll take it," Boone said. "Ma, if you need things from town, now's the time to say so."

"I could use some raisins," she said. "If you fetch some, I'll make you a raisin pie, Boone. Other than that, you or this ranch has given be 'bout everything I need."

"I'll bring 'em," he told her. "We'd best get heading that way if we're goin'."

Jacob finished eating and drank the dregs of his coffee. "I'm ready."

Garrett came to his feet. "So am I."

"Let's get mounted and ride."

They set out at a trot with dawn painting the sky with vivid shades of rose, gold, and orange behind. Once they were off the ranch, Boone picked up the pace to a canter. Although they managed to talk a bit as they traveled, it wasn't until Boone halted for both a swig of water and to roll a smoke that Garrett asked a question.

"So, I've been here long enough to figure out some of the dangers," he said. "You got shot, Moses near died sick, Zeke got beat half to death and stabbed, Katie's brother ran afoul of rattlesnakes, plus there's always ways to get hurt around horses or cattle. Even a spider laid you low. Seems like the weather can turn faster than you can say Jack Robinson. Most of it's no different than anyplace else, but what about Indians? I recollect hearing something about some massacre last spring from some folks in San Antonio, but none of you have mentioned it. Ought I be worried? Are we likely to get scalped or killed with an arrow, Boone?"

Jacob tensed and lit his own cigarette. He knew the answer, but the question brought back unpleasant memories and a terrible time.

"I don't reckon," Boone said after a long pause. "But what you heard was true enough. That raid took 18 lives and wounded more, but it twasn't all Indians. A lot of desperados got together forty strong across the river in Mexico, then rode into Texas, causing trouble. Some say it was white men who led the party, and I wouldn't doubt it none. Then there were some Mexicans who rode too, likely as many of them as Indians. Wasn't any one tribe neither but some Seminoles, Lipan Apache, and Kickapoo. Only them Apache been living in this part of the country very long. The others were run out of their home country, and I cain't fault them for being mad over it. But there ain't no excuse for what the bunch of them did."

"Came too close to rest easy over it," Jacob said. "They went to robbing and murdering innocent folk, not all that far from here. It wasn't no Indian raid, but that's how some called it."

"Good Lord," Garrett said. Jacob thought he looked more than a little pale.

"Nothing good about it," Boone responded. "Those varmints did infernal acts only the devil could inspire. They hit mostly sheep ranches, but they killed men, some boys, and a woman or two. They shot them, killed them with arrows, and stabbed them. I heard some they burned, others they tortured."

"Weren't you worried they'd hit the Double Deuce?" Garrett asked.

"Yeah, I was," Boone said. "We wouldn't have heard of it except a friend of Ezekiel's, one he worked with at the livery in Laredo, rode hard to warn us. I never told the women, for I didn't see no reason to scare the fire out of them, but we rode the ranch boundaries day and night for two weeks, until we heard the polecats retreated back into Mexico. If they'd come here, we would've fought back, likely killed as many as we could. We ain't nothing if not well armed on the ranch, and I've been to war. So had Mac, Deke, and Liam. Our side didn't lose in the war because we weren't brave nor bold. Yanks had us outnumbered, and that's what lost in the end."

"How long ago was this anyhow?" Garrett said.

"April," Jacob told him. "Last April, so nearabout nine months ago."

"Ain't you worried it might happen again?"

Boone shook his head. "Not much, no. Comanches were the Indians to fear, but their last attack was four or five years ago. Like I said, what took place last spring wasn't Indians going out against the settlers but a gang of no-good, lowdown men intent on making trouble. They got away with it, too, far as I know, but I doubt they'll be back. Army out of Fort McIntosh stepped up their patrols, and 'bout every rancher knows. I make sure the hands keep their eyes peeled for anything suspicious. Forty mounted men on horseback are gonna kick up enough dust to see coming for a fair piece. I wouldn't mention it to the women, though, or they'll fret."

"With good reason," Garrett replied. "Ma don't know, so I won't tell her."

Boone offered his canteen, then finished his smoke. "Then let's ride if we're heading to Laredo. I'd like to get there today and get back before dark if we can."

They cantered, then increased speed to a gallop so that they rode in Laredo by mid-morning. The Wilson brothers slowed to a walk as they navigated down the street where the Out of Luck stood. Frame buildings lined the narrow street, which was muddy with deep puddles. A few brick buildings sat between the others. Signs advertised grocers, boticas, a hotel, some dining establishments, saloons, barbers, and more. Garrett's gaze traveled from side to side as he took it all in.

"There's the Out of Luck," Boone said, his tone conversational. "That's where I got shot while playing faro, and where we stayed where the proprietress thought I was dying. Over there, that's the livery where Zeke worked for a spell, and up here. See that saddler's shop? We rented the rooms above right before Rachel and me got hitched. She stayed there whilst I was in jail, then once I was free, we lit out for the ranch. I'd had enough of Laredo by then."

The jail loomed ahead. "That where you were locked up?" Garrett asked.

"It is," Boone said. "Let's go look at the rest of the place, maybe ride along the river, then we'll get what we need from the mercantile. Cain't get much – it'll have to fit in the saddlebags or be tied on since we didn't bring a wagon."

"We gotta take that letter to Katie's auntie," Jacob said, and Boone nodded.

At the Rio Grande, they rode along the eastern bank, and Boone took off at gallop, whooping and waving his hat. Jacob followed suit. He liked rivers and such. He often missed having one nearby at the ranch. If they had more time, he'd like to wet a line and do a bit of fishing.

"The other side is Mexico," Boone told Garrett. "Lots of Mexicans on this side, too."

"What are they like?" Garrett asked. "I ain't never seen the like. After what you said about that raid, I'm wondering if they're outlaws and such."

"Naw, most of them are good folk," Boone said. "Like anybody, mostly. If Graciela is still working for Katie's Aunt Clodagh, you'll meet her. She used to work for Mary over at the saloon. She taught Rachel how to make those frijoles and was a good friend to us when we were staying in a room above. We'll stop by the boarding house last, I reckon, unless you want to visit the Out of Luck.'

After their ride along the river, Boone headed for the mercantile where they traded. He bought the raisins Ma had requested along with a few pounds of salt and coffee. Katie had asked for tea, so he bought that too and added some candy for the children: licorice, lemon drops, and peppermint sticks. Then Boone insisted that Garrett choose a pistol. Garrett balked a little.

"I'm a better shot with a long gun," he protested.

"You'll need an iron on your hip out here," Boone said, and talked him into a Colt revolver along with a holster.

As the clerk totaled the bill, Jacob noticed some new candy stock.

"You ought to get your babies a chocolate bar," Jacob suggested. "Or I will."

"It's a mite expensive," Boone replied. "If you want,

though, I'm sure they'll enjoy the treat."

Jacob bought several, one for each of the children big enough to eat it. After all, he figured, why not – he had his wages, few needs, and little reason to spend money. With that in mind, he offered to buy dinner while they were in town.

They ate fried fish at one of the cafés, served with fried potatoes, hominy, and coffee.

"That catfish is right tasty," Jacob said. They had plenty of meat on the ranch, but the fish, fresh out of the Rio Grande, was a rare treat. Back home in Kentucky, there had been many rivers to fish.

After the meal, the next stop was the boarding house on Grant Street. Jacob led them there since he was the only one who'd been there before. The small frame house hadn't changed, nor when she opened the door to them, had Clodagh O'Neill. Katie's aunt showed her age, though, more than she had before her nephew's death. Her auburn hair had numerous white hairs showing, and new lines cut deep into her face. From her visit to the ranch for Connor's funeral, she recognized Boone.,

"Oh, come in, come in, Boone Wilson," she said. "What brings you to town?"

Boone swept off his hat and gestured that his brothers do the same. "Katie sent a letter, and I came to get a few supplies," he said. "And show my brother Garrett here the sights of Laredo. He just arrived last month from Kentucky, the last of my brothers to come."

Garrett bowed to her like a gentleman, which amused Jacob, but he said nothing.

"How fares my niece?" Clodagh asked as she ushered them into her parlor. "Would you like to eat or have some tea?"

"Katie's well," Boone told her. "She's in the family way, looking for a baby this spring, late March or April. Ezekiel's about to bust his buttons over that. I thank you for your kind offer, but we need to head back to the ranch 'fore long. I'd like to make it home before dark, and night comes early this time of year."

Graciela came from the kitchen, wiping her hands on her apron. She smiled when she saw Boone.

"Mister Boone, it's always good to see you," she said. "You look well."

"I've been mostly fine," he told her. "Had a little trouble with a spider bite, but it's near healed. I ought to steal you for the ranch. I miss those tamales you make – never tasted any better."

She blushed and grinned. "I'd make you a batch if you could stay."

"Cain't," he said. "Wish I could."

"Before you go home, Mary wants to see you," Graciela said. "She asked me to tell you if you came into Laredo."

Jacob listened to see what Boone would say. He wouldn't mind a stop at the Out of Luck. Although he didn't drink and seldom played cards, there was something about the saloon he found inviting. Maybe it was the music, he thought, and wondered if they could coax Boone to play the piano.

"I ought not," Boone said. "But I owe Mary friendship, so I will."

Since it was Saturday night, a crowd had already gathered at the saloon. Mary sat at her usual table in a corner, dressed in gold silk brocade. Jacob thought the gown wouldn't have been out of place at some high society ball back east. Although he'd never attended one, he'd seen wood engravings of such and a few ladies' fashion books. On a young woman, it would have been dazzling, but on Mary, hard-faced and worn, it was almost ludicrous. He didn't laugh, though. The woman paused in lifting her cigarillo to her lips and grinned when she saw Boone.

"Boone, you're a welcome sight," she cried. "Handsome as ever."

"That's a right fine dress you got," he drawled. "I got word you wanted to chew the fat with me."

She drew hard on her cigarillo, then exhaled smoke. "You've seen Graciela, then, I trust. I haven't seen hide nor hair of you in ages, so I figured if I said something to her, she'd pass it along. Sit down, and I'll have the new kitchen gal bring out some hot coffee."

"I'd be obliged," Boone said. He drew a chair and sat, so Jacob followed suit. Garrett, after a moment's hesitation, did too. The way Garrett eyed Mary and gazed around the place, Jacob had the notion he'd never set foot in a saloon until now. "You know Jacob, I reckon, and the other fella is my brother Garrett, come out from Kentucky."

Mary held out her hand, so Garrett took it. "I'm pleased to meet you, Garrett Wilson," she said. "How many more brothers you got, Boone?"

"He's the last one to come," he said. "They're all here on the ranch, and my ma too."

"Why, I'd like to meet her one day," Mary said.

Jacob imagined Jemima Wilson, who never had put a lick of rouge on her cheeks nor kohl on her eyes, sitting down to drink coffee with Mary, and shook his head. Far as he knew, Ma had never entered a saloon, let alone one that was also a house of ill repute. Jacob doubted much she would visit one at any time. She wouldn't judge Mary or the doves, he knew, but she would draw a line at setting foot inside.

"I reckon I'll keep that in mind," Boone said. Jacob heard the underlying amusement in his voice. "Did you fare well in the snow?"

"Hard on business," Mary said. "Do you or your brothers want anything to eat with that coffee? I can get Caroline to bring out some tea cakes or some such. She's new and has no clue how to make tamales, though I know you're partial to those."

"Tea cakes will do," Boone said. "We cain't linger long,

Mary. I'd like to be home before dark, though that's already unlikely."

"Stay the night," Mary said with a wide spread of her hands. "I imagine I can find you accommodation."

Boone laughed. "My wife would fret if I didn't get home."

Mary leaned forward and squinted through the smoke. "What about you two gents? You got a wife to worry back at the ranch?"

Jacob laughed. "Not yet, but I plan to wed this year, and Garrett, he's a bachelor."

"Is that right?" Mary asked.

"Yeah, I reckon I am and likely to stay one," Garrett said.

Jacob supposed his brother meant it, but he had to wonder.

After all, he'd vowed he wouldn't remarry, but he would now. Anything could happen.

CHAPTER SIXTEEN

The woman who approached with a tray moved with slow steps. Her generous lips were twisted with tight concentration as she balanced the load with obvious difficulty. The coffee pot and four cups quivered as she set them down with a sigh. She put the cups on the table one at a time. Then added a sugar bowl and a small pitcher with cream. Last, she lifted a plate with small tea cakes, each one dusted with icing sugar. She lifted the coffee pot in one hand and began pouring, then stumbled against the table. Hot coffee poured onto Boone's hand before he leapt up with a wordless cry as it spilled. Coffee puddled on the table and then dripped to the floor.

"Consarn it!" Boone cried as he sidestepped away from the mess.

"Sir, I am so very sorry," the woman said.

"You clumsy witch," Mary shouted. "You're some piece of work. You just burned one of my best customers. You're done here. Go pack your things and get out! I won't have anyone so sloppy working in my establishment."

The woman, who Jacob noted was very pretty with curly black hair, eyes as dark as a moonless night, and a heart-shaped face, began to cry. She mopped at the splattered coffee with her apron, then with a rag with her head tucked down. Not a sound escaped her lips, but her thin body trembled with sobs.

"Mary, you don't need to do that," Boone said. "I ain't hurt and I ain't mad. It was just an accident. I've met with a few myself, and it's not her fault. Let her keep her job."

"Boone, she's been as useless as a saddle on a milk cow," Mary replied. "She ain't been here a week yet and she's broke dishes as well as burned the beans. Now she's gone and scalded your hand."

"It's fine," Boone said as he held it up. "I moved quick, so it didn't burn me. If it did, I'd say so. I may have my faults, but lying's never been among them."

Mary huffed air through her nose and sighed. "I don't know why I should let her stay, but since you're asking, I'll give her one more chance, but she'd best shape up or she's back out on the street where she came from."

"She don't look like a sportin' gal to me," Jacob said. The dress she wore beneath the apron was worn, much mended, and faded, but the fabric was good quality. Her hair wasn't in the usual braids or pinned up in a bun, but was piled on top of her head in a confection of curls that ladies, not farm or working women, would wear.

"I'm not, thank you," the woman said.

Garrett untied his bandana from around his neck and began mopping up coffee from the table, then the floor. He didn't say a thing.

Mary rolled her eyes and said, "That won't do much. Barkeep! Bring over a couple of towels, will you?"

Boone sat back down and poured his own coffee. Then he picked up a cake from the plate and nibbled it. "Tastes right good," he observed.

"She's better at fancy baking than plain cooking," Mary said as she lit another cigarillo.

"Could be, but I reckon she's got a name," Boone said. "Have you lost all your manners living so long in Laredo, Mary?"

Mary fumed as Boone turned toward the young woman. "Miss, I'm Boone Wilson from the Double Deuce Ranch east of town. These are my brothers, Jacob and Garrett. I got two more back at the ranch, Moses and Ezekiel."

She stood with some dignity. "I'm Caroline Calloway, and

I'm pleased to make your acquaintance, sir."

Her voice had the slower cadence of the Deep South and a sweet sound.

"I'd guess you to be from Mississippi," Boone said, surprising Jacob. He'd never known Boone to pay mind to accents before. "Vicksburg?"

Caroline nodded, and a faint smile touched her lips. "I am indeed from Vicksburg," she said. "Might I ask how you could tell?"

"Spent a little time there back in '63," Boone replied. "Didn't end so well, but I was there."

"You're no Yankee." It wasn't a question.

"No ma'am, I'm surely not," Boone said. "Folks there were kind to us boys in gray."

If Jacob didn't know better, he'd almost vow Boone flirted with the young lady, but he did. He had no doubt Boone loved Rachel with all his heart, but he didn't understand why Boone took so much time with Caroline or why, before they left, drew Mary aside to say, "Don't let her go, Mary. I got a feelin' she'll work out for you just fine. Will you do it as a favor to me?"

Hard-eyed Mary gazed at Boone and sighed. "I will, Boone, though I don't know why."

"Because you like me, Mary."

"I do, for my sins," the much older woman said with a laugh. "Not that it's ever done me a bit of good. You don't drink nor dandle my gals, let alone me."

"I don't and won't," Boone said, but he smiled.

On the way out of Laredo, riding fast and hard because there was no way they would make the ranch before night fell, Jacob decided he'd ask his brother. When they paused for a break halfway home, he did. "Boone, why'd you take up for Miss Caroline back there?"

"I wondered the same," Garrett said. "She's a pretty little

thing, but you're long married."

"I am," Boone said. "And happy with my wife. I believe I owe her family a debt from the war. We drug into Vicksburg not long before they fell to the Yanks, and most of us by then were sick with swamp fever. Some were worse than others includin' me."

"How's that got to do with Caroline?"

"Family in one of the nice old houses there, brick with porches upstairs and down, let us shelter there," Boone said. "They tended to the ones of us that were bad sick. Caroline's too young to have nursed any of us. She would have been a child, but I recollect a little girl with big eyes and dark curls that might've been her. Mr. Calloway got us some quinine that helped, and by the time the siege ended, we were well enough to get out before the Yanks took us prisoner. I'm near sure it's her folks that did that for us. That's why. Now let's get home. I'm worn out."

He took off on Sprat at a gallop, leaving them to follow. Jacob and Garrett exchanged a look, then Jacob shrugged. Boone kept the pace most of the way home, and they trailed behind. At the ranch, they headed for the corral to unsaddle and then stable their mounts.

Zeke met them. "You're later than I expected," he said.

Boone didn't blink. "We got caught up talking at the Out of Luck," he said. "Did I miss supper?"

"Naw, Ma's at your house. She made supper for all of us, pork chops from that hog, fried taters and apples, hominy, hasty pudding, and dried apple pie," he said. "Rachel said she doubted you'd be very late, so we waited."

They gathered around Boone's table. The little ones had already eaten, so they ate the simple but delicious fare with gusto. Garrett offered his impressions of Laredo, and Jacob shared the news from Katie's aunt. Boone said little, and as soon as he'd finished a plate, he left the table to pick up his guitar. Mima and

Rob joined him.

"Are we gonna sing, Daddy?" Mima asked.

"We are, baby girl," Boone answered. "And you can sing with me on the songs you know. You might not know all these, but you can learn them, sure enough."

"Can I sing too?" Rob asked.

"You surely can," Boone said.

Jacob moved closer and once the table had been cleared, the dishes washed, so did all the family. Boone strummed the guitar and sang *Amazing Grace*. Both his children joined him, then they all added their voices. He sang two more hymns, both familiar, then switched to songs that Jacob recognized as dating to the war. First, he sang *Oh Susannah* and then the light-hearted song about eating goober peas. Even Jacob knew goober peas were peanuts. Then Boone sang *Dixie*, but he sang solo for his children didn't know the words. Then he followed it with *Bonnie Blue Flag* and *Dearest Love, Do You Remember*.

Boone wore a somber expression as he sang, and Jacob thought his brother's mind traveled back into the past. Boone glanced around and saw that he'd brought a sad mood, so he sang one more tune, *The Yellow Rose of Texas*. Mima joined Boone as he sang, and afterward, he put away the guitar.

"You little ones had best head to bed," Boone said. "I'll go myself 'fore long."

Mima put her arms around his neck and kissed his cheek. "Are you sad, Daddy?"

He hugged the girl and said, "Might be a bit, but mostly I'm dog tired. Good night, Mima."

Moses brought Mattie her shawl. "I reckon we're going home. Do you want to walk with us, Ma?"

"I'll go with Jacob and Garrett," she replied. "I doubt they'll stay much longer."

"We'll walk beside you," Ezekiel said. "Katie's tired."

Rob clamored for Boone to carry him to bed, so he did, tossing the boy over one shoulder. Mima followed and led Benjamin by the hand. Rachel picked up Sarah Rose and said, "What's got Boone unsettled?"

"The war," Jacob told her. "We met a young woman in town from up in Mississippi. Seems her family offered shelter to Boone and some of his buddies back then, although she didn't know it. I reckon meeting her brought back the past."

"He almost never speaks about it," Rachel said.

"It was a bad time for him," Ma said. "I could see in his eyes when he came home, then left again. It hurt him, deep in his soul, I reckon. Seems like he got past it, but it's natural he'd remember sometimes."

"We'd best go too so he can get some sleep," Jacob said. Next oldest, he knew how much the conflict had changed Boone, and he thanked God often that he'd not been quite old enough to go. Many had, though, his age and younger.

"Good night," Rachel said. "Don't fret about Boone, he'll do. I'll offer what comfort he needs."

On the way home, using a lantern to light the way so no one would stumble, Ma shared the plans for Sunday. "We talked about it and figured it'd be best if we eat our dinner at home, each bunch of us," she told them. "Give everybody a rest. Ezekiel shot a passel of squirrels this morning after you headed to town. I plan to fry them up unless you'd rather have them with dumplings."

"Fried is good, Ma," Jacob said. "I like squirrel either way."

Ma nodded. "I'll likely make corn dodgers and maybe bake some sweet potatoes in the ashes, too. Did Boone get those raisins?"

"He did," Jacob said. "I've got them right here."

Ma accepted them and put them away. He knew she'd wait to make raisin pie until Boone could have some. It'd been his favorite as a boy and likely still was. She sat down by the fire, then wiggled until she found a comfortable spot.

We need to get her a rocking chair, Jacob thought. She had almost worn out the one she'd had at home in Kentucky. *I'll ask if we can buy one or if we need to make it.*

She picked up her knitting and went to work on what appeared to be another pair of socks. Ma's hands were seldom idle, even near bedtime. "Tell me about town," she said. "One of these days, once I'm more settled, I'd like to go myself."

"We can take you someday in the wagon," Jacob replied. "Probably won't be until spring. I doubt Boone would've gone now except Garrett wanted to see Laredo."

He didn't mention that the proprietor of one of the saloons, which also served as a bordello, wanted to meet her. Now didn't seem like the time to bring it up if there ever was a time.

"So did this young lady from Mississippi work at the mercantile or the boarding house?"

Despite the casual tone she adopted, Jacob knew Ma was fishing for information.

"Neither one," he replied.

Garrett glanced up from removing his boots. "She's a new cook at the Out of Luck," he told their mother. He'd always been the one to tell Ma their boyhood exploits, Jacob recalled. Although they all were honest, Garrett took telling the truth to a new level. He shared all the information, good or bad.

Ma's eyebrows raised. "And that's the saloon?"

Garrett met her stare without wavering. "It is, but she's not a saloon girl, Ma, far from it."

"I wouldn't think Boone would spend time in a saloon," Ma said. "I know well enough he don't drink and he's no interest in the women there."

Jacob laughed. "You're right, but he did have a fondness for faro. That's what he was doing at the Out of Luck when he got shot those years back. From what he and Ezekiel have said, Mary, the owner, likes Boone. She let them carry him upstairs when he thought he was dying, and that's where Rachel nursed him back to health. Moses vows if it wasn't for Mary's help, he might not have got to the bottom of who really killed the blacksmith Boone nearly was hanged for murdering. She's an old woman, Ma, rough around the edges."

Jemima Wilson's stern expression eased a fraction. "I never knew most of that," she said. "She must not be all bad, this Mary. Why's this woman, what did Boone say her name was, working in such a place?"

"Caroline Calloway's her name," Garrett said. "No one said exactly why she's there, but it's not been long, a week or less if I heard right. That Mary threatened to throw her back out on the street where she came from when she spilled coffee on Boone. He stood up for her, though, and I'm glad. She's a pretty little lady down on her luck."

"I never heard about spilling coffee," Ma said. She sounded perturbed. "Though that's no crime. I'd expect Boone to take up for a stranger. It's how I raised y'all. Now I understand why he'd feel beholden if her folks sheltered him."

"He was sick," Jacob commented. "Said he was bad with swamp fever."

"Malaria," she mused. "Never knew that."

"I figure there's plenty about the war we never heard about," Jacob replied. "Might be best if we don't."

"That's true," Ma said. "Did this woman nurse him? Does she have tender feelings from it? Our Rachel won't care for that at all."

Garrett spoke up. "Boone said not. Besides, she's too young – I doubt she's as old as I am, maybe not even as old as Ezekiel."

Jacob nodded. "Yeah, I'd say so. Boone said he recollected a child, a girl with black curls and dark eyes, same as Caroline.

Likely it was her."

Ma nodded and seemed to mull it all over. "Well, I'm curious now how she ended up way out here in Texas, but I reckon I'll find out, or I won't. I'm ready to go to bed."

That was the cue for Jacob and Garrett to retreat into the bedroom they shared so Ma could have privacy to retire. They both kissed her cheek and went, leaving her to sit before the fire.

Jacob expected to go shuck out of his clothes down to his underwear, then sleep, but after he laid down, Garrett spoke out of the darkness. "Hey, Jacob."

"What?"

"It's been a day."

Resigned to not sleeping yet, Jacob propped up on one elbow. "It was and long."

"It's nearabout too much to take in," Garrett said. "First, that raid last spring has fired my imagination and not in a good way. Then, Laredo was different than I had reckoned it would be. Bigger, somehow, and crowded. Never imagined there'd be so many Mexicans. Boone walking into a saloon surprised the fire out of me. Never knew he frequented such places."

"We all been to the Out of Luck at one time or another," Jacob told him. "Ain't none of us drink or trifle with the gals. It's different here, I reckon, and Boone's been going there since he first come to Texas, trailing after Liam and Deke. He's known Mary near that long."

The way the corn shuck mattress rustled beneath Garrett Jacob could tell he sat up, so he did too. "Did Boone really stay in a room upstairs at the saloon?"

"It was long before I come, but that's what Zeke and Moses say," Jacob said. "Far as I know, after Boone was shot in the chest playing cards, they toted him up there. Boone thought he'd die, and so did everybody else, until Rachel."

"I figured he knew her before he took a bullet."

"Naw, she came here to be a schoolmarm. Deke and Mac would carry Boone down to the saloon porch every day so he could get some air, and that's where Rachel first saw him. She struck up a conversation, and when he told her he was dying, she said he wasn't."

Garrett laughed. "She does seem a tad stubborn."

"It was her who nursed him, took the bullet out, Ezekiel says. Boone likely would have died if she hadn't."

"Glad she did."

"So am I. Are you still glad you and Ma came to Texas?"

When his brother didn't answer immediately, Jacob tensed. If Garrett regretted it, there was nothing left to return to in Kentucky.

"I am," Garrett said after a pause. "I wish we'd come out sooner. I don't rightly know what took so long to decide to do it. Texas will take some getting used to, but I'll do it. I like the place already. I wish I wasn't all thumbs when it comes to driving cattle, and I can't rope worth nothing."

Relief made Jacob almost giddy. "You'll catch on to it soon. We'd best get some shut-eye."

It wasn't long until Garrett snored, but Jacob lay awake. His mind brimmed full of many things: the trip to town, Garrett and Ma's arrival, the ranch, Boone's war service, the ranch, but Maggie most of all.

Caroline Calloway was lovely, he thought. Like Ma, he would like to know her story. He wasn't smitten, though, any more than Boone had been. Jacob could appreciate something beautiful without wanting it, he thought. Pretty as she was, she couldn't hold a candle to Maggie, not in his book.

He realized he'd come back from town without any trinkets for Maggie. He'd slipped her the beads he'd bought on New Year's Eve, and he'd been pleased to see she wore them the next day.

Since tomorrow was Sunday, he resolved he'd wash up a bit and shave. Then he'd put on his best duds and go call on Maggie. Since Moses and his wife had taken up residence, he could call on her without anyone wagging their tongues. Although they would likely end up in the parlor, under her sister's eye, he would be able to see Maggie. They could talk about town, he thought, or the ranch, or most anything. And if he could, he'd steal a kiss or maybe two.

Jacob shut his eyes and willed himself to sleep so Sunday and his courtship could both begin.

CHAPTER SEVENTEEN

Since the brothers had the same basic build and height, they wore the same size clothing. Jacob borrowed a frock coat from Garrett, one he'd worn on the way from Kentucky. He had a good shirt to wear under it and a vest, or what Ma called a waistcoat. Ezekiel loaned him a silk puff tie, and Boone let him borrow his best boots. After Sunday dinner, Jacob scrubbed as much as he could using a washbasin and some of Rachel's homemade lye soap. He combed his hair and splashed a bit of bay rum, then brushed and cleaned his hat before setting out to the main ranch house. He didn't give any advance warning, just hoofed it over there and knocked on the door. If it wasn't the dead of winter, he'd picked some flowers or something along the way. To avoid arriving empty-handed, he took one of the chocolate bars he'd bought in town. Jacob had saved a couple back, figuring he might enjoy one or give the other to his mother. Now he'd present it to Maggie as a small token of his affection.

He stepped up on the porch and knocked on the door. Moses answered it with an annoyed look that shifted to surprise. "I couldn't figure who'd be chapping at the door," he said. "I was worried it might be some of Mattie's folks from San Antonio, and that got my dander up. What in tarnation are you doing coming to the door like a stranger?"

Jacob would have thought his mission was obvious since he was dressed as close to a gentleman as he'd ever been. "I'm here to court Maggie."

"I shoulda guessed," Moses said with a slight smirk to his lips. "Where'd you get the duds?"

"Mostly borrowed," he replied.

"If you'd asked me, I got some good clothes I bought when I was courtin' Maggie. Or, if you'd had the time, you could've borrowed a fine suit from Phin, but you'd had to go all the way to San Antone for that."

"Moses, who's here?" Mattie said as she came through the parlor to stand beside her husband.

"Jacob's come courtin'," he told her. "You'd best tell your sister he's here and why."

Mattie's mouth gaped wide. "*Ach du meine Güte. Jawohl!*"

"What'd she say?" Jacob asked as Mattie hurried away.

Moses laughed. "Something like 'oh my goodness, certainly'. You might as well come in, sit down, and wait. I reckon Maggie's gonna primp a bit before she sees you."

Waiting made Jacob antsy. He crossed his legs and jiggled one foot, nervous now that he'd come. He had never been ill at ease with Maggie, but the dress clothes and formal wooing changed things. It'd been one thing to cook her breakfast, do little chores for her, and talk to her in an everyday fashion. Maybe she'd find his garments lacking somehow. Jacob recalled that Liam had been a sharp dresser. His duds wouldn't compare. He stewed about it until Maggie walked into the room.

She hadn't worn stark black since Liam's funeral, although she'd said she would if she left the ranch. Jacob had never seen her wear this dress, a soft gray full-skirted dress made from a light cotton he thought was called lawn. It had long, modest sleeves and a high neckline. Buttons trailed from her throat to her waist, where a satin bow added trim. Jacob noted she wore the brown agate beads he'd given her and thought that was a good sign.

He stood as she entered. "You look pretty," he told her, then realized it was an understatement. Her golden hair was pinned in her usual braided style, but she'd added a bow that matched the dress.

"Thank you," she said and nodded. "You look quite

handsome, Jacob. I've never seen you in fine clothing."

His face became warm. "I reckon I clean up all right."

Maggie looked at him for a long moment, and he worried he'd said the wrong thing. Maybe he should have tried to quote poetry or at least a song, he thought. Her lips twitched into a smile, and then she laughed. "You do, dear heart."

When she laughed, he did too, and the awkwardness vanished like smoke.

"Come, sit down, Jacob," she told him. She settled her skirts and took her place on the settee. He sank down beside her, careful to keep some distance between them. "I'm so glad you came to call."

"I brought you chocolate," he said, pulling the candy from the pocket of his frock coat. "I would've liked flowers, but it's not the season."

Her eyes glowed. "I like chocolate!"

"I bought it yesterday in Laredo," he said. As he relaxed, conversation was easier. "Boone and I took Garrett to see town. We picked up a few things while there."

"I heard," Maggie told him. No one had secrets on the ranch, especially not when she shared the same home as one of his brothers. "How was it?"

Jacob told her about the journey, their visit to the mercantile, how they rode down to the river, dined on catfish, and delivered a letter from Katie to her aunt. Then, he mentioned their visit to the Out of Luck and the young woman they met.

"She's the cook there now, although she didn't seem suited to it. She's from Vicksburg," he told her. "Seems that Boone was there at the last of the siege, right before it fell to the Federals. Caroline – that's her name, Caroline Calloway – would have been a child, I reckon, but Boone thinks her family gave him and some other soldiers shelter. He had come down with swamp fever, and they got him through it. Remembering all that put Boone in a state. He was discombobulated a fair bit, and last night, after supper, he sang songs from the war. He usually don't say much about those times."

"What does she look like?" Maggie asked, and from the sour expression she wore, he realized she might be jealous.

"Aw, she's not too hard to look at," he said, downplaying Caroline's looks. "I believe Garrett might be taken with her, though he's not said much. I ain't seen any woman prettier than the one sitting beside me, not in Laredo and not anywhere else. You put them all to shame, honey."

Her face lit up like the Christmas tree they'd had in this very parlor. "Do I?"

"You do, Maggie."

She reached for his hand and held it. "Is your brother smitten?"

Jacob shrugged. "Likely."

Then he shared the story of the spilled coffee and how Garrett undid his bandana, then used it to mop up the mess. "He never said a word, though, while he did."

"He seems quieter than the rest of you."

"Ma always said still waters run deep," Jacob told her. "It fits Garrett to a T. I ain't saying he's gonna head to Laredo to start romancing her. We have no idea how she ended up there or why. I reckon there's a story, and in time, we'll know. He'll mull it over a spell before he does anything."

Her small hand was enveloped by his. Jacob liked the weight of it tucked into his palm. On impulse, he lifted it to his mouth and kissed it. Maggie blushed and shivered a little.

If he didn't stop, he'd keep on until he kissed her lips, so Jacob ceased. That turned out to be a good choice because Moses and Mattie joined them with little Ellie. Moses asked about town, although it turned out he'd already talked with Zeke earlier in the day. He'd heard about the mysterious Southern lady and

Boone's reaction.

Ellie chattered, although no one could understand much of what she said. Maggie scooped her niece onto her lap, heedless of her fine dress, and Jacob realized she must miss her own children very much. He missed his, too, although probably not the same way she must. Raising the girls had been Sally Ann's responsibility more than his. After one bad year, back in 1870, the crops had been good. So, he'd been out working the tobacco crop or training horses.

Despite the loose-fitting dress Mattie wore, Jacob noticed the swell of her belly beneath it. Spring would be an interesting time, he figured, with both Mattie and Katie due to have babies. He'd like to see a spring wedding for himself and Maggie, but all those things had best to happen before they trailed cattle. It wasn't likely that all five of the brothers would drive cattle, but some of them must.

"Does your mother like Texas?" Mattie asked, breaking him away from his thoughts.

"She does," Jacob said. Then he wondered for the first time how Ma would feel when some of her sons were gone for months. She'd deal with it, though, content with the knowledge they would be back soon, not absent for years. "She's getting settled in, I reckon. I'd like to see about getting her a rocking chair. She had one back home she was partial to, but they couldn't bring it on the train."

"Jack McGee's a fair hand with wood," Moses said. "I'll ask if he can't make one before it gets busy around here come spring."

"Boone will want him to help with that church, if he's serious about building one," Jacob replied.

"Oh, he is, I do believe," Moses said. "I like the notion myself. Would be right nice to have somewhere to have church sometimes, whether we could get a preacher or not."

"Boone thought we could have school there as well," Mattie said. She touched her belly as she spoke. "That's a fine idea. I know Rachel's taught her two oldest to read and write, but before long, there'll be more children to learn."

Jacob nodded. "That would be a good thing, too."

He struggled to keep his mind focused on the conversation. He had little interest at this moment in building a church or school or even a rocking chair. All he wanted was to spend more time with Maggie, alone. That might give him a chance to hold her hand again or sneak some kisses. Although past thirty, Jacob had a young man's eagerness to spoon, which surprised him. He had married young, still in his teens, and until these past months, when it dawned on him what he felt toward Maggie was more than friendship, he'd almost thought his interest in such things had vanished. It hadn't, though, or if it did, it had returned as powerful as ever.

The fancy garments stressed him. His collar was too high for comfort, and he wanted to unbutton the top buttons. Inside the parlor, it was warm, and he'd become hot in the shirt, vest, and frock coat. The silk tie choked him, and he ached to undo it, then cast it aside. Jacob longed for his usual dungarees with the denim worn soft and comfortable. His usual shirts, made from cotton or calico, fit better than the woolen dress shirt that made him itch.

Judging by the shadows, it had to be near four o'clock. Dusk would fall in an hour or so, and it would be full dark in two. Sunday suppers were usually simple, but Ma would put food on the table by then, and so would Mattie. So far, she hadn't made a move toward the kitchen, although Jacob wished that she would. Then he might snitch a few more minutes alone with Maggie.

Garrett burst into the room without knocking, face frantic and eyes wide. He left the door open behind him.

"We got trouble on the ranch," he cried.

Jacob leapt to his feet. "What is it?"

He imagined the worst, wildfire, desperados, someone sick or hurt, or a stampede.

"Two men, riding in fast and hard on paint horses," Garrett cried. "I do believe they're Mexicans with the big hats and the blankets."

"*Serapes,* not blankets," Moses said. "Best fetch Boone."

"What if it's a raid?" Garrett asked.

Jacob cringed, afraid his brother might mention last year's massacre in front of the women, who had no idea it had happened.

"With two riders? It's not," he said.

"I surely hope it's not," Garrett said. "I'll get Boone."

He turned to go, but as he did, Boone strolled through the door, unruffled and unsmiling.

"I'm here," he said, unnecessarily. "What's this ruckus? Young Davy tore over to my house like the ranch was burning down and told me I'd better head this direction."

"Two riders are headed this way," Garrett said. "I reckon they're Mexican, maybe, by the hats they wear and some of their gear."

Boone quirked an eyebrow and asked, "Does it matter? I reckon it's more important what they want. I'm fixin' to find that out."

Jacob heard the hoofbeats approaching and moved to the window. He saw the pair as they slowed their horses, then halted. One of them tossed his reins to the other and dismounted. As he made his way toward the door, Boone opened it.

"*Hola!* " he cried. "What brings you to the ranch?"

Garrett's mouth drooped wide. "Does he know them?"

Jacob laughed. "He might, might not."

"Does he speak Spanish?"

"Naw, no more than a few words," Jacob told his brother. He had a feeling Texas was more of a revelation to Garrett than he'd guessed. "You'll notice he also has a hand on his Griswold."

Boone's stance appeared relaxed as he stepped onto the porch to greet the men, but his right hand rested on the pistol.

"Mister Boone, we come to work," the man who had dismounted said. "I'm Matias Alvarez Torres. You know our sister, Graciela. We are experienced *vaqueros*, my brother Diego and me."

Moses had sent Mattie and Maggie away from the parlor when the riders arrived. He returned with a smirk and poked Garrett in the back. "Trouble on the ranch, you said?" he asked, his voice thick with laughter.

Garrett flushed. "Coulda been."

Jacob offered his support. "It might've, that's true, but thank God it ain't."

"I do believe I met you once or twice," Boone drawled, his Kentucky accent very noticeable. "Come in and we'll talk."

The second man dismounted and tied the horses to a small tree. Both stamped their feet to remove any mud or dirt before entering the house, they followed Boone into the parlor. Once inside, they removed their sombreros and held them over their chest.

"We want to work on the Double Deuce," Matias said.

"I could use you," Boone told them. "What experience do you have?"

They listed several ranches, ranging from one within the area and two others farther away. Neither sounded familiar to Jacob, but Boone nodded.

"What brings you here in the middle of winter?" he asked.

"We been working up north of San Antone," Diego told him. "On the Lighting Z. Mr. Zimmerman kept us after last year's cattle drive, but he died last week. We've been wanting to be closer to our sister, Graciela, and she's in Laredo. After our mother died when we were small, she raised us like we were her sons. We came because the Lightning Z is being sold, and our sister said we should see if you need hands."

"What happened to Ernst Zimmerman?" Boone asked. He took a seat and rolled a smoke as he spoke.

The brothers exchanged a glance. Matias sighed. "He had an apoplexy and died right before Christmas. His widow packed up and left. Wasn't no money to speak about, and some German banker out of San Antonio bought the ranch. He hired a ranch manager, and he was a cruel man. Treated the livestock better than he did us, so we left."

Boone lit his smoke. "Let me guess," he said in a sharp tone. "I don't reckon this here banker might be named Guttersnipe Hammerschmidt."

Both Torres brothers nodded, and Boone sighed. "That don't surprise me one bit. I'll take you on as hands, both of you. There's room in the bunkhouse. I'll pay wages once a month, but I don't take anything out for your eats or a place to sleep. I know some ranches do, but I won't. I will expect you to trail cattle come spring, and I'll pay a mite more then. I won't tolerate drinking on this ranch nor foul language. You'll work hard, but so do I. If you can abide with all that, you're hired."

"*Gracias,*" Matias said, and Diego echoed him.

"*De nada,*" Boone replied. "Garrett, you want to take them over to the bunk house. I'll be there directly to tell Otis myself, then I'll head on home. Gents, you can start in the morning. I take it those are your horses out there, so you've got that. Are you armed?"

"We each have a rifle," Diego said.

"That'll do for now."

Garrett nodded and headed outside with the two new hands trailing behind.

Moses shut the door and turned to Jacob.

"You're welcome to stay and eat. I think Maggie hopes

you will. It ain't much, just some fried cabbage, a few pieces of bacon, and some biscuits."

"I will, thanks," Jacob said. He'd planned to leave, but he'd stay for Maggie.

Once the meal was over, he decided he'd best head home. Dark had fallen, but Maggie walked him to the door. Jacob drew her out onto the porch where the shadows were deep.

"Are you glad I came?" he asked her.

She put her hands on his shoulders and smiled. "I am, Jacob, very glad. I enjoyed the afternoon despite the interruption."

He laughed. "I'll come tomorrow if I can, though I'll likely be busy."

"I'd like it if you could," she replied.

Encouraged by that, Jacob pulled her into his arms and kissed her the way he'd wanted to all afternoon, his lips slow and warm against her mouth. She returned the kiss and grasped the edges of his frock coat. He stopped before he became tempted to go any further and held her close. The rose scent of the sachet powder she wore wafted into his nose, and he savored it. Maggie fit against him as if she were tailor-made for him. He held her longer just to enjoy the feeling.

He folded the fingers of his left hand against her cheek.

"Good night, Maggie," he told her.

"Sleep well, Jacob," she replied. "*Schatz.*"

Although he wasn't certain of the exact meaning, he knew it was an endearment and that sent a rush of warm sweetness like honey through his blood.

"I'll see you tomorrow, dear heart," he said and took his leave.

Jacob walked through the darkness and didn't hurry. His thoughts centered on the woman he'd just left. Her taste lingered on his lips, and her fragrance in his nose. When he reached the dog trot cabin, Ezekiel sat on the steps.

"Airish, ain't it to sit out?" Jacob said. Although temperatures were not as cold as they had been over Christmas, it was cooler at night.

Zeke shrugged. "It ain't too bad. You're late if you're lookin' for supper. We ate most of it, and Ma put away the rest."

"I ate over to Moses' place," Jacob told him. "Where's your wife?"

"Fast asleep," Ezekiel said. "The longer she's in the family way, the more tired she gets. Ma says that's how it is, though, but I worry."

"Gettin' like Boone in your old age," Jacob joked. Ezekiel wasn't yet 23 years old and wouldn't be until March. He knew, though, why the kid would fret. Jacob's wife had delivered three fine girls, then lost the fourth and died soon after, wracked with childbed fever. This wasn't the time to mention that, though. "I reckon Katie'll be fine."

Ezekiel nodded. "I hope and pray. I think maybe she'll have the baby sooner than we thought. She's bigger in the belly now, a lot more than Mattie."

"Won't that be good? Better before we trail cattle."

His youngest brother's expression turned sad. "It would. I don't rightly know how I'll bear it if I gotta go and the baby ain't here yet."

Jacob put a hand on Ezekiel's shoulder. "You'd manage, like we all do," he said. He hoped to marry Maggie before they hit the trail, but whether they did or didn't, they would make it work somehow. Wilsons always did.

CHAPTER EIGHTEEN

Two days later, Jacob marked his 33rd birthday. He didn't expect any fanfare, but Ma surprised him with a birthday kiss on his cheek. She served his favorite buckwheat pancakes for breakfast with a side of sausage, which he preferred over bacon. Garrett and Ezekiel both wished him happy returns of the day, but Boone stunned him.

He showed up to work at the corrals, ready to check and pick the horses' feet. It was a routine task, but necessary. Boone met him there and, with a slantwise grin, said, "Take the day off, Jacob. Ain't much work anyhow."

Jacob protested, aware there were many chores to be done, but Boone shook his head.

"Naw, you'd best head up to Moses' place. I hear that Maggie fancies a picnic out by the pond, and the weather is fine."

Two weeks ago, the weather had been chilly and frightful, but on the 7th of January, the sun shone from a sky with no more than a few clouds. A warm south breeze wafted across Jacob's face, and he grinned.

"Are you sure, Boone?" he asked. "I can get a few hours work done before it's noontime. I don't mind."

"I do," his oldest brother replied. "I didn't get a gift for you, but I surely can give you the day to go courtin."

"I don't need a gift."

"You could use a day with Maggie, I reckon," Boone said. "Lord knows if I had the chance to go picnic with Rachel, I'd do it. Cain't because of the babies, but I surely would if we could."

Boone's offer touched him, so he nodded. His lips stretched into a grin. "Awright, you talked me into it. Thank you, brother."

"*De nada.*"

Jacob opted to change into a fresh shirt, a candy-striped button-down style, and to shave. When he had finished, Ma stopped him.

"Let me trim your hair," she told him. "You look a sight with it grown out the way it is."

He'd rather not wait, but since it was still early in the day, he agreed.

Ma had him sit at the table where she snipped at stray locks of hair with her best scissors.

"I'm no barber, son," she said. "But it's an improvement over looking scraggly. You're a fine-looking young man when you clean up a bit."

Katie came across the dog trot to offer Jacob a set of sleeve garters. "Aye, he is," she said with a smile. "'Tis because he looks a little like Ezekiel."

Jacob laughed. "Being as he's the least one, I'd say he takes after me, Katie."

"That may well be," she replied. "But though I'm fond of ye, Ezekiel has my heart."

She rubbed her growing abdomen with a small, almost secret smile. "This one, he'll look like his daddy," she told them.

"You're lookin' out for a boy, then?" Ma asked.

"'Tis one," Katie answered. "I'm baking bread the day, so I must get back. Enjoy your day with Maggie, Jacob."

"I reckon I will," he said, wondering how everyone already knew about the outing. There were few, if any, secrets among the Wilson family.

Ma turned to him once Katie had gone. "She seems right sure it'll be a boy, but it may be a girl. If it is, I hope she's not disappointed."

"She won't be," Jacob said. "But she has a knack for knowing things, so she's likely right. Does she look closer to her time than they've said?"

Jemima Wilson narrowed her gaze. "She does, and that's a fact. Ezekiel asked the same. I doubt she'll last until late March or April. My guess is that she has the child closer to your brother's birthday."

"That's in two months."

"It is," Ma said. "You'd best head up to the main ranch house if you're takin' your Maggie on a picnic."

Jacob hitched up an open wagon and wished it were a buggy. Buggies weren't practical on the ranch. The traces that passed for roads heading to Laredo or San Antonio were too rough for anything but a heavy wagon. If it were just him, he'd walk and carry the food, but he figured Maggie would enjoy the ride.

The delectable aroma of fried chicken wafted out to greet Jacob as he parked the wagon at the ranch house. He licked his lips in anticipation, then swung down from the seat. Maggie came out to the porch, a wicker basket over one arm. She wore a bright calico dress he didn't remember ever seeing and a big smile.

"Happy birthday to you, Jacob."

"Thanks. Let me tote that," he said and took the basket. He set it in the back of the wagon, tucked snug into a corner of the bed, then offered his help so she could climb into the seat. Before he could pick up the reins, Moses exited the house.

"Happy birthday, brother," he called. "It's a downhill drag now, ain't it? Over thirty makes you an old man, and you're what, is it thirty-three?"

Jacob grinned. "You ain't so very far behind me, Mosey."

"Six years, I do believe."

"He's a man in the prime of life," Maggie said. "And a fine figure of one at that."

She's got it bad, Jacob thought with joy and a measure of pride. But so did he.

"Come eat supper with us this evening," Moses said, laughing. "Maggie said she'll make that rouladen you so liked in honor of the day."

"I'd like that," Jacob said. "Though this fine fried chicken smells like heaven to me."

"She had me kill one of her best young chickens for that," Moses said. "Had me up at the crack of dawn to do it. Then she took up the kitchen, so I had to wait for my breakfast, all the time smelling chicken frying."

"I made you biscuits," Maggie said, her cheeks flushed red. "And I had the coffee ready when you brought me the bird."

"You did," Moses agreed. "That's true enough. Enjoy your day, both of you."

Mattie came out on the porch, wrapped in a shawl with little Ellie to wave. Her earlier objections to Jacob courting Maggie appeared to have vanished, and he liked that very much. To him, they were already one family, and it had become even more vital when the Baumanns had disowned their daughter. The combination of his birthday, Maggie's compliment, Moses' light-hearted picking, and Mattie's wave gave the day a holiday feel.

Jacob clicked his teeth, and the team set forth, slow and steady as he guided them to the pond. The sunshine, the pretty woman seated beside him, the rare weekday free from chores, the anniversary of his birth, and the delicious aromas rising from the basket put him in a pleasant mood. He felt like a king or at least a prince. A deep happiness filled his heart, and he couldn't keep from smiling.

"I'm right glad you thought up this picnic," he told Maggie.

She tilted her face up toward him with a perplexed look. "I didn't," she said. "Boone said that you craved a picnic for your birthday. He came by the house and told me so yesterday. I thought it was a grand idea, so I said I'd be happy to accompany you."

Surprise filtered through his bright mood. "I'm glad you did," he said. "I don't have a notion what was in Boone's mind, though."

Jacob did, though. He figured his brother knew how much he wanted time alone with Maggie, and he'd devised a way to provide it. A suspicion that his whole family was part of the plan crept into his mind as he thought about how his mother had trimmed his hair and did her best to help him look handsome. Katie contributed the sleeve garters, and Moses added good wishes with a side helping of teasing. Mattie and Ellie's cheerful waves factored in too.

The earlier objections, mostly based on his timing, so soon after Liam's death, had faded, but until today, his folks had done their level best to make sure he and Maggie were chaperoned.

Since Moses and Mattie had moved into the main house, he hadn't had any early morning conversations over coffee or unscheduled visits with Maggie. Now the day stretched out full of promise and time to spend with her.

I reckon they want me to ask her to get married, Jacob realized. They'd talked about wedding. Maggie brought up the subject first, asking if he would marry her to keep her family from toting her back to San Antonio. Long smitten with the pretty woman, Jacob had agreed but admitted he would like to make her his wife regardless. He hadn't asked her, however, and he decided this would be the day he did.

The pond, framed with cedars still vivid green despite the winter, appealed more than ever. Sunshine sparkled and danced across the surface. None of the stock was here to drink from the water, although the weeds had been trampled flat in the spots they preferred. Jacob halted the wagon and locked the brake in place before helping Mattie step down. He noted that she wore ankle-high boots and was glad. If she'd worn fancy shoes, he wouldn't have asked if she wanted to walk a little before they ate.

He offered her his arm, and she accepted it. They strolled around the perimeter of the water, inhaling the fragrance of the cedars and the loamy smell of the pond. Jacob relaxed more than he had in days, and they talked. Their conversation covered little things, everyday happenings on the ranch, and larger stuff. He told her about growing up in Kentucky and what prompted him to ride out for Texas. Maggie told him about her often strict upbringing in town and how she savored the freedom found on the ranch.

"We had to behave so properly," she told Jacob as they walked. "Papa wouldn't allow us to laugh or even smile at the dinner table. There were things that we, as young ladies, could not talk about, and we had to go to dances and musicales and such."

"I'd like to dance with you," he told her.

"You wouldn't like the way we danced," Maggie replied. "There were waltzes and minuets, no two-stepping and no square dances."

"None?" he asked, surprised. Jacob could recall some happy times at a square dance, often in someone's barn. They had used the Wilson tobacco barn out of season for dancing.

She shook her head. "No. I wouldn't begin to know how to allemande left or do-si-do. I only know those words because I've heard people talk about square dancing."

"I could teach you, if there ever was one to go to," Jacob said. "Or to two-step."

"Can you waltz?"

"I reckon I can, a little," he told her. "Ma taught us so we'd be ready if we ever needed that skill. I might be a bit clumsy, but I can."

"I'd like to waltz with you, Jacob," Maggie said. "I wouldn't need a fancy gown or flowers in my hair or musicians, just your arms around me and the two of us dancing, one, two, three, four, one, two, three, four..."

He almost took her into his arms, but the footing on the pond bank was uneven, and he suspected it wouldn't be good for dancing. Later, though, if he could, they would waltz, and he would do his best not to step on her toes.

"Maggie," he said, serious now. "I want to ask you something, and it's mighty important."

She faced him and gazed up into his eyes. "What is it?"

Jacob took her hands in his. "We've talked about it and around it, but will you marry me, Maggie?"

He held his breath as he waited for her answer. After a long moment, she nodded.

"I will, Jacob, gladly."

"I don't want to wait the year," he told her. "I'd like to wed before I go trail cattle come April."

"I'd like that myself," Maggie said.

"If Boone gets his church built, we could marry there, but if not, I'm willing to say I do anywhere."

"I feel the same."

Jacob wanted to holler and whoop, then he did. He lifted her up and swung her around.

"We're goin' to get married," he cried. "Maggie, I love you."

Once he set her down on her feet, she stood on her toes and kissed his lips in a swift buss.

"Jacob, I love you too. It's different than with Liam."

That gave him pause. "How so?"

"More," she replied. "Stronger, better. There's a poem I'd like to quote."

"Go ahead."

"I love thee with the breath, smiles, tears of all my life," she said, and he recognized the poem by Elizabeth Barrett Browning.

"And, if God choose, I shall but love thee better after death."

A grin stretched his lips. "I've heard that, back in school."

It didn't seem the time to mention Sally Ann had been right fond of it too. Instead, he pulled her tight into the circle of his arms and kissed her. He'd kissed her a few times before, but not like this. His mouth claimed hers with possession, heady with the knowledge she would be his wife. Maggie gave back the kiss with the same urgent fervor, and he didn't hurry.

"Woman, you've made me a happy man, but I'm getting mighty hungry. How about we eat?"

Maggie nodded. "Let's."

Jacob intended to spread a quilt on the ground and sit there, but it remained soft and more than a little bit muddy, so they decided to eat in the wagon bed. It would keep her dress clean and be a bit warmer. Once the quilt was down, Maggie sat down and settled her skirts while he sat cross-legged. She brought the food out along with two plates. In addition to the fried chicken, which was still warm, there were corn dodgers, German-style potato salad, pickles, hard-boiled eggs, and dried peach pie. There was a paper twist with some salt, and she'd brought along some butter.

He began with chicken. It remained crisp and tasty. She'd coated it with both flour and cornmeal the way Jacob preferred, then seasoned it. The potato salad was unfamiliar to him, but he was game to try it and liked it, although he thought it was a touch vinegary. The pickles had a good crunch, and he ate two of the four eggs with a bit of salt. He polished off both drumsticks, one of the thighs, and a breast before he groaned.

"It's good, Maggie, but I gotta quit or I won't have room for peach pie, and I do love some pie."

"Don't forget Mattie's making rouladen for supper tonight," Maggie told him.

Jacob sighed. "I hope I'll be hungry by then."

After he'd eaten a slice of the peach pie with a flaky crust and sweet fruit, he lay back in the wagon bed as Maggie packed away the leftovers and dishes. "Think I'll take a little rest if you don't mind."

"It's fine with me," she said. "I do believe I'll join you."

His heartbeat increased when she stretched out beside him on the quilt. Jacob lay on his back, hands beneath his head, and breathed in unison with Maggie. With his stomach full, he drifted into a somnolent state, but he managed not to fall asleep. He ached to take Maggie into his arms, but he knew it would be easy to fall into temptation, so he kept his hands under his head.

"Look at the clouds," Maggie said. She sounded as drowsy as he felt. "Did you ever try to see shapes in them?"

"Yeah," he replied. As boys back in Kentucky, they spent a few happy hours gazing skyward, spotting animals and more in the cloud formations. "We used to do that right regular."

Maggie giggled and pointed. "That one looks like a bear. See the shape of the head and ears."

"It's a bear all right," he agreed. "Looks to be a grizzly. Now over to the west, that's a donut, right down to the hole in the middle."

They idled away the afternoon, seeing faces and shapes in the clouds. Jacob sat up after a short time so he wouldn't doze, and they sat together, with their backs against the front of the wagon. The wind turned chill, so they used the quilt to wrap around their shoulders, and he cuddled Maggie close. He kept one arm wrapped around her and indicated clouds with the other until the sun sank toward the western horizon.

"We'd best head back for supper," Jacob told her, reluctant to end the day. "Moses and your sister will be looking out for us."

"They will," Maggie replied. "It's been a wonderful day, though."

"Best day in ages and ages."

"And it's far from over."

Jacob figured it was. They would eat with his brother and his wife, then maybe they'd retire to the parlor, but he wouldn't have another chance to be alone with Maggie. He'd never told Ma he wouldn't be home to eat and realized he ought to have sent word. She might hold the meal, expecting he'd return after the picnic. Maybe Boone invited her and Garrett over, he thought and hoped so.

At the main ranch house, he helped Maggie down, then took the wagon and team to the barn. Jacob returned on foot in the twilight and wondered if he'd been born early or late. He would ask Ma, he thought, although it didn't matter. Since he wasn't company, he headed around to the kitchen door and walked inside.

Mattie almost dropped a tray of biscuits fresh out of the oven. "Ach, you frightened me," she said, pressing one hand to her heart. He noted the swell of her belly beneath her apron, not as large as Katie's. "I didn't think you'd come in the back way. Go back around and come in the front."

He started to protest, then shrugged and turned around. Jacob tramped around and knocked. His mother opened the door and smiled.

"What took you so terrible long?" she asked. "We all been here waiting."

"For me?" Jacob said, surprised.

"Yes, son."

He stepped inside and his gathered family, all of them, shouted "Happy birthday" so loud his ears rang.

Mattie served the beef rouladen along with so many other dishes that Jacob lost count. Over the meal, he and Maggie shared their news. No one protested but offered congratulations. He ate the hearty food and finished off with two slices of apple stack cake his mother had made in honor of his birthday.

By then, he'd eaten far too much, and his stomach grumbled.

"I gotta go home and sleep off all this food," he told them. He spread out his right hand across his belly and groaned. "It's been a fine birthday, one of the best."

Boone's family had already gone, taking his mother along.

Maggie walked Jacob to the door. "I love you," she told him. "I'm glad your birthday was a good one.

He kissed her. "I love you, dear heart. I'll likely see you tomorrow."

A bellyache kept him awake for a long time, but it would pass, he thought, but his love for Maggie would endure forever.

Joy outweighed the pain in his gut, and he drifted off to sleep at last with a smile.

CHAPTER NINETEEN

Although there were frigid days, by mid-February, the church had begun to take shape. The building site was within view of the main ranch house, situated between it, the bunkhouse, and their homes. Once finished, it would sit beneath a tall sugar hackberry tree. With Otis Webb, the cook that the hands called Spider, leading, it would get built. Most of the hands were more familiar with building since they'd finished Boone's house. The church would be more of a chapel since there would be no minister on a regular basis. Boone planned it to be small, to seat no more than fifty or sixty.

Since winter chores were lighter, both Jacob and Garrett spent a fair amount of time working on the church. Garrett proved to be far more skilled at carpentry than he was as a cowboy, although he had learned to rope and to cut an animal from the herd.

"You're a fair hand at that," Boone commented when he rode up to the church at the end of a long day.

Garrett nodded. "I was a better farmer, but there's no real use for that here."

"I've studied on that some and I think tobacco would grow here if we wanted to try," Boone said. "Down the road a piece, I reckon we might."

If nothing else, Jacob thought, it would keep them in baccy. It would also serve to give Garrett a role he could do well.

"I'd like to try it," Garrett said. "But this land's never been under a plow, except for a garden."

"That's where we'd start," Boone told him. "Maybe next fall, we could give it a try, plow some ground, then plant come spring. By then, you'll figure out if you're any good at being a hand or if you'd rather farm. Ranch might be in better shape then, too. Leastways if Jacob weds Maggie, we likely won't need to worry about the German folks trying to horn in on the Double Deuce."

"Do you reckon they still would?" Jacob asked. He had a major investment in both the ranch and Maggie.

"I surely hope not," Boone said, pausing to light a smoke. "But I wouldn't doubt they might. Germans seem to be all fired, stubborn, and hard to stop. Yanks had some German soldiers, and they'd fight till the last dog was hung."

The possibility Maggie's folks might still hold enough of a grudge to threaten the ranch tied a knot in Jacob's gut. "Seemed like they wrote her and Mattie both off," he commented. "I figured it was over."

Boone shook his head. "I wouldn't count on it, and I don't mean to make you fret. Once you're married, I doubt they'll try, but that part about Gesundheit being a widower now stuck in my craw. If Maggie had married him, her folks wouldn't have told her children she's dead. They'd have welcomed her back like the prodigal daughter. I don't trust that polecat, not at all."

"You're scarin' the fire out of me, Boone," Jacob said. "Should I be on the lookout for him?"

"Wouldn't hurt and I'd keep your pistol handy just in case," his brother replied. "Just got a feelin' he might turn up to be the hero and bring Maggie back to San Antone. He lost out on Mattie and didn't show up till she was married to Moses. You ain't married yet."

"Maggie wouldn't go with that rascal," Jacob stated.

"Not willing, naw, she wouldn't. He might try to carry her off, though, that's what worries me."

Garrett had listened without speaking until now. "Boone, I reckon we'd all stop him if he tried."

"I know that well," Boone said. "But it's a fact I'll rest easier once they're wed. I gotta head to the house. Rachel promised she'd make beef stew for our supper. I'm hollow as a gourd and need some vittles."

"Back bothering you too, ain't it?" Garrett asked.

"A mite," Boone said after a pause. "How'd you figure, though?"

"I could see the way you're favoring it. Ma didn't raise any dunces."

"No, she did not. Otis, when you reckon this church will be ready to use?"

The older man squinted at Boone in the fading light. "It'll be a spell yet. If the weather's good, maybe by middle March, maybe early April. I got the boys working fast as they can, but they ain't carpenters by trade."

"Will it be done before we trail cattle north?" Jacob asked. He would be married before he went on the drive, or he wouldn't go.

Spider shot him a look. "I'm shootin' for it to be, but time will tell."

If it wasn't, then Judge Masters could ride out to officiate, Jacob thought. Or the priest. Neither he nor Maggie was Catholic, but he wouldn't mind.

By the time he started for the cabin, it was full dark. Weary to the bone, Jacob knew he wouldn't make it over to visit Maggie. He'd had coffee with her early, though, and that would do for this day. Ma had the meal on the table when he and Garrett arrived. She'd made soup beans using pintos and seasoned them with ham. A pan of cornbread sat beside the pot. Once they'd said a blessing and sat down, they tucked into the food with gusto.

"You got a good scald on these beans, Ma," Jacob said as he finished a bowl. "They're right tasty. I'm fond of those frijoles Rachel makes but I cotton to these more."

Ma beamed. "I reckon I ain't lost my cookin' skills."

"No, ma'am, you have not," he told her. "This is fine eating, warms me up right good. It got cold workin' on Boone's church."

"I hope it won't snow again," she said.

"It ain't too likely. Don't snow here all that much, not like back home."

Garrett buttered another piece of cornbread. "When's the next time someone needs to head to town?"

Although he made his voice casual, Jacob knew his brother wanted more than a trip to Laredo. "I don't rightly know. We don't go all that much unless there's a need."

"Thought we might need to pick up more nails, maybe, or something for the church."

Jacob smothered a snicker. Garrett knew as well as he did that they were less than halfway down into a keg of nails. "I cain't think of anything much, but Boone might."

"Ezekiel and Moses won't want to go," Ma said. "They'll stay close to their wives till they have the babies. Moses has got right fussy about what he wants Mattie to do and not do. Zeke, he's even worse."

"I thought I might pick up something for the kid's birthday if we made it into the mercantile," Garrett said and fooled no one.

"Or you might see if that pretty little gal's still working for Mary," Jacob said. "Miss Caroline Calloway."

Garrett's gray eyes flashed fire like flint and steel. "I didn't say nothin' about her, though I might call to see how she fares next time I'm in town."

"I reckon that would be a fair thing to do," Jacob replied.

"It would," Ma said. "I've not met the young woman, but it sounds as if she might need a friend or two."

Jacob nodded. He did know of something Boone wanted from town. Boone had asked him a few days earlier about finding a small, gentle horse for Mima. She'd outgrown the pony, and her riding skills were Boone's pride. The girl had graduated from riding in circles around the corral. Her daddy wanted to surprise her with a horse of her own, but he needed a small saddle. Once Mima had one and the horse to match, she could ride the ranch with Boone's permission and family supervision.

He had his eye on a Morgan filly that would serve the little girl well. Jacob had named her Peach Blossom, and Mima knew the horse. Blossom was about two years old, sweet-natured and gentle.

"There might be one thing Boone wants enough to send someone to town to fetch," Jacob said.

Garrett's eyes brightened with interest. "What's that?"

"A saddle for his baby girl. She's outgrown the pony, and there's a sweet filly perfect for Mima."

"Why, he should have done that at Christmas time," Ma said.

"Too much happened for him to think it through then," Jacob said. "Liam died, you came from Kentucky, and that big snow. He dotes on Mima, and I doubt he'd want to wait till next year or even her birthday come September. I'll ask Boone first chance I get. He knows the saddler well enough – he and Rachel rented rooms above his shop when they were first wed."

Garrett beat him to the draw and asked Boone the next day.

"I hear you're in need of a saddle for Jemima Ann," he said. "I reckoned I could make the trip into Laredo to fetch one back."

Boone leaned against the corral fence, watching Jacob work with the horses. He straightened up, winced, then shook his head. "Word travels faster than a stampeding herd on this ranch. I had in mind to get a saddle, but first I gotta find the horse."

"Jacob has a filly in mind, he says," Garrett offered.

"Do tell," Boone said. Then he shouted, "Jacob, show me this filly I hear you picked out for my baby girl."

"I'll fetch her out directly," Jacob replied.

Before the end of the morning, Jacob brought out Peach Blossom, a liver chestnut filly, a Morgan with Boone's own Sprat as the sire and a Morgan mare from a nearby ranch as the dam.

"Likely lookin' Morgan filly," Boone said with a slight grin. "I'm fond of chestnut horses. What's she called?"

"Peach Blossom," Jacob said. "Mostly I call her Blossom."

"Why not Star?" Boone asked. "She's got one on her forehead and blaze on her face."

"And four white stockings on her feet," Jacob replied. "She's gentle-natured and Mima's already fond of her."

"Surely you ain't told her she's getting a horse?"

"Naw, that's yours to do, but she likes to visit the young horses. Blossom's not yet two, but she'll take a handful of hay from Mima's hand."

"Jemima Ann would like to have a horse, although I don't want her riding without one of us along. She's too young yet to let her go where she wants," Boone said after he'd inspected the horse. Blossom nuzzled him, and he rubbed her nose. "Likely we'll need to order a saddle to get one the right size unless Abernathy has one already made. She'll outgrow it soon enough, but then the boys can use it."

Most folks would teach a girl to ride side saddle, but Boone had insisted from the first time he put his daughter on a horse that she would ride astride or not at all. It wasn't uncommon among ranch folks.

"Rob's been riding Bluebell, and 'fore long it'll be Benjamin," Boone said. "Awright, I suppose you can head to Laredo Friday or Saturday to see about a saddle. If you can pry Zeke away from Katie, take him along. He knows Abernathy about as well as I do."

"I figured on going too," Jacob said.

"I reckoned you would. Go early and don't tarry. I got fence that needs mending in two or three places. Need to fix it while this stretch of weather holds. I want that church finished, too, and you got a stake in that, Jacob."

His lips shaped a grin. "I do, at that. Sooner it's built, sooner I can get hitched."

"Best figure out where you'll take up housekeeping when you do," Boone said.

Jacob hadn't even thought. If the small cabin were available, he'd take it in a heartbeat, but Deke and his bride called it home. The idea of bringing Maggie to live with him, Ma, and Garrett on one side of the dog trot cabin lacked appeal. The main ranch house had been Maggie's home before it had been Mattie and Moses. Maybe they could share for the time being.

"Maybe I can borrow Otis and a few hands to build somewhere close," he said. "I reckon we should share the house with Moses and his wife for a spell."

Boone laughed. "You might could."

At first light on Friday, Jacob, Ezekiel, and Garrett headed for Laredo. They didn't take a wagon this time, preferring to move faster on horseback. The saddle would be small enough to carry back, and the list of other items was short. Ezekiel had first demurred and said he couldn't leave Katie, but his wife insisted that he go. Ma asked if he would bring back some outing flannel so she could make diapers in advance for the new babies.

"Sure, and I'll be grand," Katie told him. "Ye mustn't fret, Ezekiel. The babe won't come until he's ready and 'tis not yet time."

Zeke put his arms around his wife. "I hope you're right, Katie, darlin'."

"Ye know I am."

Their first stop was at Abernathy's shop. Jacob worried they would have to order a child-size saddle, but the saddler had a perfect one.

"Family ordered it for their daughter," he said. "I made it, then they couldn't pay. The man's wife died of a fever, and he owed near everyone in town. It's a fine saddle, and it would be just right for a little gal. How old did you say she was?"

"Seven but tall for her age," Jacob told him. "We'll take it, but I'd like to pick it up before we leave town, so we don't have to tote it everywhere. I'll pay for it now, though."

With the saddle secured, their next stop was the mercantile, where they bought outing flannel as well as some linsey-woolsey, calico, muslin, chambray, and some dimity. Ma asked for all of it, along with needles, pins, and threads.

"I reckon she plans on doing a fair amount of sewing," Ezekiel said once their goods had been wrapped and bought.

"She's a dab hand at it," Jacob said. "And Lord knows we all could use a few new garments."

He'd purchased a few things for Maggie as well, hoping the others didn't notice and tease him. His favorite item was a silver wedding band, made by a local silversmith. Although a lot of women didn't wear wedding rings, he figured Maggie would like it when the time came to wear it.

"It's near noon," Garrett commented, squinting upward at the sun overhead. "I reckon we've the time to get some grub before we head back to the ranch."

Jacob maintained a sober expression, but he ached to grin. "There's a couple of little restaurants where we could go," he said, knowing Garrett angled to visit the Out of Luck so he could ogle Miss Calloway. "Or we might go by Clodagh's boarding house and see if we can get some tamales from Graciela."

"I was thinking we'd try that saloon," Garrett said, his face as bland as plain bread without butter.

Ezekiel and Jacob exchanged a glance. "We could," Zeke said. "Mary's always glad to see us, even if we don't partake in her gals or liquor."

"Then we'll go to the Out of Luck," Jacob said. "We'll pick up that saddle then, after that, we'll head home. I'd like to get home early if we can."

"I would too," Ezekiel said. "Katie vowed she'll be fine whilst I'm gone, but I'd rather be with her, the shape she's in and all."

They entered the saloon, and Mary waved to them from her table. Two men already sat there, and Jacob recognized one as Dr. Trelawny, the doctor Boone had dragged out to the ranch, thinking an amputation was in order for his damaged fingers. The other was a stranger, but since he wore a star pinned to his jacket, he figured him for the latest sheriff.

"Come join us," Mary cried. "There's plenty of room."

The three brothers sidled over and sat down. Garrett turned the chair around and sat backwards, an old habit.

"Dr. Trelawny, Sheriff Lancaster, these are three of the Wilson boys from the Double Deuce Ranch," Mary said. "Jacob, Ezekiel, and Garrett."

"We're acquainted," the doctor replied. "Glad to see your fingers have healed well."

Jacob flexed them and nodded. "They did. Sheriff, I don't reckon we've met."

The lawman extended his hand to shake. "I'm Yancy Lancaster, and I've been sheriff here a fortnight, I believe. The other sheriff up and died right after Christmas, I was told. I've not met you before, but I've heard of Boone Wilson."

"That's our oldest brother," Zeke said with pride. "He's the ranch boss now, but we all got a stake in it. What kind of eats you got today, Mary?"

The crusty old woman rolled her eyes. "Donuts," she told

him. "We got donuts, but we also have some fried ham with potatoes. Caroline can fry up some eggs to go along if you're interested. And beef stew. No tamales, and I know you're partial."

Ezekiel shrugged. "I'll take the stew if it's fresh."

"Made yesterday," Mary answered. "It'll be better the second day. What about the rest of you lot?"

They all ordered the stew, which came with sourdough biscuits. Caroline Calloway brought it to them on a tray and managed to serve them without any spills.

"Where's the coffee?" Mary asked with a bite in her voice. "These cowboys like their coffee since not a one of them drinks."

"I'll fetch it, Miss Mary," the young woman said.

Garrett came to his feet. "I'll lend a hand."

Mary's eyes widened, and Jacob stifled a laugh. "I reckon I will too," he said.

He wasn't going to miss this conversation, not for love or money.

In the kitchen, Garrett grabbed the coffee pot as Caroline picked up a stack of tin mugs.

"You don't belong here," Garrett said. "What brought you to this wild place?"

The dark-haired beauty paused. "I came as a picture bride, supposed to marry the sheriff, the one who died. Even if he hadn't, though, I wasn't going to wed him. He lied to me in his letters, said he was a young man, and he was near old enough to be my grandfather."

"What'd he die from?" Jacob asked, curious.

"He had an apoplexy," Caroline told them. "The very day that I arrived here on the stagecoach."

"That's ill luck," Garrett said. "Why didn't you turn around and go home?"

Her mouth turned down, and she blinked back a few tears. "There's no home back in Vicksburg where I could return," she told them. "And I have no means to travel. I couldn't have come here if Abner – that was the sheriff's name, Abner Thompson – hadn't sent me a train ticket to San Antonio and money for the stage to come here. He might have been a kindly man, but he was an old one. I wouldn't have come if I'd known, but then I couldn't have stayed in Mississippi either. I don't know where I'd be if I hadn't left."

Garrett stepped closer and used one finger to wipe away the stray tear that trickled down her cheek. "I've money enough to pay your way back if you wanted to go."

"I thank you for that," Caroline said. "But there's no one in Vicksburg and no home. If it weren't for Mary, I'd be on the street or worse. I never dreamed I might end up working in a saloon of all places, but at least it's the kitchen and nothing more. We'd best get the coffee served or she'll be shouting at me."

On cue, Mary bellowed from the saloon. "Where's that coffee, Caroline?"

"I'm coming, Miss Mary," she called.

Garrett shifted the coffee pot from one hand to the other. "You're too fine for this place."

Caroline shrugged. "I've no other place to go or be. Mary's bark is worse than her bite. She has a good heart beneath all the bravado, I do believe. You're kind, Mr. Wilson."

"I'm Garrett," he told her. "There's five of us. You might as well know which name to call me."

"Thank you, Garrett Wilson."

She took the cups from Jacob and carried them to the table. Garrett followed with the coffee pot. By the time they sat down, the beef stew had gone cold, but they ate it anyway. Once they finished, after conversing with the other two men, they rose to leave, but Garrett lingered.

"If you have need of me, send for me to the Double Deuce," he told Caroline.

The woman offered him a faint smile. "I'll remember."

Once they had Mima's saddle, Jacob tied it behind him, and they rode home, saying little.

Jacob didn't talk much either, but his thoughts were full, and somehow he suspected Garrett's were as well.

CHAPTER TWENTY

If he lived to be an old man, which he hoped to do, Jacob would never forget the joy that lit Mima's face when she realized Blossom was now her horse. The little girl's eyes twinkled like the brightest stars in the night sky, and her lips spread wide in the biggest grin he'd ever seen on her face.

"Peach Blossom belongs to me?" she asked, turning back to face Boone and Jacob, where they stood.

"She does, baby girl," Boone replied. "Your uncles made a trip to town to fetch back a saddle just your size so you can ride her. You went and outgrew that pony."

"Rob can ride Buttercup if he wants."

Jacob laughed. "You know your brother does, Mima. I figured he'd be here today."

Boone spoke up. "He's got a snotnose, so we're keeping him home. He'll ride soon enough."

Boone tended to be overcautious with his children, but Jacob couldn't fault that. Ma had been the same, and save for the baby who died of diphtheria before Boone was born, she hadn't lost a child. Jacob nodded and said, "I bet he's chomping at the bit to get out of the house."

"He is, but I'd rather he stays home and be mad than get sick."

Mima stretched on tiptoe to rub the horse's nose. "Daddy, can I ride outside the corral?"

"I reckon you can, but only if I'm with you or one of the uncles is," Boone said. "You may be old enough for a horse, but you're nowhere near big enough to ride off alone. If I catch you riding without one of us, you'll get a whipping."

"I won't, Daddy," she promised. Then she abandoned the horse to run to Boone. She threw her arms around him in a tight hug. As tall as she was, Boone lifted her up and spun her in circles, laughing. "Can we go ride now, please?"

"We ain't goin' very far, but we'll ride for a bit," he told her. "Jacob, you want to ride too?"

"Might as well," he answered. "Where you thinkin' to go?"

"To the pond, maybe a little further. Let's get this baby girl in the saddle."

Once they were all mounted, they set out with the horses at a walk. Mima complained, and Boone, with a grin he tried to hide, answered, "Jemima Ann, we gonna walk before we trot or canter. You're good on a horse, I'll give you that, or you wouldn't be one now. But I'd rather not see you fly off and get yourself hurt. If your mama didn't strip my hide, your granny sure would, and I'd be plumb mad at myself."

"I won't," the stubborn child said.

"You cain't know that. Every one of us Wilson men's been thrown or hurt by horses, and you've seen it yourself, baby girl."

Mima stared down at the reins. Jacob watched and saw she knew when to quit.

"All right, Daddy," she said. "But 'fore long I'll be galloping. You just wait and see."

"I'll be right proud when you do," Boone told her.

They skirted the perimeter of the pond, which brought fond memories of the recent picnic with Maggie, then rode a little further. Then they headed back. Because Mima sat straight in the saddle and moved as if one with the horse, Boone allowed them to pick up the pace to a trot. Once back at the corral, he directed his daughter to take care of Blossom.

"This is your filly," Boone told her. "She's gonna be your horse for a long time. I've had Sprat since right after the war, rode him to Texas from Kentucky. He wadn't much older than Peach Blossom, and all these years later I'm still ridin' him."

"How long has it been?" Mima asked.

Boone paused to consider, then said. "Nearabout fourteen years, I reckon. And Sprat's still got plenty of years left. That's 'cause I take care of him and I expect you to do the same with your horse."

"What do I do?"

"First thing, you keep her to a walk the last little bit of the ride," he said. "That's to let her ease off after riding. Now, here in the corral or the barn, we're gonna undo the cinch. That's the strap that holds the saddle on her. See, it goes under her belly. I'll do it for now, but as soon as you get a mite bigger, it'll be your chore, not mine. Pay mind to how she acts – which you don't know what to look for yet, but I surely do, and you'll learn. See how she's blowing? That's to cool down and calm down. Next, we're gonna take off the saddle, bridle, and bit, then put them in the barn. You gotta tend to the saddle, too, keep the leather clean and use some oil so it don't dry out."

"I want to do it myself, Daddy."

Jacob laughed. "Your child's as stubborn as you, Boone."

Boone ignored the comment. "Make sure she can drink some water, not too dang much or she'll founder. After that, you gotta brush her down, see? You can do this, Mima, but you gotta take care. Last thing, you can comb out her mane and tail. You mind yourself around the tail. Don't spook her, or she might kick out to hurt you. She wouldn't be meaning to, but it can happen."

"Like that one time you got a black eye from Sprat kicking," she said.

Boone laughed. "Yeah, like that time. It can hurt you a whole lot more than that, though."

As the girl combed her horse, talking to her in a soft voice that the animal appeared to like, Boone checked the filly's legs and picked out the hooves. "In time, you can do all this yourself, but not just yet," he told her. "She looks fine, I don't see any trouble with her at all."

Last, he instructed her to give Peach Blossom some hay. "You can feed grain, too," he said. "Don't need to right now, though. Now if it wasn't going on to evening, I'd say leave her out in the corral, but since it is, we're gonna put her in her stall."

With all that done, Boone tended to Sprat. Jacob had already taken care of his mount.

"Now we head home to wash up and eat some supper," he said. "Jacob, I believe Ma and Garrett are joining us, so you might as well come too."

"I will, thanks."

It was a simple meal, leather britches beans seasoned with ham, cornbread, and fried potatoes, but it tasted fine. Mima was almost too excited to eat as she chattered about Peach Blossom and her ride. Rob sulked until Boone told him he would soon be riding Buttercup and that one day he'd get his own mount, too. That promise perked him up, and after the meal, Ma told stories. She shared some of the Jack tales, the adventures of a poor young man from the mountains who managed to survive and thrive with his wits.

"Well, there was the time that Jack's daddy bought him a new shotgun and he took it out the first time, brought home a passel of meat. I reckon you're wondering how he managed that – here's what happened."

Jemima described how Jack fired at a gray squirrel perched on a rock. "The shotgun killed that squirrel deader than dead, but it got two rabbits sitting nearby, too. The blast knocked Jack back into the creek, and when he came up out of the water, his pockets were filled with bass. A button flew off his shirt and hit a deer passing by with enough force that it killed it. A bit of antler from that buck flew through the air and hit a bull in a nearby field. It went down, and so Jack brought home a squirrel, two rabbits, a mess of fish, a deer, and a bull. His daddy was right proud," Ma concluded.

"Tell another one," Rob cried.

She told two more, Jack And The Bean Tree and Jack And The Northwest Wind. Although the children clamored for more, she shook her head. "It's likely past your bedtime," she told them. "I got more stories, but we'll save them for another time. I'm headin' home myself so come give Granny a kiss."

Garrett stood and offered to accompany his mother home. Jacob lit a smoke.

"I'll be right behind you," he said. "I won't be long."

As soon as Garrett and Ma were out of the door, Boone turned to Jacob. He drew deep on his own cigarette and said, "What's got into Garrett? I don't reckon he said more than three words all night long."

Jacob laughed. "He's been like that since we came back from Laredo. It's that gal, Caroline. I do believe he fancies her, Boone, but he's been a bachelor so long he ain't sure what to do about it."

Boone shook his head. "They say the quiet ones think the most, and that's Garrett. Did y'all find out any more about how she ended up in the Out of Luck?"

"A bit," Jacob replied. "She told us she came as a picture bride, was going to marry the old Sheriff, the last one who died. But he'd lied and said he was a young man when he wasn't. Besides, he died of apoplexy the very day she arrived. Miss Caroline says she's got no home to go back to, so she stayed. Mary gave her employment and kept her off the street, but that young lady, she ain't fit for saloon life even if she's just in the kitchen."

"I reckon not," Boone said. "She's got ladylike ways. I figure she was raised in one of the fine old houses in Vicksburg, but her folks must have fell on hard times after the war. Does

Garrett want to court her?"

Jacob shrugged. "I've no notion, but I think it's likely. Knowing Garrett, though, it's liable to take some time."

Boone crushed out his smoke and sighed. "Maybe we'd best build two cabins or another dog trot cabin just in case. Sooner or later, someone would live in it. Never dreamed when I first come here we'd all be here or in need of homes. I might have started building sooner if I had."

"It'll work out, one way or another," Jacob said, glad his brother hadn't forgotten about his need for a home.

"It surely will. That little gal of mine, she can ride, can't she?"

Jacob grinned. "Yeah, she can, Boone. She sits horse as well as any of us did at her age."

"Better," Boone said. "I'm fixin' to turn in myself, but I'll see you in the morning. There's plenty of work to get done, besides, Mima probably will want to ride that horse."

Every day, one or the other of them rode with Mima. The first chance she could break away from home, she headed for the corral. Rob, who got over his cold with no complications, often came begging to ride Buttercup. If Jacob was working with the horses, the pony ride was simple, but it took more effort to break free to accompany Mima. After the first two weeks, she often rode with them to whatever place they had work to do. With grudging admiration and more than a little concern, Boone allowed her to sometimes pick up the pace to a trot.

March came in like a lamb, so Jacob expected it would go out like a lion. The old folk weather lore had proven right more than once. He just wondered if it would be rain, thunderstorms, or snow to end the month. Two days before Ezekiel's 23rd birthday, the kid woke them up early, pounding on the door.

"Katie's in a bad way," he hollered as Ma let him inside. "She's either got the worst belly pains ever or she's going to have the baby."

Jacob trailed his mother across the dog trot to find Katie in bed, clutching her huge abdomen, her features taut with pain. She made no sound, but it was obvious she hurt.

"It's time, isn't it?" Ma asked, her voice smooth. She put her hands on Katie's belly.

"Aye, 'tis," Katie gasped. "I tried to tell this *amadon* so, but no, he thinks 'tis something I ate or that I'm ill. His son is coming."

Ezekiel stood by the bedside, frowning. "Isn't it too soon?"

Both his mother and wife shook their heads. "It's not," Ma told him. "Babies come when they're ready, and I figured she'd have the child sooner than you thought."

"Should I go fetch Mattie?" he asked.

"No, don't bother her," Ma replied. "She's in the family way herself and doesn't need to be here. I'll bring the baby."

A worry line furrowed Zeke's forehead. "Do you know how?"

Ma laughed. "You don't remember how many babies I brought into this world back home? Or that delivered six of my own?"

"Yeah."

"Then I know what to do. I hear in a pinch, so do Boone and Moses. Son, you might as well go and work. You won't help being here."

"I'd rather stay."

Katie grimaced, and a low moan slipped through her lips. "No, ye must go," she gasped.

"When will the baby get born?" Ezekiel asked, his eyes on his mother.

"It could be here by dinner time or supper time or tonight," Ma said. "First ones sometimes take their own time about arriving. Go, and I'll send someone to fetch you when it's here."

"I'll go if I bring Rachel over first," Zeke said.

"I can fetch Rachel," Jacob told him.

Ezekiel pressed his lips together tight, then leaned down to kiss his wife. She grasped his hand tight for a few moments. "Don't ye fret," Katie told him. "I'll be here when you return with your son in me arms. I'd know if I wouldn't be so, I'm telling you true."

"I love you, woman," Zeke told her.

"And don't I love ye more than anything?" Katie returned. "Now, go."

Ezekiel went. Jacob lingered for a moment until Ma said, "If you're bringing Rachel, go fetch her. You'd best let Boone know, too. It's early yet, so he's likely still home."

Jacob, without the benefit of breakfast, set out for Boone's place. He found Rachel serving johnny cakes with bacon. Boone glanced up from his plate with a wary look.

"If you're here this early, something's happened," his brother said. "What?"

"Katie's having her baby," Jacob said. "Might I beg a cup of coffee? Ma is with her and I ain't had breakfast, not even coffee."

"You don't have to ask," Boone said. "You can eat, too, there's plenty."

"Ezekiel would like Rachel to come help Ma in a bit."

Rachel wiped her hands on her apron and nodded. "I can, Jacob, but I'll have to bring the children with me."

"Maggie could tend them," he said. He didn't have to ask – he knew she would. It also would give him a chance to deliver them to her care, so he'd see his sweetheart.

"I could go help," Mima said. "Or if I wasn't needed, I could go ride."

"Jemima Ann," Boone said. "It might not be the day for it."

Disappointment shifted her face to a frown.

"I'll take her riding, if she wants," Jacob said. "Once everyone else is squared away. Zeke's gone to work. Ma and Katie insisted."

"It's for the best," Boone said. "He'd rather that than catch the baby. That's awful hard on a man's nerves."

Rachel laughed. "You did it, Boone."

As she stood beside his chair, Boone circled her waist with one arm. "That's how I know, honey."

"Quit spooning and get those children ready," Jacob said with a twinkle in his eyes. He anticipated the day when he could be affectionate with Maggie.

Maggie met him at the kitchen door and took Sarah from his arms.

"Ezekiel came by," she told him. "He wanted us to know Katie's in childbirth. I figured you might bring these little ones to me so I'm ready."

"Rachel said to tell you Sarah can drink from a cup now and eat a bit," Jacob told her. "Mima's going with me to ride for a spell, then I'll bring her back if you don't mind."

Her smile radiated love. "Of course not. Have you eaten? I can make you breakfast."

"They fed me at Boone's," he told her. He wanted to give her a kiss, but he couldn't, not with the children clustered around her. "I'll be back for them after the babe's born."

Moses strolled in, his galluses undone. "I hear we'll be uncles again 'fore the day is out," he told Jacob.

"We will," Jacob said. "I'm riding out to check on a couple places of the barb wire. This little miss is gonna ride with me."

"I figured that as soon as I saw her britches," Moses replied. "Rob, if I get time, I'll let you take a few turns on the pony today."

"Thank you, Mo Mo," the little boy cried. "I'd surely like it."

"Then we'll do it, little cowboy."

By mid-morning, he and Mima had ridden out to the boundary fence on the north side of the ranch. Jacob had tightened some wire, which he'd noticed tended to go slack and require maintenance. Mima dismounted while he worked. Her eyes, as gray as his mother's and Boone's, took in everything. He doubted she'd ever been this far from the main ranch, so the scrub, the flat country, and the native vegetation must be new and exotic in her eyes. The girl marveled over the prickly pear cactuses she saw and asked about the soap bushes. Jacob answered when she had a question and listened to her chatter, his mind on his work.

It was almost noon when he heard the rapid hoofbeats striking the ground. The sound came from the north, away from the ranch. Jacob stood up and stiffened, wary. "Mima, why don't you mount your horse?"

She glanced at him, puzzled. "I can, but why?"

"Someone's comin' this way fast, and I don't know whether or not they're a friend. I want you out of the way and ready to ride if I say so."

Mima obeyed. By the time the lone rider came into view, she was astride Blossom with the reins in her hands. Jacob cupped his right hand above his eyes to get a better gander. Judging from the way the rider sat the horse, it wasn't any of his brothers or any ranch hand. Jacob noted the blonde hair beneath the bowler hat the man wore. No cowboy or capable rider would wear such fancy headgear riding out on the range. He narrowed his eyes and peered hard, then came as close to swearing as he ever did.

"Thunderation!" he cried. Gunther Hammerschmidt approached on a speckled Appaloosa, his expression sour as spoiled milk. Whatever his motive, it wouldn't be a good one. *Boone was right,* he thought. Last – and the only – time he'd ever seen this character before had been when he and his henchmen jumped him in San Antonio. They'd mistaken him for Moses, which amused Jacob, for he and Ezekiel had more of a resemblance. Moses looked like Boone. "Jemima Ann, when I say the word, you ride for your daddy fast as you can."

Despite the traces of fear reflected in her eyes, an unholy joy lit her face. "Alone?"

"Yeah, baby girl. I know you can do it, but wait till I say go."

As he watched, the man halted his horse short of the fence line and dismounted. He stood about 100 feet away.

"Guttersnipe Hammerschmidt, you'd best stop right there and come any further," Jacob said. "You're not welcome on this ranch, and you'll be escorted off the property. You have no business here, so I reckon you'd better go."

The red-faced German glowered as his anger hung heavy in the air between them. "I've come for Magdalena. Since Mattie spurned me and my wife, who was a sorry sort at best, died, I'll take her as my second wife. Little difference between the two women or any woman, but she's fair and will do."

"Maggie and I are promised," Jacob told him. "We'll be wed soon. She wants no part of you nor anything to do with San Antonio."

Hammerschmidt laughed, but it wasn't pleasant. "She'll change her mind once she's back in a house with servants, with food served three times a day, pretty clothing to wear, and parties to attend. I'll tell her children she's not dead, that it was a mistake. She'll be happy enough."

"She won't." Jacob spit out the words like bullets firing from a weapon. "She's marrying me and no other."

Gesundheit - Jacob had taken up Boone's insulting way of never saying the man's given name correctly - stared at him, then cackled. He realized the man was insane, and wariness coiled deep in his gut like a rattlesnake about to strike.

"If I can't have her, no one can," Hammerschmidt cried. He lifted a short Winchester .22 rifle and pointed it at Jacob. "Not you, not me."

Jacob shouted. "Jemima Ann, go now! Fetch Boone."

The German fired, and if Jacob hadn't sidestepped his horse, the bullet would have hit him square in the chest in a killing shot. Because he moved, it tore through his upper left arm, just below the shoulder. Hot pain seared his flesh as if he'd been branded. Behind him, Mima screamed.

"Jay!" she cried, and he heard her sobbing.

"Go," he hollered. Jacob feared the crazy man might shoot Mima next. "Go now."

This time, the girl obeyed. Blossom galloped away with a rapid gait, the sound of her hooves and Mima's crying diminishing as she moved away. Jacob prayed she'd reach Boone with speed, and his brother would find him before he bled out.

Warm blood flowed down his arm, wet as it soaked his clothing and stained the saddle. The intense pain from the corner of one eye, Jacob saw Hammerschmidt raise the gun again, and he tried to move. If the German fired again, he might well hit him in the chest or head.

Instead, the German turned the rifle around and placed it beneath his chin, then pulled the trigger. The front of his face vanished into red gore, and bone fragments flew. The report from the shot echoed in the air. Intense pain centered in his upper arm and radiated to his shoulder. Jacob trembled as he tried to nudge his horse forward, hoping he could ride back home under his own power. Instead, as his head spun, he lost his balance, toppled from the saddle, and struck the ground hard.

His last conscious thoughts before he slipped into darkness were a fervent hope his brother would find him in time and a prayer that Mima made it home.

CHAPTER TWENTY-ONE

Boone rode with Diego and Matias as they drove part of the herd from one pasture to another. The hungry stock had munched most of what they could find, so it was time to move them elsewhere. It was a routine task, and the new hands had proven their skill long since. He thought he heard a distant gunshot, then another, but dismissed it. On this sunny March morning, he didn't figure much could go wrong. He'd sent Ezekiel on ahead to make sure the wire was holding up before they left the cattle in the field, aware that the kid was preoccupied about the birth of his first child. Moses was with him, for moral support, while Garrett was shoeing a horse who'd thrown a shoe.

He'd almost forgotten about the shots when he heard galloping hoofbeats headed his direction, then his daughter's voice. Boone caught sight of her, riding hard and fast alone, and anger boiled within. He'd told her not to ride alone, and since she'd broken her promise, he'd have to give her a whipping. That was something he hated to do and hadn't done more than twice in her life.

"Whoa, Jemima Ann!" He shouted as she approached. "What do you think you're doin'? You've winded that young horse, and it's pure luck she ain't thrown you. Where's Jacob?"

"Daddy," she gasped as she wheeled the horse to a stop. "Daddy, he's shot. He sent me to fetch you, but he's hurt."

His chest clenched tight as he reached over and grabbed her reins. "What do you mean, he's shot? How'd that happen?"

"That man," she wheezed. "That German, that Gutter... Gutter...Gutter snipe."

He'd never known her to stutter, but she did now.

"Hammerschmidt?" he asked, frantic. "He's on the ranch?"

Mima nodded and began to cry. Boone pulled her from her filly to his saddle, then he held her close. "Hush, baby girl. You done good, riding back to get me. Let's go find Jacob."

She sobbed against his chest as he barked orders. "Diego, take her horse back to the corral and find Garrett. Tell him to meet me at the dog trot cabin. Matias, ride with me."

"*Si*, Mister Boone," the hand said and crossed himself.

Boone fired his pistol three times in the air, hoping it would alert Zeke and Moses.

"Mima, you gotta tell me where you were at when Jacob was shot, so quit cryin'. We gotta go help him."

Although she wasn't that familiar with the ranch, his daughter directed him back to where they'd been when Hammerschmidt arrived. Boone saw the blood puddling beneath Jacob, and fear clutched him hard. He handed Mima to Matias and dismounted, kneeling beside his brother.

Jacob lay face down in a pool of blood, but when Boone turned him over with gentle hands, he saw the bullet wound in Jacob's arm. Boone pulled off his neckerchief and tied it tight above the gaping hole where the bullet had entered. "Jacob," he cried. "Jacob Wade Wilson."

Jacob's breathing was shallow, but his eyelids flickered when he spoke his name, although he didn't open them. "He's alive," Boone said. "We gotta get him back."

Jemima screeched. He turned to see her pointing across the fence. "He's dead."

"Naw, honey, Jacob ain't dead," he said. Boone didn't mention that he was close enough to swap howdys with Death or that he wasn't certain he would survive. His brother had lost a lot of blood. "We just need to get him home…"

"Daddy, look!"

He turned his head and gasped. On the other side of the

barbed wire, Hammerschmidt, his head destroyed, lay near the fence. His horse cropped at the grass a few feet away. He still held the rifle clutched in one lifeless hand.

"Good Lord," Boone said and removed his hat. After a pause, Matias did the same. Boone loathed the man and wasn't sorry to be shed of him, but he still had proper respect for death. Besides, there would be a reckoning. They couldn't just leave him lay there as buzzard bait, tempting as it might be. They'd have to get a lawman. For now, though, Jacob was the priority, and Guttersnipe could lie in the dirt.

Ezekiel and Moses rode up at a canter, then stopped when they saw the scene.

"What in the name of God Almighty happened?" Moses asked.

"From what Mima said, Gunther came to the ranch, wanting Maggie," Boone said. "Then he shot Jacob. She rode back and got me, like Jacob told her.. It appears that Hammerschmidt took his life, but I don't know. Right now, we gotta get Jacob home. He's shot through the arm, and he's bleeding worse than a pig on hog killing day."

"He's alive?" Ezekiel asked in a hoarse whisper.

Boone shot him a look, then glanced at Mima. "He is, for now. Let's get him home."

The little girl wore a frightened face. "Z, can I ride back with you?"

"Of course, you can, baby girl," he said. "C'mon, then."

"Once you see if your child's born, bring Maggie," Boone said. "He'll want her there when he wakes, and we'll need her. I know she was watching my children, but I'll do that if need be. Moses, let's figure out how to get him home 'fore he bleeds out."

He recalled a verse from the Book of Ezekiel used to stop blood and said it aloud, " And when I passed by thee, and saw thee polluted in thine own blood, I said unto thee when thou wast in thy blood, Live: yea I said unto thee when thou wast in thy blood, Live."

"Amen," Zeke said.

Taking him home by wagon would have been best, but Boone doubted they had time to wait for one. He decided he'd carry him the same way he had Zeke after he'd been beaten and stabbed, but when he suggested it, Moses spoke up.

"You'll wreck your back if you do, Boone," he said. "Won't do anyone any good, especially not Jacob. I'll take him."

Boone opened his mouth to argue, took another look at how pale Jacob was, and yielded.

"Alright, then. Let's get him back."

They rode as fast as they dared, arriving back at the dog trot cabins by mid-afternoon. Ezekiel had arrived first and sat on the step, smoking, but leapt to his feet when they rode up. He yelled, and Ma came outside. Although her face was calm, Boone noticed the way she wrung her hands with nervous agitation.

"Come help with him," Boone called as he dismounted. "Is your kid here yet?"

Despite the circumstances, Ezekiel smiled. "He is, and he's a fine, big boy. Rachel reckoned near ten pounds."

"Congratulations," Boone said and meant it. At least one joyful thing had come out of this day. "Let's get him inside."

Garrett came down the steps and joined them. Three of them managed to lift Jacob's limp body from Moses' horse and carry him into the cabin.

"Put him on the table first," Ma told them. She had it cleared, with warm water and clean rags ready. "I'd best get him cleaned up and see what damage was done. Has he roused?"

"Naw," Boone said. "He's lost a fair amount of blood."

Mima burst into the cabin. "Where's Jay? I want to see him."

Rachel followed. "You need to wait, Jemima Ann."

She stopped and put her hand to her mouth as her eyes roved over Boone and his brothers. At the sight of his blood-drenched garments, she gasped. Her face lost all color, and she swayed. Boone, once he'd laid Jacob where Ma directed, rushed to her. He feared she might swoon.

"It ain't my blood, honey, none of it. I'm fine."

"Boone," she said. "Oh, Boone, I thought it was."

He steadied her by putting his arms around her. "It ain't. It's all Jacob's. How's Katie and the baby?"

"They're good," she said, her voice quavering. "I'd best take Mima and get the other children so Maggie can come. Jacob will want her, I'm sure."

"I'm staying," Mima declared. "I can help."

Rachel glared at her daughter. "You need to come home. Boone, tell her."

Boone met his daughter's eyes. "Let her stay, Rachel. She saw him get shot, and she's a fair hand at tending sick folks. If you want, I'll go fetch the children and bring Maggie."

She touched his blood-soaked shirt. "You'd best change first or you'll scare the dickens out of them."

"I'll go with you, Boone," Moses said. "I'd like to see my Mattie, and besides, I reckon we gotta tell them what happened with Hammerschmidt."

Boone exhaled a long breath. "Yeah, we do. And somebody's gotta fetch the sheriff from Laredo."

"I can go," Garrett said. "We met him last time we went to town. Want me to bring him back?"

"I reckon that'd be best," Boone said. "Matias, go find Mac or Deke, then see if they can help bring Hammerschmidt's body back. We cain't leave it out there."

Ma glanced up from tending Jacob. "Whoever's not going anywhere, come give me a hand. I'm gonna have to cut this shirt off, it's stuck to him with all the blood, then I need to wash this wound, see how bad it is."

"I'm still here," Garrett said. "And Boone's girl can lend a hand."

Boone and Moses changed clothes, leaving the blood-stained garments in the bucket Ma indicated. They might be ruined, but she said she'd give washing them a try. Rachel sat down hard and then asked, "What did happen with Hammerschmidt? Should I worry he's coming after the rest of us?"

"He's dead," Moses said. "He won't trouble anyone."

Rachel's eyes widened. "Boone, I hope you didn't kill him."

He knew she remembered those dark days when he'd been accused of a murder he didn't commit and locked in jail waiting to be hanged. "Naw," he said. "He took care of that himself."

"He died by his own hand?" Rachel's voice shrilled.

"After he shot Jacob, yeah," Boone said. "That's why we need the sheriff."

"What will you do with Gunther's body?" Rachel asked.

Boone shrugged. "I don't rightly know yet. Bury him if need be."

Efficient and capable, Ma had Jacob stripped down to nothing but his long underwear bottoms. She'd washed the blood away from the wound, which still seeped a little blood, then cleaned it. She bandaged it with some of the flannel she'd meant to use for diapers, torn into strips after smearing it with comfrey paste and more.

"Let's get him in bed," she said. "Then you two can take off, and I'll get him settled."

His brothers moved him the short distance to the bed.

"He's cold," Moses said.

"He's in shock. I saw it plenty in the war," Boone said. "Wish he'd rouse a bit."

"He will," Ma said with certainty in her voice. Boone

wasn't sure if it was genuine or hopeful. "Go on, do what you must. Garrett, go fetch the law. Little Mima and I will take care of Jacob."

Boone knew she would, so he nodded. He and Moses stabled their horses, then went to the main ranch house. Garrett saddled up one of the best horses on the ranch and headed toward Laredo with haste.

"You're early," Mattie cried. She had two-year-old Ellie on one hip. "Why, supper's nowhere near finished..."

Her voice faded as she saw their grim faces, but it was Maggie who asked, "What's wrong?"

"Jacob's hurt," Boone said, trying to soften the news. "We brought him to Ma, but he'll want you. I told Rachel I'd bring the children back. Zeke and Katie's baby came into the world, too."

Maggie asked, "How is he hurt?"

Boone couldn't stop a huge sigh. "Hammerschmidt shot him, Maggie. I don't know all the details, but my Mima was there and saw. She wasn't there for what happened next, which is a blessing."

"What was that?" Mattie asked.

"The German shot himself," Boone said. There was no way to sugarcoat it. "He's dead. I got to deal with that after I see how Jacob's doing."

The sisters exchanged shocked glances. "*Ach du lieber Gott,*" Mattie said. "You can leave your little ones here, Boone. I'll mind them till Rachel comes."

"Sweetheart, I'll stay to help," Moses said. He took Ellie from his wife and hugged her. She prattled to him, nonsense words. "Where's the boys and Sarah?"

"She's asleep and the boys are playing in the parlor," Mattie said. "I can mind the children. You'll want to see how Jacob fares, too. I'd go if I wasn't in the shape I'm in. Did Katie have the boy she was looking out for?"

Boone smiled a little. "She did. I have no notion what they're calling him, and I ain't yet seen him. I'm going to get some of the hands to go bring Hammerschmidt's body in before some varmint gets at him, then figure out the rest. I appreciate it, Mattie. Maggie, I'll walk with you to the cabin if you want."

"Thank you, Boone," she said. She gathered some things in a basket, then they set forth. He thought she would ask more questions on the way, but Maggie didn't; she just marched onward with purpose. Moses took the basket from her without asking.

When they reached the cabins, Boone took Maggie aside.

"Why don't you go admire Katie's new baby?" he said, wanting a few moments to judge how Jacob fared before Maggie saw him. She gulped, then nodded.

"I will, then," she said. "Tell Jacob I'll be there directly."

Boone entered the cabin. His daughter sat at Jacob's bedside.

"How's he doin'?" Boone asked, his voice ragged. He had to know before Maggie came.

"He's awake, Daddy," Mima said. "He drank a little bit of Auntie Katie's Irish tea."

Ma stepped to Boone's side and put one hand on his arm.

"He's weak," she said. Her worried eyes met his. "Cain't lift his head or talk loud enough to hear. He's cold, but he's sweating, and his heart's beatin' too fast. We got a few sips of tea with plenty of sugar down him. It seems the bullet went through, so that's a blessing. He needs to lie still, and we need to get something in him to replace the blood he's lost. I'm making beef tea, but it won't be ready for a good while yet."

Boone peered down at his brother. Jacob didn't turn his head, but he moved his eyes, searching until he located his brother.

"Boone," he mouthed, his voice too low to be audible.

"I'm here," Boone replied. "You need to save your strength right now. You come near to bleeding out before I got you home."

Jacob moved his lips, and Boone thought he was trying to say, "I figured."

Maggie entered, smiling, but her happy expression wilted when she saw Jacob. She caught her breath with an audible gasp. "*Liebling,*" she cried. "Oh, Jacob."

At the sound of her voice, Jacob opened his eyes wide.

"Let Maggie sit there, Jemima Ann," Boone told his daughter.

The child stood and offered the chair. Maggie sank into it and reached for Jacob's hand. He was tucked beneath the covers, but his right hand was free because Mima had been holding it. When Maggie wrapped her fingers around Jacob's, he made a small sound, and she kissed his hand.

"Maggie," he said, but it was no more than a breath. "Maggie."

"Sh," she told him and put two fingers across his lips. "Rest, my love."

"Hurts," he whispered.

"I know, Jacob," she told him. She glanced up at Ma and Boone. "Is there any laudanum?"

"There's a bit," Ma replied. "But he needs to get something in him before we give him any. I've beef tea seeping. As weak as he is right now, with laudanum, he might not wake up again. I do have some willow bark tea steeped."

"Give him some," Boone suggested. He could see the harsh lines of pain etched on his brother's face. He'd been shot, more than once, and he'd seen men suffer gunshot wounds. "He needs it."

"You'll have to help me lift up his head or prop him higher," Ma said. "He'll choke if we don't."

Boone agreed but added, "Best if you get a spoon. He's

likely too weak to drink, but he can take it from a spoon."

If Jacob couldn't, he would likely die, and Boone knew that very well.

With Ma on one side and Boone on the other, they managed to raise Jacob's head with gentle hands and great effort. Maggie dipped a spoon into the cooled willow bark tea and put it to Jacob's lips. He managed to get some down, one scant spoon at a time. She coaxed him to swallow each sip until he'd taken enough to make a difference. The effort taxed him, and once he'd finished, he closed his eyes.

"Is he asleep?" Maggie asked.

"I surely hope so," Boone said. Either Jacob slept or he'd lost consciousness. His body needed the rest either way.

Boone took his daughter to see Ezekiel's baby. Rachel let them in with a smile.

"He's a fine boy," she told him after a swift kiss. "Come see. Ezekiel's with Katie."

His brother sat on the side of the bed facing his wife. Katie had the baby in her arms, smiling down at him with the face of a Madonna.

"I thought I'd get a look at my new nephew," Boone said. "Mima wanted to see the baby, too."

Zeke stood and faced them. "How's Jacob?"

"Alive," Boone told him. "Terrible weak."

Ezekiel frowned. "Is he gonna make it?"

"I reckon so," he replied. "He's got to rest and get his strength back. Long as the wound don't get infected, he's got a good shot at it. What's this boy's name?"

"'Tis Sean Seamus Connor Wilson," Katie told him.

"That's a big name for such a little feller," Boone replied with a grin.

"We'll call him Johnny," Ezekiel said. "Or I will, leastways."

"Hello, Johnny Wilson," Mima cried.

They all laughed. Rachel linked her arm with her husband.

"Let's go get the other children and go home," she said. "You look worn to a fare thee well. I'll make something to eat, and you can get some sleep."

Boone felt pulled in two directions. He ought to stay and help with Jacob, but fatigue dogged him. "All right, honey," he said. "We'll go get Rob, Benjamin, and Sarah. Then I gotta check to see if the hands brought the German back here. After that, I'll eat a bite and rest a spell. Sooner or later, though, I'll be back over there to help Ma."

"Maggie's capable," Rachel said. "Jacob'll need you more tomorrow than today."

"I'll have to talk to the sheriff tomorrow," Boone said with a sigh.

"Yancey Lancaster?" Ezekiel asked. "The new one?"

He nodded. "I sent Garrett to fetch him. It's best so there's no confusion over what happened to Hammerschmidt. Did he seem like a fair man?"

"Far as I could tell."

Boone gave a nod. "You got a fine son, Ezekiel. I'm headin' home for a bit. If anyone needs me, come fetch me."

Then, with his wife and daughter, Boone went to gather the rest of his family.

He could use a hot meal and more than that, a sound sleep.

CHAPTER TWENTY-TWO

Jacob couldn't think straight, no matter how hard he tried. From shoulder to fingertips, his left arm hurt with such intense pain that he thought he might die of it. Opening his eyes had been a challenge. Moving his head or anything else was impossible. He had no strength left to summon and felt as feeble as an old man. His mouth ached from being dry, and he had no volume when he tried to speak. When he first roused, he couldn't remember what had happened to put him in bed, if he'd been sick or hurt. His mind couldn't stay focused, and his thoughts flew like birds before an approaching storm. The first thing he realized was that his niece sat beside him, her hand holding his.

She'd been there, he recalled, when whatever happened did. A vague image of her galloping away on Peach Blossom surfaced, then bits and pieces floated through his head. He'd been fixing the fence, and that man, the German, the one Boone called Guttersnipe or Good For Nothing or Griping Guts, rode up. He'd intended to make trouble, wanted to take Maggie, and they argued.

He shot me, Jacob thought. There had been two shots, though, and someone else got hit. He couldn't recall. It wasn't Mima because she sat beside him with a worried look in her gray eyes. With effort, he sipped what he thought would be coffee but turned out to be tea, the kind Ezekiel's wife liked, laced with so much sugar he near spit it out. He worried, then, that it might have been Boone who took the second bullet and was hurt, but when he tried to say his brother's name, Boone was there.

So was his ma and his other brothers. Their voices weaved in and out of his consciousness, but they all sounded worried. It dawned on Jacob that he was the reason for their concern, and he wanted to speak up to reassure them, but he couldn't. He tried to cut his eyes around the room, but his range was limited. He didn't see Maggie, so he got anxious. If the German had taken her against her will, he would track him down and get her back. Or he would as soon as he had the strength to get out of bed.

It seemed like a very long time, but he couldn't keep track of time in his current state, but then she was there. Her voice flowed into his ears as sweet as water in a drought, and he tried to talk to her. She forced some bitter willow bark down him. He recognized the taste and didn't want it, but he knew it would ease some of his hurts, so he took it from a spoon.

The struggle wearied him, and once he'd finished, Jacob closed his eyes. Sleep came, and for a time, he drifted in a place without pain. He roused to the sound of Boone's voice and others, so he listened.

"I'll need to talk to the girl, Boone," an unfamiliar voice said. Jacob had no idea who it might be.

"She's just seven," his brother said. "You saw the man's body. Is there any doubt he died by his own hand?"

"There's not, but I'd like to hear what she has to say."

Jacob, even half awake, recognized the frustration in Boone's voice.

"I'll fetch her – she's just across with the new baby."

Baby? Katie must have delivered the child, Jacob thought. Ezekiel must be busting his buttons over it. Mima's young voice filtered into his consciousness.

"Jemima Ann," Boone said. "Sheriff Lancaster wants you to tell him what happened, out at the fence line."

"I will," she replied. "I want to see Jay first."

She approached the bed, and he forced his eyes open a little. The little girl leaned down and kissed his cheek. "I'll stay and tend you after the sheriff's done with me," she told him, and he tried to smile. Jacob wanted to hear her story, so he forced himself to focus.

"I went out ridin' with my uncle," Mima said. "That's him, Jacob, there in the bed. He had to fix fence, so he let me go so I could ride Peach Blossom. That's my filly. We'd been there a fair bit when we heard someone riding hard in our direction, so Jay told me to get on my horse. He said when he told me to ride to fetch my daddy, that's Boone Wilson. I did what he said, then the man came. He was that German, the one who caused trouble here before. He said he'd come to get Magdalena, that's Aunt Maggie, but Jay said he couldn't have her. The German man said he'd give her servants and fine dresses, but Jay told him to go, that he couldn't be on this ranch. He wasn't quite; he stayed on the other side of the fence."

Her words helped Jacob remember with more clarity.

"Then what happened?" the voice he now knew was the Sheriff, the one they'd met in Laredo, asked.

"That Hammerschmidt," she fumbled over the long, unfamiliar name, "he raised up his rifle and said if he couldn't have her, neither could Jay or anyone else. Jay's sweet on Maggie and they're gonna get married, I reckon. He shot Jay, and if he hadn't made his horse sidestep, it likely would have killed him. I was scared out of my wits, but when Jay hollered to ride, I did."

"After that, was there anything else?"

"I heard another rifle shot," Mima said. "I didn't dare look or go back. I knew Jay was hurt bad, for he was bleeding something awful. I did what he told me to and fetched my daddy. When we got back, Jay was lying in a puddle of blood, which worried me. And the other man, he was laying on the ground, rifle still in his hands, and he didn't have a face anymore."

"Surely that's enough," Boone said, his voice a deep growl. "She saw more than any young gal should."

"It'll do," Lancaster said. "I thank you, Miss Jemima. You

helped me figure it all out – Hammerschmidt shot your uncle, then himself, over a woman. Boone, there's no charges against anybody. I'll take the body if you don't mind and haul it to Laredo. If he's got folks that want him to bury, they can come fetch him. If not, we'll put him in the ground.

"I'd rather you do take him," Boone said. "Thank you for coming out to hear what happened."

"It's what I'm meant to do," Lancaster said. "It's my pleasure to meet you. I've heard a great deal about you, and I know Mary's fond. I hope that your brother fares well. If you have need of me for anything else, send for me."

"I will do, and I'm much obliged to you," Boone said. "I'll see you out."

Jacob's mind drifted as Mima wiped his face with a damp rag. He stirred when Boone returned and, with Garrett's help, raised him up until he was propped against a stack of pillows. The motion intensified his pain, and he moaned.

"Easy," Boone said. "Ma said your head had to be higher or you might choke. She wants to give you more beef tea."

"Boone." This time, he managed to speak his brother's name aloud, although it was barely a whisper.

"Hush," Boone said. "I'm here and I'll be close. You're gonna be all right, Jacob, but you near bled out. You cain't move around till you get some strength back. Long as that bullet hole don't get infected, you'll be fine."

Good to know, Jacob thought, but he had another question, the most important one.

"Where's Maggie?" Jacob could almost hear himself this time.

Boone grinned. "I figured you'd ask. She's asleep over at Ezekiel's, stayed up with you all the night. I don't reckon much of anything will keep her from coming back the moment she wakes."

Ma brought a cup of hot beef broth to the bed. "Do you want me to help you with this or little Mima?" she asked. "I suppose Boone could if you'd rather."

"I'll pour it down his throat," Boone said with a laugh. "You'd best do it, Ma, or let baby girl. She's capable."

"I'd say she is," Ma told them. "Any child who could ride back over half the ranch to fetch her daddy is resourceful. 'Course she is your daughter, Boone, so I'd expect no less."

"I can do it, Granny," Mima said.

"I'll lend a hand," Ma replied.

With his mother supporting his head and his niece holding the edge of the cup to his lips, Jacob managed the beef tea. That small task sapped his energy, and he lay back against the pillows spent. The warmth of the broth in his belly felt good, though, as he half-dozed, waiting for Maggie.

When she came, she didn't disappoint. She kissed him, her lips light against his, then sat beside him, across from Mima. Maggie seemed unable to keep from touching him. She combed his hair, caressed his cheek, and held his hand. She helped him drink more beef tea later in the day, and she remained constant at his side.

After three days, he could manage a whisper loud enough to be understood, although they all fussed and told him to be quiet. In a week, he could manage to eat more than broth or soup. After two weeks, he ate anything he wanted, but he hadn't yet been out of bed. By then, he was going more than a little crazy, so his brothers hauled in the wooden armchair and helped him sit.

That left him shaky, but Jacob was glad to be upright.

Ezekiel and Katie brought his newest nephew over, and he held the chubby baby boy.

"He's handsome," Jacob said. "He must take after me."

"Aw, now he's the very look of his da," Katie replied with a smile. Jacob and Zeke had a strong resemblance as it was. "He's a grand wane, our Sean Seamus."

"Johnny's a fine boy," Ezekiel said. "He came close to being born on my birthday."

"I missed your birthday," Jacob said. "Happy birthday, weeks late."

"Thank you. I'm just glad you didn't die on my birthday," Zeke said. "That would have been a sad thing. Are you gonna be fit for the trail?"

Jacob hadn't considered it. "I hope I am," he said, but he wasn't sure. "What day is it?"

"March 15," Ma said. "The Ides of March."

"You missed Rosey Posey's birthday, too, Jay," Mima said. "She's two now."

"That don't seem possible," Jacob answered, though he knew it was.

Six to eight weeks remained until they trailed cattle. He hoped to be on his feet before then, and he'd like to be married before he rode. He hadn't seen Maggie yet today and was curious why until she arrived.

"Mattie's in labor," she told them. "Garrett's gone to find Moses. I can't stay very long, Jacob."

"I'll manage," he told her.

"You're sitting in a chair," she cried. "Oh, it's good to see. How do you feel?"

"Puny," he admitted. "Better, though. I'll be glad once I'm up and able. Soon as I am, I want to marry you."

Maggie's smile brightened the cabin. "I'm willing. Boone's church should be done by then. I'll be back soon as I can, *liebling*."

Ma put a large pot of beans on the fire to cook, despite watching all the children in the family, young Johnny, Ellie, and Boone's children. Mima tended Ellie and her brothers while offering Jacob help.

"Is having all the young 'uns underfoot too much?" Ma

asked. "I can take them over to Katie's if it is to mind them. She's gone to be with Mattie, Rachel, too."

"Naw, I like it," Jacob said and meant it. The children were noisy, but they brought life, and he enjoyed it. He had been answering questions from the boy and promised Rob that as soon as he was able, he'd get him riding the old pony.

"I'll get you back on Bluebell," Jacob promised. "And as soon as you're old enough, I reckon your daddy will find you a horse too."

"I'm six now."

"You'll be seven in less than a year, then."

He'd have to mention this to Boone ahead of time so the boy wouldn't be disappointed.

Now that he had improved, his appetite had returned. "Ma, are those beans for dinner?"

"Supper," she replied. "I'll make biscuits and gravy for dinner. These children will eat biscuits, with or without gravy. I've got syrup too for those with a sweet tooth. I might have fried bacon, but I know you're a fool for sausage."

"I'm a mite old to spoil," Jacob said, but he liked it. Apparently, flirting with death encouraged folks to coddle him.

Ma paused and wiped her hands on her apron. "You're mine, Jacob Wade, so you won't ever be too old. Hold little Johnny whilst I start cooking. Just don't drop him."

She thrust the infant into his arms. He held the baby and marveled at how small he was. It had been a long time since he'd had his children with Sally Ann, all girls. He wouldn't mind another child or two with Maggie. He would welcome her children if they returned as well. She said little, but he knew she pined for them, but they had been told that she was dead.

Ma's biscuits were perfect, crisp on the tops, fluffy in the middle, and the gravy she made, with plenty of homemade sausage, was delicious. Jacob ate two portions, then wished he hadn't because he grew tired.

"Jay, do you want to lay back down?" Mima asked. "I reckon Granny and me together can get you to the bed."

Although he'd hoped to sit up till evening, Jacob knew he'd best rest. "I reckon so. I can wait for Boone or one of the others, though."

"They won't be back till supper time," Ma said. "Don't fret – we'll get you back to bed, son."

By the time they had him tucked back under the covers, pillows piled behind his head, drowsiness threatened to overtake Jacob. He slept despite the children's chatter and occasional crying. It had to be past dark when he woke. Ma had the lamps lit, casting shadows against the walls, and Boone sat at the table, smoking.

"'Bout time you roused," he said. "Feared you'd had a setback."

From his jolly tone, he hadn't thought anything of the kind.

"How late is it?"

"I don't rightly know," Boone replied. "Past supper time, anyway, but there's plenty left if you're hungry. The rest of them went to see Moses' new baby."

"Boy or girl?"

"Boy. They couldn't agree if they'll call him Matthew or Mathias, but I figure it will end up being 'Matt'."

A month after he'd been shot, Jacob was on his feet. His arm still pained him on occasion, but the wound had healed. Ma's vigilance kept it from getting infected. He tired quicker than normal, and he hadn't gained his full strength back, but he could sit a horse. Although he and Boone had been debating whether he was physically able to trail cattle, there was no doubt that he and Maggie would marry soon.

Spring had barely begun when he'd been hurt, but now,

when he ventured out first to the breezeway between the cabins, then out onto the ranch, Jacob found everything green. The hardwoods had leafed out, and wildflowers appeared. Although he wasn't good at naming them, he could recognize pink evening primroses, bluebells, blue-eyed grass, sunflowers, daisies, and butterfly weed. Their bright colors among the green vegetation were beautiful. He picked some for Maggie the first time he ventured away from the cabin.

Boone came by on Saturday night, smelling of horse, leather, sweat, and tobacco. Jacob had worked with the horses until noon, keeping short days until he had more stamina. He'd idled away most of the afternoon with Maggie, watching her tend her fledgling garden. Afterward, they sat on the porch sipping lemonade until he headed home.

"I got a piece of news you'll like," Boone told him. "The church is finished, windows and all. Thought we'd have an Easter service. If you'd like, there could be a wedding too."

Joy flamed like fire through Jacob's heart. "I would, very much, Boone, long as Maggie's willing. I'll ask her tomorrow."

Boone nodded. "I saw Ma was across the way with little Johnny. I believe Katie asked her to supper."

"Have you had supper? I ain't."

"Naw, but I believe Rachel left some cornbread and fried ham. There's enough for you if you want."

"Sounds mighty fine."

Once they'd eaten, they sat out on Boone's steps in the pleasant cool as dark fell and smoked.

"Jacob, how are you farin'?" Boone asked.

"Fair to middlin'," he replied. "Wound's nearabout healed. I still get tired too easy, but I'm good."

"Reckon you're able to trail cattle in a few weeks?"

"I aim to," Jacob said. "I'll hate to leave Maggie so soon after marrying her, but I don't see much else that can be done."

"I've been worried you're not yet strong enough," Boone told him, rolling a fresh smoke. "It can get rough on the trail, as you know. You've been there. I gotta find a few more hands 'cause a few need to stay here, and I reckon one of us ought to be here. If you think you'd best stay, I'll go. I ain't wanting to, and Rachel's not fond of the notion. But if this ranch is gonna prosper, I may have to do it."

Jacob imagined spending the rest of spring into summer with his Maggie and liked it. He envisioned quiet evenings and precious mornings. He couldn't wait to wake with her beside him, although they would share the ranch house with his brother Moses' family. Garrett would be on the trail, and afterward, he'd said he could abide in the bunkhouse for a time. If Jacob had those months, he could become strong again. He would turn brown working out in the sun. He would watch over his brother's families. Images of him working with Rob on the pony, riding with Mima once again, and bouncing the youngest ones on his knee filled him with a wonder and joy.

But if he stayed, Boone would have to go. "I'd like to stay, Boone, but I need to go. I cain't take you from your family. I'll be all right, and it'll be a sweet reunion with Maggie when we get back."

"Jacob…"

"Moses or Ezekiel got more reason to stay than I do," he continued. "They have young babies. Boone, I just wouldn't feel right."

Boone met his eyes and shook his head. "We'll study on it some more before we decide," he said. "It'll work out, whatever we do."

"Will you stand up with me when I get married?" Jacob asked.

"I'll be proud to," Boone said. "I'll see if we can get either a preacher, a priest, or Judge Masters out here to do the wedding."

"Thank you, brother," he replied. "Boone, you mean the world to me. Always did and still do."

"That goes back at you," Boone said. "I got the gray hairs creeping in to prove it."

He slung one arm across Jacob's shoulders in a rare show of affection, then they smoked one more cigarette before ending the evening in harmony.

Jacob lay awake longer than he intended, his mind full of the possibilities that lay just ahead and his heart brimming with love for Maggie as well as his family.

CHAPTER TWENTY-THREE

Easter morning dawned fair, the sky a soft blue highlighted with touches of gold and rose. Jacob awoke early on his wedding day, and the beautiful sky seemed like a blessing from above. He thought of the Scripture that read "for now we see through a glass, darkly" and thought this morning's radiant dawn must be a foretaste of heavenly glory. Last night, he had spent some time reflecting about the day he wed Sally Ann and their life together. He'd loved her without doubt, but she was gone, and he remained. Their daughters were growing up far away, and he'd come to Texas for a new beginning. He'd found that in Maggie.

Jacob wasn't one to compare one love to another, but he knew he loved Maggie with his whole heart. What began as admiration for a lovely woman had become friendship, then something more after she was widowed. He'd liked Liam and mourned him, but his death brought something he hadn't expected – the chance to fall in love.

Their love was far from conventional. Maggie had asked if he would wed her before her husband was in the ground, afraid her family would try to force her back to San Antonio. Jacob had already been smitten, but he'd never imagined the situation would change and that he could court Maggie. He had no idea until then that Maggie would ever offer anything more than friendship.

Today, he would marry her.

In a few weeks, he'd ride out trailing cattle to Kansas on the annual drive, but he'd be back within three months. Someday, maybe they would have enough hands that they could trail cattle and he could stay home, but until then, he'd do whatever it took to keep the ranch going.

Jacob took an early morning bath, then dressed in his best, which consisted of borrowed finery from Moses, including the suit he'd worn to court Mattie in town. As a family, they walked together to the new church. Judge Masters had arrived the day before and would officiate at the wedding. In the absence of a preacher, Jack McGee had offered to speak about Jesus and read from the Bible. Ma wore her best dress. It was one she'd carried all the way from Kentucky. Katie and Ezekiel were well-dressed, and their baby wore a new garment. Garrett wore his best clothing. When they met Boone's family, Boone had dressed in pin-striped trousers and a new shirt. His boys wore smaller versions of the same. Mima grinned from ear to ear, proud of her new calico dress. Rachel wore the gown she'd been married in almost eight years earlier.

The last to join them were Moses and Mattie, along with their two children. Some of the hands trailed behind, and the church was full. There were six pews on each side, and Jacob chose a seat at the back beside Judge Masters. Maggie, who had accompanied her sister's family, wore a navy dress with a white lace collar. Jacob thought it was one Mattie had worn, maybe as her wedding dress. Ike Masters confirmed it in a whisper.

After Boone led the small congregation in singing some hymns, including 'Christ The Lord Is Risen Today' with Mima beside him. Everyone present remained in place for the wedding. Jacob took his place at the front of the church, with Boone beside him. Maggie, with a bouquet of wildflowers clutched in both hands, made her way down the aisle to stand beside him.

The Judge read a passage from the Book of Ruth, one Maggie had chosen:

"And Ruth said, Entreat me not to leave thee, or to return from following after thee: for whither thou goest, I will go; and where thou lodgest, I will lodge: thy people shall be my people, and thy God my God."

"Our bride chose that for this day," Masters intoned in the somber voice usually reserved for court. "And her groom picked this one from Ecclesiastes: Two are better than one; because they have a good reward for their labor, for if they fall, the one will lift up his fellow: but woe to him that is alone when he falleth; for he hath not another to help him up. Again, if two lie together, then they have heat, but how can one be warm alone? And if one prevail against him, two shall withstand him; and a threefold cord is not quickly broken.""Both have been wed and widowed," he told those gathered. "They seem to have a fair grasp of what marriage means. So, unless anyone objects to this wedding, we'll ask them to say their vows."

No one spoke up, so he asked them to repeat their vows and then say "I do." Maggie complied, but Jacob said the words, then broke tradition. "I just want to say a few words," he said. "We've been together already in sickness and in health. She nursed me, with the help of my Ma, my niece, and my family, or I wouldn't be standing here today. I reckon we'll have good times and bad like all folks, but I vow to love and cherish Maggie to the end of my life. Maggie gazed at him, her eyes radiant with love, then he repeated the vows and said, "I do."

Boone handed Jacob the ring he'd bought in town, and Jacob slid it onto Mattie's left hand.

"With this ring, I thee wed," he said.

"By the power invested in me by the State of Texas, I pronounce you man and wife. What God has joined, let no man put asunder," Ike Masters said. "You may kiss your bride, Jacob."

He'd kissed her many times, but now, on this day when they became one, his lips touched hers with gentleness. It was sweet and brief, but now they had all the time there was to kiss and be together.

The hands cheered, and the family surged forward to

congratulate them.

"Come on back to Boone's," Ma said. "Rachel and I cooked a fine meal yesterday. It should be ready to eat."

There was a ham, sweet potatoes, Irish potatoes with gravy, deviled eggs, cornbread, leather britches beans, and a spice cake with vanilla frosting. The wedding feast was held at Boone's because he had the most space. Ma had arranged to spend the night there so that on the wedding night, the newlyweds would have the cabin alone.

"We ain't gonna shivaree you," Boone told Jacob as the couple prepared to leave. "I don't find it fitting, though some do. But I'll wish you all the happiness in the world, Jacob, Maggie."

Jacob hugged Boone, speechless with tears in his eyes. "Thank you. I'll be at work tomorrow morning."

"Naw, take a day off," his brother told him. "I reckon you don't get married often. Tuesday will be soon enough."

Mima presented them with a sampler she'd stitched that proclaimed, "Bless this house". There were a few small gifts, but once they gathered them, Jacob took Maggie's hand.

"Let's go home."

"Take cake for the morning," Rachel said, with a smile. "I've got it ready."

With the dessert and the presents, they departed in a chorus of well-wishes.

Jacob walked hand in hand with Maggie. Once they passed out of view, he paused and put his arms around her. He kissed her long and deep. "I love you, wife," he told her. "I'll do my best to make sure you're well provided for and that you're happy."

Maggie gave him back the kiss and rested her hands on his shoulders. "I am happier than I think I've ever been, Jacob. I never dreamed I would be, but I am."

"Even without your children?" That was a question that had niggled and worried him considerable.

She nodded. "I do miss them, but they're lost to me. I thought maybe we'd have a few ourselves before we reach old age."

His breath caught in his chest. "I'd like that, truly I would, Maggie."

"Then once we're home, let's get started on trying."

She didn't need to ask twice. Moses and Mattie would stay with Ma for a few nights to give the newlyweds privacy. At the ranch house, decorated for their wedding day with wildflowers, Jacob saw no need to wait for night. He shucked out of his finery, hung it up on pegs on the wall with care, and came to her.

"Love me, Maggie," he said. "Let me love you."

He never thought about his first wedding night or of Sally Ann. For now, this woman filled his senses and his heart. They came together without rushing, moving slow and with a sweetness he hadn't expected. Afterward, he cradled her close in the bed they would now share, in the second room of the cabin, and whispered words of love.

On Monday, they never left their home, although she cooked for him, and they ate the cake they had carried back. For one day, they shared a private world populated by two. None of his brothers visited. Ma didn't visit, although she would tomorrow. They talked, they read, they sang a little, and they loved. His heart, broken when Sally Ann died, had healed through Maggie's love.

Jacob prepared to ride in two weeks when Boone had determined they would set out on the Great Western Trail to Dodge City. He figured on being gone three months or so. Maggie had accepted his upcoming absence, although she'd fussed a little, worried he wasn't quite back to full health.

Boone thought the same, and on the Friday before they would head out on Monday, he pulled Jacob aside. "I been watching you close," he said. "You ain't ready to trail cattle for the next three months. You still give out awful easy, and you ain't got your full strength back.

"It's been near two months," Jacob protested. "I'm fit to go, Boone."

His older brother shook his head. "I ain't taking that chance. If we get down the trail a bit and you take sick or get weak, I cain't leave you, but I couldn't bring you back, neither. I don't fancy dropping you off in some little burg along the way. Or, worse, leaving you to fend for yourself in open country. You're gonna stay here, Jacob."

"Boone…"

"Hush," he said. "It ain't going to be an easy task to be the one here, neither. I'm leavin' you to watch after my family, Moses and Ezekiel's families, and Ma. A couple of the hands will be here, too, though I'm taking most of them. Deacon Lee's gonna stay now that he's got a wife, and he'll be a help to you. I'm leaving Otis – Spider Webb — here. I'll take Cookie, probably be his last time, but he's eager for it. Jamie, Dawson, and Red will be here, too. That's six counting you – it ought to be enough. If it ain't, go see if you can hire some hands over at Laredo."

"I didn't think you wanted to ride the trail," Jacob told him.

Boone sent a piercing look in his direction. "I ain't keen on it, but this ranch has to prosper or we're all out of a living. Makes a difference with Liam being gone. Ezekiel's gonna be trail boss, though. He done good last year and he'll do fine again. I'm countin' on you to keep everyone here safe, Jacob."

"Who's gonna manage the remuda?" That had been his job since he'd come to Texas.

"Garrett," Boone answered. "He's good with the horses, and he's become a fair enough hand. He can manage, or I wouldn't put him in charge."

Jacob wanted to argue, but he didn't. He wished Boone

could stay. It had been a few years since Boone took the cattle north. He knew, though, he wasn't fully healed. He lacked his usual strength and stamina. The idea of being left along the trail horrified him. Besides where he might end up, he knew Boone would worry endlessly. It would also leave them short a hand.

"All right, Boone, I'll stay behind," he said with a sigh. "I'd rather you stay and me go, but I'll do what you want. I owe you, though, for this."

"You don't," Boone said. "It's what's best for all of us. You can work with Rob and that pony. And you can oversee Spider once he starts to build. It'll give you the chance to tell him what you want for your place. We'll be back in three months, give or take, by the end of July or the first of August. I can send a letter or two as we travel, but you cain't write back 'cause we'll be on the move."

When Jacob shared the news with Maggie, she smiled.

"I'm glad," she told him. "Oh, I know Boone will suffer away from his family, and they'll miss him dreadfully. We all will, but you'll be here. You'll have time to heal and get strong again. Mattie and the children can remain here, with us."

"I ain't gonna have much spare time," he told her. "I'll be tending to Boone's family, Katie and young Johnny, Mattie with her two, and Ma. There's still gonna be chores around the ranch, and I'll have to watch over the hands that stay."

"Who's staying?"

"Deke," Jacob said, counting them off on his fingers. "Spider, so he can build more cabins, and the young boys, Jamie and Pete. Well, Pete ain't so very young – he worked at the livery in town when Zeke did, but he's not as experienced."

"It'll be fine," Maggie said and kissed him. "You'll see."

Monday dawned warmer than it had been yet that spring. Ezekiel and Boone were in the lead as the hands rounded up most of the cattle for the journey. Garrett had sixty horses to drive and tend. Cookie with young Nick, who'd helped Spider last season, drove the chuck wagon, outfitted with plenty of grub. Jacob rode with them when they set out as far as the fence line. Matias and Diego would ride drag, but neither complained. As new hands, it was expected.

Boone hung back when they reached the fence line. "Mind yourself and the family," he told Jacob. "They're more precious to me than my own life."

"I will, Boone," Jacob promised.

"I know or I wouldn't go," he said. "You might check on Rachel in a bit. She cried when I left, and that ain't like her. Ma's gonna move in while I'm gone to help her with the children."

"She told me," Jacob said. "Mima said she'll be helping me out. I reckon you knew that."

"My baby girl does beat all," Boone said with pride. "She'll do her best. If she hadn't ridden for me, you'd likely died out here."

"I would've. Watch yourself, Boone, and the brothers. I'll see you in three months."

"I'll be countin' the days till then," Boone said.

"*Vaya con Dios*," Jacob said, having learned the phrase from Matias. "Take care, brother."

"You do the same," Boone said and rode away at a gallop to catch up with the herd. He'd ride point beside Ezekiel all the way.

Jacob remained and watched till the last of them passed out of sight. He said a prayer for their safe return, then wheeled his horse back to the ranch. Although he wanted to see Maggie, to let her offer wise words that would reassure him he'd made the right choice in staying, he headed for Boone's house.

Ma was there, her apron in place, bustling around the step stove in the kitchen.

"I guess they're gone," she said when she saw him. "Your

Maggie's gone up to spend some time with her sister. Katie's with Rachel, for now, with little Johnny. If you're hungry, I'll have some vittles ready before long."

Jacob nodded. "Where's Rachel? Boone was fretting cause she cried this morning."

"She did," Ma said. "Took me aback until I knew why."

His belly tightened, and he asked, "Why?"

"She's in the family way again, but she didn't want Boone to know. Said he'd stay if she told him, so she didn't."

Concern shot through him. A lot could happen while Boone was gone, he thought, and he didn't like the idea that he would be the one to answer for it. "How far along?"

"Two months, maybe more," Ma said. "By the time they're back, though, she'll be showing."

"Boone will have a conniption fit when he finds out."

Ma smiled and touched his cheek. "Aw, as long as it's all good, he'll be happy. If he's riled, it won't last long."

Jacob glanced into the front room but only saw the little boys. "Where is she?"

"She's working the garden with Katie," Ma told him. "Mima, too. I reckon we'll have some fresh green onions and lettuce with supper. You might as well bring Maggie over. I'll fix kilt lettuce."

"Sounds good," Jacob said, although right now he was anything but hungry. The burden of watching over the entire family in Boone's absence weighed heavily, even more so since he'd learned Rachel was expecting. "I'll head over to Mattie's. I'll fetch them all back to eat if there'll be enough."

"There will be," Ma said. "But supper is still hours away. It's still morning, Jacob, so you might want to wait."

He realized it was. Less than an hour had passed since he'd bid Boone farewell and watched the herd head north. It was going to be a long day, he thought, and then amended that. It would be a long three months.

Fatigue settled over him like dust out on the trail. As much as he had railed against it, Boone had been right. He hadn't recovered from the gunshot wound or near bleeding out.

"I didn't sleep worth a flip last night," he told his mother. "I was thinking about them leaving and me staying."

"You'll do well," Ma said. "Though you'll miss your brothers just as I will. I'm glad you're staying, though, Jacob. I enjoy your company."

Because they'd left later than usual, May arrived by the end of the week. Back in Kentucky, it would still be spring, but here, summer had arrived. What rain they'd seen that spring vanished, and under the bright sun, temperatures rose until it was hot. Each morning, the women headed to the garden to hoe, weed, and pick. Jacob sometimes tagged along to make sure they didn't get too heated. He insisted that they stop before noon. If he didn't go to the garden, he took Rob to the corral to ride the fat old pony to the boy's delight. Like his sister, he proved to be a good horseman.

When he rode around the ranch, Mima often saddled Blossom and accompanied him. He'd worried that seeing him shot and returning to find Hammerschmidt dead in a grisly fashion might have made her enthusiasm fade, but it hadn't. She remained eager to ride and talked about her dream of one day going on the trail. Jacob didn't tell her, but he couldn't imagine a day when Boone would ever allow that.

Without his brothers, he had some lonely moments. Jacob enjoyed spending time with the women and the children, Maggie most of all. No matter how long his day stretched, he always returned to the cabin at night. Sometimes Ma prepared the meal, some nights Maggie did. Katie usually helped, but young Johnny kept her busy. He kept an eye on Rachel, mindful of her condition, and did all he could to make her life as easy

as possible. Jacob made sure she had plenty of firewood for the
stove and any chores that needed to be done around the house,
he did.

Boone sent a letter from Fort Griffin that arrived just over
a month after they'd departed.

Dear Family,

*I write to you at the first chance to tell you so far, so good. We've
reached Fort Griffin, although the herd remains outside the fort itself.
We haven't lost any hands yet and hope we don't. We've all been well for
the most part. Garrett got into a mesquite thicket, but I taught him how
to pry the thorns out before they made him sick. It's been hot, though
we've had a few storms, one that scattered the cattle in every direction,
but we got them back. The lightning was fierce.*

*I hope this finds all of you well. I miss you all, especially my
dearest wife, Rachel, and my children. Mima, you help your uncle Jacob
as much as you can. Tell the boys to mind their mama and granny.*

*If the weather holds and we don't meet with any unfortunate
events, we should be home near the end of July, maybe early August.*

I send my love and will be happy to be home on the Double Deuce.
Boone

"It's a fine letter," Ma said after Jacob read it aloud and
passed it around the supper table. They had all gathered at the
main ranch house.

"It is," he replied. "I'll be glad when they're back."

Rachel's eyes filled with tears. "We all will be. I miss
Boone."

Two more months, nearabout, Jacob thought. Then they
would be back, safe and sound. He could surely hold the ranch
together that long. His days in the saddle and outside had turned
him brown. His strength had almost returned, and by the time
Boone was back, he'd be hale again.

No matter what, however, he vowed he would never be left to hold down the ranch alone again. He would ride with his brothers, but he wouldn't stay behind. Through the long, hot summer days, he worried plenty, but he took pleasure in his family. Some evenings, he spent with Boone's little ones, reading a story or two out of Mima's fairy tale book or the Bible. Sometimes, though he lacked Boone's sweet voice, he sang with them. Ma and Katie often carried the tunes while he joined in, and often Mima led them.

Maggie brought him a contentment he'd never known, rich and full. He treasured her and couldn't imagine how he'd ever managed without her. The verse that often came to mind from Matthew said, "For where your treasure is, there will your heart be also." Maggie first, then his family equaled his treasure, so his heart was happy. It brimmed full on the Double Deuce, and he thought that it always would.

Lee Ann Sontheimer Murphy is a former newspaper editor and reporter who makes her home in the Ozarks. As a widow with three grown children, her focus is on writing romance novels that range from sweet to heat, from contemporary to historical. She has written more than twenty-five novels and novellas, along with a variety of non-fiction and freelance works. A native of St. Joseph, Missouri, where the Pony Express began and outlaw Jesse James met his end, she is a graduate of Crowder College and Missouri Southern State University. She lives in what passes for the suburbs in far southwestern Missouri, a little north of Arkansas and just east of Oklahoma.